BLOOD SURRENDER

"Don't talk, Deirdre," Sam said. "You've done nothing but talk about being a vampire since I've known you. Show me what it's like."

I hadn't had a willing victim in a long time. There was a heady, sensuous feel in this man giving himself to me.

I put my mouth to his neck. My tongue emerged to lick his skin, drinking and savoring the tang of sweat and salt. He moaned and held me closer to him. His hand came around behind my head and he tangled his fingers in my hair, holding my mouth to him.

I continued to lick the surface of his neck in preparation of my bite. My hand reached over and pulled at his hair, bending his neck further down so that I could feed without stretching. I continued to lick him. Then I took my mouth from his neck for a minute and licked my lips before bringing my teeth full into Sam, causing him to cry out. It didn't matter whether it was passion or pain, we were both too far gone to care.

My fangs split through the surface of his skin and I sucked on him, drawing his blood deep into my mouth, taking swallow after swallow. His body pounded against me as I drank, and from his heavy breathing I knew that he was close to orgasm.

And still I drank from him, deeply, taking much more than I needed, more than I meant to take. . . .

BOOK YOUR PLACE ON OUR WEBSITE AND MAKE THE READING CONNECTION!

We've created a customized website just for our very special readers, where you can get the inside scoop on everything that's going on with Zebra, Pinnacle and Kensington books.

When you come online, you'll have the exciting opportunity to:

- View covers of upcoming books
- Read sample chapters
- Learn about our future publishing schedule (listed by publication month *and author*)
- Find out when your favorite authors will be visiting a city near you
- Search for and order backlist books from our online catalog
- Check out author bios and background information
- Send e-mail to your favorite authors
- Meet the Kensington staff online
- Join us in weekly chats with authors, readers and other guests
- Get writing guidelines
- AND MUCH MORE!

**Visit our website at
http://www.zebrabooks.com**

BLOOD TIES

KAREN E. TAYLOR

Zebra Books
Kensington Publishing Corp.

http://www.zebrabooks.com

ZEBRA BOOKS are published by

Kensington Publishing Corp.
850 Third Avenue
New York, NY 10022

Zebra and the Z logo Reg. U.S. Pat. & TM Off.

First Printing: October, 1995

Printed in the United States of America
10 9 8 7 6 5 4 3 2

In loving memory of Lawrence W. Gallagher, a teller of tall tales, slayer of serpents, and transplanted Texan extraordinaire. I miss you, my brother. Walk softly.

Acknowledgments

This one was a tough one, so the list is long. Most importantly, thank you to John, Cherry, and Steven, for not yelling too much and for their almost infinite supply of patience and humor. Thanks to Pete, Brian, and Geoffrey for their love and cooperation throughout a very long and lonely process. Thanks to the friends who asked "how's it going?" and thanks to those who did not. Hugs and thanks to the many friends on GEnie (if I mention you all, I'll never finish) who were always there to encourage and commiserate. And to all the many wonderful people who wrote letters wanting to know what was going to happen next— here you go!

One

He moved through the narrow streets like a shadow, in stealth and darkness, stalking an unsuspecting prey. I followed close enough to keep him in my sight, but also hidden, my presence merging with the night. His muscles coiled beneath the black sweater, his legs, taut and powerful, and his silvery hair glistened in the moonlight. I held back a gasp at the magnificence of this creature; I did not want to be heard. But my caution made no difference, he was oblivious to my presence. He remained a mysterious and nameless figure intent only upon the quick footsteps of his chosen victim, leading him around a corner and down a darker alley. I hurried to catch up with them, not wanting to miss the moment of capture.

Standing at the head of the alley, I squeezed tightly against its rough brick wall, watching in fearful anticipation. My legs trembled and the breath froze in my throat. Then, when I thought I could stand the waiting no longer, he struck, suddenly and ferociously. His hand snaked out and grasped the young man's shoulder, spinning him around, silencing his protests with a single glance. His mouth came down on the man's neck and my hand traveled to my own throat; my pulse pounded in excitement, my breathing quickened, my tongue darted out to lick my lips. The tangy, acrid smell of blood exploded in the air; its odor, enticing and invigorating.

He drank hungrily, silently, but his pleasure was almost tangible, as easily heard as the strangled moans of his victim.

"Ahh." The slight whisper escaped my lips involuntarily and although it was barely audible, he heard and pulled away to face me. His mouth was bloodied, his canines, sharpened and lethal, and the ecstasy of feeding shone on his features. I do not need to fear him, I thought, he is of my own kind. But the internal reassurances did no good, and, in spite of myself, I shrank away from him, in awe and fright. A look of puzzlement flashed across his face, then he smiled and his eyes, with their intense blue glow, met mine and broke the spell under which his presence had held me.

"Mitch." I murmured his name and slowly moved toward him, claiming my place at the man's neck. Delicately, I placed my bite within the marks he had left and pulled deeply on the strong, rich blood. As I drank, Mitch stroked my hair with one hand. His other arm held me and the victim in an iron embrace until I finished my feast. Then with a few hoarsely spoken words, he calmed the man, urged him to forget, and gently deposited the now sleeping form on the sidewalk.

We linked arms and walked back down the alley to return to the pub. I nestled into his strong arm and glanced up at him, smiling. He kissed the top of my head and I sighed. Mitch had adjusted to his new life better than I had ever expected.

"So how'd I do?" It had been his first solo stalking since his transformation and the apprehension he had shown before we came out was now replaced with an exhilaration I knew all too well.

"At first I thought you would have been better off with someone older, someone slower perhaps. But you picked well, he was young and strong and you . . ." I sighed again. "You were perfect, Mitch. No, more than that, you were magnificent. You took my breath away."

"Well," he shrugged and pulled me closer to him, "I had a wonderful teacher."

"Yes," I said, "I suppose I should offer professional tutoring in bloodsucking. Such a valuable skill." I tried to make my voice light and teasing, but the acid of the words splashed through.

We walked in silence until we were about a block from the pub. Mitch stopped and turned me around to face him. "What's wrong, Deirdre? You've been edgy and nervous all day. It's crazy, but I can't help but think it has something to do with me. Are you tired of me this soon?" The anger and hurt in his voice made me want to cry.

"No, my love," I reached a hand up to stroke his cheek, "it's not you. I wish I knew what it was. I'm tired. Perhaps that's all it is."

"But we slept all day and just fed pretty well. You should feel great; I know *I* do."

I gave him a sidelong glance. "You slept all day, you mean. I don't sleep much anymore."

"Why not? Do I snore?" His voice was slightly indignant.

"No, that's not it," I said with a small laugh, then sobered instantly. "I feel uneasy, like something is nagging at my mind, but I can't pinpoint it." I glanced up at the night sky, mentally numbering the remaining hours until dawn. "We'll have to leave here soon, you know."

"I know. Pete's expecting us back at the pub soon so he can go home. It was nice of him to stay, while we ran out for a bite." He winked at me and I smiled, but shook my head slightly, for both the bad joke and his misunderstanding of my words.

"No, I meant that we will need to leave England soon."

"But we just got here. And everything is just starting to fall into place, the house, the pub, and you and me. What else could we possibly want?"

"More than four hours of darkness at night would be nice. You've never spent an entire summer at this latitude. I have and it's an experience I am not anxious to repeat."

"Oh, yeah." He paused a minute and ran his fingers through his hair. "I was never real good at geography. Where should we go, do you think?"

I shrugged. "Any place is as good as another, I suppose, as long as we get at least seven hours of darkness. Any less than that and we might be in for trouble. What would you think about Spain?"

"Sounds fine to me." Mitch's face lit up with a mischievous grin. "I hear they have some great beaches there. You know, the ones where you can get a really good tan."

A sharp wave of panic struck me. I remembered too clearly my own initial longing for the sun; how, after over a century of living in the night only, I still missed the warming rays and the brightness of summer days. "No beaches, Mitch." My voice was imperative and harsh. I reached over and grasped his arm tightly. "You have to promise me, no beaches."

"Okay, okay." He disengaged my fingers from his arm, but kept my hand in his. "Bloody hell, Deirdre, I was only joking."

"Please, Mitch, never joke about that."

He must have heard the despair in my voice and said no more, but pulled me close to him, rocking me slightly for a few seconds. "Feeling better?" His breath tickled my ear and I smiled into his sweater.

"Yes, thank you. Now, we'd better get back to the pub."

"Dottie, and Mitch, my boy," Pete's boisterous voice greeted us as we opened the front door. "Back so soon? I was just saying that you'd be a while longer. Trying to make a liar of me, are you?"

I shook my head slightly and smiled, knowing that it did no good to interrupt him. Mitch laughed, clapped Pete on the shoulder and stood next to him behind the bar.

"Sure," Pete continued, "and now I suppose you'll be sending me home right as I was in the middle of making the acquaintance of a new visitor; telling him the story of how you returned here with a new name, a new husband, and without an extra ounce of fat on your bones. Not that they're not fine bones, mind you," and he nudged Mitch, giving him a small wink, "but you both could do with a little fattening up."

I tensed slightly at his mention of a visitor and glanced around the bar, seeing no one but the regulars. Catching Mitch's eyes, I shrugged and asked the question I knew Pete was waiting to hear. "What new visitor?"

He looked around in confusion. "Why, he was just here, wasn't he, boys?" The men around the bar nodded and Pete continued. "Probably stepped off to the gents; he'll be turning up soon, no doubt. Real eager to see you, he was. Says he knew you both in the States." Pete's eyes narrowed in a fake scowl, "Seems to me, Dottie, that last time that happened you took off and left me for another man."

"But I came back, Pete."

"And that you did, Dot." He drew himself a glass of stout, and walked around the bar, lighting a cigarette. "But this wasn't the same man that dragged you away before. This one is older and has a trace of accent, not American, mind you, but someplace foreign."

As he settled himself onto a stool to finish his drink, I moved back behind the bar with Mitch. "Do you remember his name, Pete," I asked with a smile, leaning toward him, "or did you forget to ask?"

"Now, Dottie, don't give me grief, I get enough of that from the missus owing to my poor memory. Vincent, it was, or something close to that."

"Victor Lange."

I knew Mitch well enough to hear the undercurrent of tension in his voice, but Pete merely nodded and announced triumphantly, "Yes, that's the chap. Know him, do you?"

"Unfortunately." This time, the anger in Mitch's voice was unmistakable.

"Well, fortunate or not," Pete said, glancing curiously at Mitch, "he's here somewhere." He drained his glass, stubbed out his cigarette and stood up. Taking off his apron, he tossed it to Mitch, then reached over to give me a delicate pat on my cheek. "Now, Dot, don't you go running off on me again without notice."

Although I knew Mitch and I would both be leaving soon, I nodded my head, thinking that we had less than a month before the nighttime hours would begin to dwindle enough to force us to move on. "Well, Pete," I began, "we won't . . ." But the rest of my answer went unsaid. The air seemed to thicken over me; the hair on the back of my neck rose. I could hear nothing, but felt the presence of someone standing close behind me, as clearly as if a hand had been laid on me. I quickly looked over my shoulder and around the room, but could see only those that had been there a second earlier, no one else.

Mitch walked over next to me and wrapped an arm around my waist, his familiar touch calming me only slightly. "Don't worry," he said, "we won't leave you in the lurch. Now if you don't go soon, your wife'll be mad."

Pete's contagious laugh roared over the pub and almost rid me of the unsettling feeling of the invisible presence. "Right you are, my boy. See you tomorrow night."

The rest of the evening passed uneventfully. I was still nervous; I thought that the patrons spoke too loudly and that the smoke of their cigarettes was unnaturally heavy, curling thickly through the dark corners of the room. I breathed my relief when last call had been made and the doors were finally locked. Mitch silently poured me a glass of port, handed me Pete's cigarettes and began to clear the tables.

When I finished the wine, I lit one of the Players and sat at the bar to watch Mitch wash the glasses and the steins, admiring the grace of his movements and the strength of his hands. He looked up at me, his eyes met mine and he smiled. "What?"

"Nothing," I said. Suddenly the nervousness fell aside and I felt at peace with myself for the first time since Mitch's transformation. "I just like to watch you. You do that so well."

Mitch laughed. "I know, you brought me all the way here just so I could wash dishes for your pub."

I returned his laugh. "That's right, my love, regular dishwashers don't come cheap and you know how Pete is about spending money."

He gave a noncommittal grunt and completed his work behind the bar. Then he pulled out a glass for himself and filled it and mine with tawny port. He took both glasses and sat down at the closest table. I followed and sat down next to him.

"So," his voice had lost all of its humor and was intense and serious, "what exactly was that?"

"You mean right before Pete left? I don't know. I've never experienced anything like it."

"Wasn't Max, was it?"

After having lived with the ghost of Max for over two years, I discarded that theory immediately. "No, it didn't have his imprint, somehow."

"I didn't think so."

I turned to him in surprise. "You felt it too?"

"Yeah." He ran his fingers through his hair in a tired gesture. "But it was vaguely familiar." Then he shrugged and touched my hand. "Another thing, what the hell is Victor Lange doing here? And where in bloody hell do you suppose he disappeared to?"

I shook my head and my eyes drifted to a corner of the bar, where the smoke of the night had collected and the darkness was impenetrable. Rubbing a hand on my face, I looked again and a shiver of amazement flowed over me. "Why that son of a bitch," I whispered in a trembling voice, "he never left at all. He's been here all night."

"What?" Mitch looked at me in surprise then glanced over his shoulder. When the figure behind the bar began to materialize into an almost recognizable form, Mitch jumped out of his chair, knocking his glass to the floor in the process. Its crash was the only noise for what seemed a long time. Then there was the sound of footsteps and suddenly Victor stood in front of us.

"Good evening, Deirdre," he nodded, "and you too, Mitch. It's good to see you again."

Mitch and I just stared at him; neither of us ever had any inkling that what Victor had just done was even possible. Mitch cleared his throat and tentatively held out his hand. Victor shook it, grinning.

"Jesus, Victor," Mitch said with a touch of both anger and awe in his voice, "how the hell did you do that?"

Two

"Forgive me for the theatrics," Victor began, ignoring Mitch's question. He brushed a spot of invisible lint from his impeccably tailored jacket, and sat down at the table. "I did think that our meeting would best be conducted in private. We have a lot to discuss, we three."

I glanced at Victor uneasily, then glanced away, feeling, as I usually did in his presence, shoddily dressed in my jeans and black sweater. He exuded an elegance and a confidence as easily felt as the power and magnetism of his being. Mitch was still staring at him and I could almost hear the questions racing through his mind. Was what Victor had done possible for us? And if so, how was it accomplished? But where I shrank away from the inhumanity of such a trick, Mitch, I knew, would pursue this new power effortlessly and relentlessly, as he had so readily embraced the unnatural life he had been given.

I shuddered and looked down at the tabletop. Victor reached over and lifted my chin. "Cat got your tongue, Deirdre? I do apologize for the abruptness of my appearance. I didn't mean to alarm you."

"No," I found my voice and was amazed that it sounded even and calm, "it was just a surprise, seeing you appear like that. After all, we had been told you were here."

"Yes, well," Victor looked over to Mitch, "what if you pour me one of whatever you two are having and we'll get down to business."

Mitch walked back behind the bar to get the bottle and another glass for Victor. My mouth curved in an almost smug smile as I watched him; Victor might be elegant and powerful, but he could never be a match for the utter intensity and sensuality that Mitch possessed. A low noise escaped my throat, almost a purr, and I blushed, but Victor merely laughed.

"He is developing nicely, my dear. You've done a good job with his training."

"What do you mean?"

"Come now, Deirdre," Victor admonished, "I do have eyes and my senses are even more finely honed than yours. The glow of transformation still lingers over him. He will do well, and for what it's worth, I approve."

Mitch came back to the table and handed Victor his wine. "And exactly what is your approval worth, Lange?"

Victor looked up at him calmly. "Quite a bit, actually. As head of the Cadre, I have the final decision on most transformations, especially one such as yours, since you now both fall into the house of Leupold. Never underestimate the ties of blood, Mitch. As you grow older, you will eventually lose your human family, but your blood clan will continue. And," Victor gave a low chuckle, "like it, or not, I am the head of that clan."

"I'd like it a lot better if you could teach me that little trick you entered with." Mitch sat down and leaned back casually in his chair. "How on earth do you do it?"

Victor gave me a puzzled look. "Deirdre should be able to teach you. It merely requires concentration and practice— years, or more properly, decades of practice. I wish I could take the time to teach you, but I'm afraid my business here is not pleasant and my time is short. I am needed back at the Cadre before tomorrow evening." Victor stood up and brushed at his pants again. "And, although I hate to interrupt your honeymoon, the two of you must accompany me."

"Must we?" Mitch still sat in his relaxed pose, but the glitter of his eyes and the set of his jaw betrayed his animosity.

Victor glared coldly at him, and leaned over the chair, his posture threatening, his tone of voice even more patronizing than usual. "You do remember when you promised to perform a service for the Cadre at our discretion? Well, quite simply, Greer, we are now calling in our marker, and as you value your life and Deirdre's, you will not refuse. A private jet is waiting for us at the airport and we will leave in an hour and a half. Be there."

Victor turned to me and the anger in his eyes faded, replaced by something that could have resembled tenderness. Taking my hand, he kissed it; then he spun around and was gone.

Mitch looked where he had been standing and shook his head. "Do you suppose he's actually gone?"

I laughed. "Your guess is as good as mine, my love. Shall we close up now and go home and pack?"

"Just drop everything and do as we were ordered? Give me one good reason why we should have anything to do with Lange."

"I can give you several reasons, Mitch. We did promise to do the service for the Cadre, whatever it may be. I know that we were hoping never to have anything else to do with them, but so be it." He nodded reluctantly, and I continued. "And Victor is right about the bond between the three of us, there is no way to deny that." I stood up and smiled at him, reaching out for his hands. "Plus, if you stay in his good favor, he might even teach you his little parlor trick. I have no inclination to dissolve myself. And even if I did, I have no idea how to go about it."

"Okay, okay, you've convinced me. But you'll have to break the news to Pete." He pulled me to him and kissed me, his lips cool against mine. Then he held me out and studied my face. "Deirdre, if whatever we are called to do is dangerous," and he gave a small humorless laugh, "as I'm sure it will be, I want you to promise that you'll let me bear the brunt of it. Don't take any chances; I don't think I want to exist eternally without you."

"Nor I, without you."

"So then, we're agreed."

"No," I shook my head with a small smile, "not at all. But let's not fight until we know what the situation is."

"Okay, I guess I can live with that, but only for a while. And we'd better hurry, I'd hate to keep Mr. Lange waiting."

We made it home, and were almost through with our packing when I finally asked, "Why do you hate Victor so much?"

Mitch looked up at me from his suitcase. "It's not really Victor, you know; I could almost like him if it weren't for . . ." He paused for a minute, staring at me. Then he looked away, "It's the whole hierarchy of the Cadre. They sit in their underground warren, spinning their devious little webs, meting out their arbitrary justice." He folded his last pair of jeans, crammed them on the top of the suitcase and snapped it shut. "They almost succeeded in making me crazy, they would've left me in that institution for the rest of my life and not thought a thing about it. They could very easily have doomed you to a hundred years of starvation and never once bothered to ascertain the fairness of the sentence. They're immoral, inhuman parasites, living off of innocent people and I wouldn't care if the entire lot died tomorrow."

Well, I told myself, as I watched him stack our cases by the bedroom door, you asked for it. But

I said nothing, and walked across the room, picked up the phone and dialed Pete's home number.

"Pete," I said when he answered, "it's Dorothy. I'm afraid I have some bad news for you."

"Leaving again, are you?" He sounded more amused than angry.

"Yes, I'm sorry."

"And didn't I know it when that Vincent chap turned up asking for you. I suppose you'll be taking your husband with you too, leaving me with no help at all?"

"Yes."

"Dottie, darlin', you know if you didn't own half the pub, I'd be firing you right now."

"I'm sure you would, Pete. I'll call you when we get there."

"I'd appreciate that. But don't you worry, I'll do fine."

"Thank you, Pete. You take care now."

"And the same to you, my girl. Godspeed."

I hung up the phone, stood for a minute with my back to Mitch and wiped away a few tears. A horn beeped on the street and still I didn't move until Mitch came up behind me and wrapped an arm around my neck, kissing me softly on the ear. "We'd better get moving, Deirdre, the taxi's here. Are you ready?"

I nodded and we went downstairs. We locked the house, loaded the boot of the taxi and made it to the airport with five minutes to spare.

The plane Victor had chartered was a small, sleek Gulfstream; Mitch and I were the only passengers evident. The seats were plush and comfortable and I settled in by one of the windows. Mitch sat next to me with a grim smile, outwardly relaxed and at ease, but I could feel the keyed-up tenseness of his muscles as he stretched his legs out. Even though Victor was nowhere in sight, the plane began its acceleration down the runway almost immediately and made a smooth leap from the ground into the night sky.

My sigh from the window was easily audible; Mitch reached over and took my hand. "Nervous?"

"No," I said softly, turning to him, "not at all. I love to fly. But I was just wondering what it would feel like without the plane, how it would feel to just be picked up by the wind and carried away." I gave a small laugh to compensate for the emotional outburst. "I guess we would find out soon enough if we were to crash."

"Do you think we'd survive?"

"You know, I have no idea."

Mitch was silent for a while. "My guess is we would. Unless," and he chuckled a little, "we happened to land on a picket fence somewhere."

I studied the view from the window. "I think we're safe from that. We're over the ocean already. But I suppose if you really want to know, we could ask Victor. I wonder where he is."

Mitch gave a noncommittal grunt. "What is it with you and him, anyway? All of a sudden the two of you seem pretty chummy. You jump to his commands, express concern over his whereabouts. Personally, I don't know why he even bothers with the damn plane at all; why doesn't he just turn into a cloud and float back?"

"Mitch," I turned from the window again and looked into his eyes, "don't start. There is nothing between Victor and me. I married you and intend to stay married to you. I'm here to fulfill my commitment, nothing else. After that, we're free to do whatever we like, go wherever we want."

"Okay," he shrugged, giving me a boyish grin, so at odds with his silvered hair, "I'm sorry. I just don't like the guy."

"I think you have made that more than evident." My mouth twisted in a dry smile. "But," and I reached up, kissing him on the cheek, "just put up with it for a while, for my sake."

Mitch returned my kiss, then moved away from me and laughed. "I will say one thing for Lange, though," he gestured around us, "he sure knows how to travel. This is quite a setup; how much do you suppose this put him back?"

"Actually, Mitch," the door to the cockpit opened and Victor came out, "I own this plane. And, believe me, the convenience far outweighs the cost." He went to the back of the compartment and opened another door. "Now that we are safely airborne, may I offer you a drink?"

Before Mitch and I even had a chance to agree, Victor had poured drinks and brought them over: red wine for me and a scotch on the rocks for Mitch. When I saw Victor's choice for Mitch I started to laugh.

"What?" Mitch looked at me after taking a long drink. "Is something funny?"

"No, but Victor has a surprisingly good memory. He actually remembered what you drink when you're angry."

"Oh," Mitch shrugged sheepishly, "I see."

"Not that you don't have the right to be angry." Victor's voice was smooth and conciliatory. "After all, you've hardly been away for more than a few months, and I have called you back. I do apologize for the inconvenience, but I want to assure you that this trip is necessary. And it was not just my decision to call you, it was a unanimous vote from all the founders."

Mitch gave a snort. "And what could possibly be so difficult for that esteemed group to require our involvement?"

"We have our reasons, Greer, as I will explain, when you give me the chance." Victor gave him a warning glare then turned to me. "In the first place, at least six murders have occurred that lead us to believe that we are faced with a dangerous rogue vampire. Since we became acquainted with you, Deirdre, most of us have come to the realization that we have been weakened by our ritualized training.

"You," Victor nodded at me, "have the advantage of being able to approach situations such as this from a fresh viewpoint. Being a rogue of a sort yourself, we hope that you can outthink our culprit, or at least anticipate his moves. In addition, Mitch, there is your police training— a highly valuable asset in this situation. Although,

I must admit that your transformation has come as something of a surprise. We had hoped that you could cover the daytime and root this vampire out of his lair. But I suspect your new skills will only enhance your old detective instincts."

Mitch shrugged. "And?"

Victor looked down at his hands for a moment. "And as you know, the Cadre has strict rules governing the killing of one of our own. None of us can attempt to catch and kill this vampire, without incurring the impact of our laws. But you two, since you are not officially part of the organization, can be given special dispensation in this one case only."

"How convenient," Mitch drawled. "I remember it otherwise."

Victor bared his white teeth in a threatening smile. "Different circumstances, Mitch. We're not talking here about an established house founder, but about an undisciplined murderer."

"And Max wasn't?"

"Max would have been dealt with our way. Let's not begin to rehash a situation that, regretful as it may be, is now over and done with."

Hearing the pain in Victor's voice, pain not diminished by the time that had passed since Max's death, I looked over at Mitch and pleaded with my eyes for him to drop the subject. Then I took his hand in mine and turned again to Victor. "All of that seems reasonable to me, Victor. We will do our best to help you."

"Thank you, Deirdre. I knew you would. But I'm not quite through with the story. And this part may not be pleasant for you, my dear, but it is the most telling reason we wanted you." Victor stood up, opened the overhead compartment, and brought out a large manila envelope. "The murders began to occur shortly after you and Mitch left town. Obviously, you personally cannot be held accountable for the deaths, but it seems that you are involved. All of the victims were last seen at the Ballroom of Romance."

"What a surprise." Mitch gave a small, derisive snort. The Ballroom had belonged to Max, been passed on to my ownership through his estate. And it carried nothing but bad memories for us both.

Victor sat back down and passed the envelope to Mitch. He took it, but did not open it. Instead he set it down on the seat next to him, as if leaving it unopened could delay the inevitable decision to cooperate with the Cadre. "You're involved with the Ballroom, too, Victor," Mitch said evenly. "After all, you've been managing it for Deirdre in her absence."

"Actually, I turned it back over to Fred. After you left town, there was no need to keep him in exile and he does a good job."

"But," I said, "Fred is not a rogue."

"That is true," Victor chuckled, shaking his head, "and Fred, even with all his faults, is definitely not responsible for the deaths. We have," he cleared his throat, "screened all the Cadre members, none of them are involved."

"So where does the Ballroom enter into this?" I did not really need to ask; from the sickening twist of my stomach, I realized suddenly that I knew who the rogue was. I glanced over at Mitch, and his grim nod confirmed my thoughts. But neither of us said a word, we just let Victor continue.

"Ever since the unfortunate occurrences there, rumors have abounded that the club is haunted." Victor raised an eyebrow in a half-smirk. "Humans, who can figure them out? Business is better than it's ever been since the rumors started, even the murders haven't kept them away, but only added to the mystique."

"Haunted?" Victor's choice of words threw me off balance. "How could it be haunted? Max is gone." Mitch looked away from me, and drained his scotch, tensing at the tone of sadness in my voice. I couldn't help myself; not a day had gone by since his true death that I did not miss him.

"Deirdre," Victor's voice wavered only slightly, "it's not Max who haunts the Ballroom of Romance. It is Larry Martin."

Three

"Of course," Victor went on, "haunting is not the proper terminology, since our murderer is not a ghost. Apparently, as they say, reports of his death were greatly exaggerated and this, too, seems to involve you both. And although we know who the rogue is, we do not know why he is now a vampire," Victor's voice became stern, "or why his transformation went unreported."

I shook my head and sighed. We should never have gone away, should not have allowed Larry to prey upon the city. And now six people were dead due to our selfishness. I squirmed in my seat, avoiding Victor's gaze. We were almost as guilty as the rogue himself. "Sins of omission," I murmured.

Mitch got up, went to the bar, and poured himself another scotch. Draining it in one drink, he turned around and looked at Victor, who rose from his seat deliberately and slowly to meet his gaze. Except for the smooth, low hum of the engines, the plane drifted in silence, a silence at first merely uncomfortable, then growing fearsome, threatening, as they continued to stare at each other. The muscles in Mitch's neck seemed to rise to the surface his skin, twisting and coiling. Victor's breathing accelerated, small drops of blood-tinged sweat began to appear on his forehead. And I was rooted in my seat, unable to move, unable to speak. The tension in the compartment expanded, growing so great that it seemed the plane must explode. I held my breath, suspended between their power, caught in their gazes like a fly in a web. Then suddenly, when I felt that neither of them could sustain a second more, Victor threw his head back and laughed, joined surprisingly by Mitch only a second later.

"*Touché,* Mitch," Victor rasped with a tone of admiration in his voice. "And I am not easily impressed. So, now that that's out of the way, will you help us?"

Mitch continued to laugh, a thick, harsh laughter I had never heard from him before. He stopped and he smiled. His canines were elongated and his eyes glowed with what seemed to me an inhuman passion. "With the greatest of pleasure, Victor."

I sat silent for the remainder of the flight, not joining in the tentative camaraderie that seemed to have been established between Victor and Mitch. Instead, I drained two bottles of wine in the absolutely futile attempt to block out the sight of the two of them, both so powerful and terrifying. Every so often, I caught Mitch's reflected gaze in my window, but I kept my eyes on the night sky above us and the ocean below.

Mitch had finally opened the manila envelope and glanced at the pictures within. He made a move to hand them to me, but I shook my head and looked away. He shrugged at my seeming lack of interest then turned back to Victor. "These are police photos. Do you mind if I ask how you got them?"

"We have friends in high places. You didn't seriously think that an organization such as the Cadre could exist without some local support."

"I never heard of you."

Victor laughed. "High places, Mitch. I hope I give no offense in saying that the knowledge wasn't allowed to filter down to the level at which you worked. But these same friends were partly responsible for our calling you in. You are a highly respected member of the department."

"Were, you mean. I can hardly resume my regular job now."

I flinched slightly at the regret in Mitch's voice, but Victor didn't seem to notice.

"While your return has not been discussed officially, I'm sure that something could be arranged should you desire it. But first things first; I think that you owe me an explanation about our rogue."

I did not elaborate as Mitch told the story of Larry and how we suspected he had been transformed, how the gunshot from Mitch that had "killed" Larry had also punctured my shoulder and our blood had been mixed, how Larry must have slipped out of the morgue before the mandatory autopsy could be performed, and how the disappearance of the body would just seem like another lost piece of paper in an overwhelmed system of police red tape. Mitch and I had never spoken much of those circumstances, but it was obvious that he had spent a lot of time in thought about Larry. Not that I was surprised, since it was Larry's nearly fatal attack on him that caused me to change Mitch into what he was. I suspected that he had nightmares about that night; I myself had been haunted for over a century with the details of my own change. But at least, I thought, with a twisted smile, Mitch has the advantage of knowing who to blame.

"Deirdre?" Mitch's concerned voice brought me out of my reverie, and I noticed that we were alone in the compartment again. "We're about ready to land. And," he checked his watch, "we've got only about an hour before dawn. Let's hope they're not too stacked up or we'll have to spend the day in here."

"I'm sure Victor will take care of that."

"No problem," Victor's voice called out from the cockpit. "We're cleared for landing. Anyway, there's more time than that, you forgot to set your watch back. Here we are."

The plane touched down, and when it finally slowed to a stop, a familiar figure emerged from the cockpit and walked up to us. Mitch's face twisted into a jealous grimace, but I found to my surprise that I was happy to see him. "Hello, Ron." I said warmly. "Victor never mentioned that you were here." Ron had acted once as a spy for the Cadre, reporting on my activities, but he

had also been a good friend to me during a time
when I felt I had no other.

Ron smiled. "Well, someone had to fly the
plane and Victor needed to talk to you." He gave
Mitch a quick, furtive glance, then put his arms
around me briefly and kissed my cheek, dropping back a respectful distance after he had finished. "Welcome back, Deirdre, it's nice to see
you."

"Thank you, Ron."

Ron held out his hand to Mitch. "Hello,
Greer," he said brusquely. "Forgive me if I skip
the kiss."

Mitch shook his hand warily. "Fine by me."

"Now, let me unload your luggage and we'll
be on our way. There's a limo waiting."

Mitch draped his arm around my shoulder and
we walked to the door of the plane. Victor stood
waiting for us, and opened the hatch. A set of
stairs had been wheeled over and we exited into
a clear, starlit night. When we got to the tarmac,
Mitch put his head up, took a long whiff of the
air and smiled. "It's nice to be home," he said,
with a note of contentment in his voice that I
hadn't heard in months. "I missed this dirty old
city."

"I have prepared a room for you in the Cadre
headquarters." Victor turned around from the
front seat of the limousine. "You need not stay
there for the duration of your mission, but I
thought it would be easiest until you had a

chance to make your own arrangements. From what I understand, Mitch, your son has moved into your apartment."

Mitch nodded. "Yeah, he called and told me. How did you know?"

Victor shrugged. "Very little escapes my notice when it concerns the security of the Cadre. Not knowing how much he knows about us, it seemed a good idea to keep an eye on him, now and then. He knows of your transformation, doesn't he?"

"No," Mitch's face darkened slightly, "actually, I haven't broken the news to him yet."

"Ah, well," Victor said, "you'll have plenty of time for that later on."

Mitch gave a noncommittal nod and looked out the window. I held his arm and rubbed my head against his shoulder. The upcoming confrontation between Mitch and his son had me worried; Chris had a difficult enough time coming to terms with what I was; I suspected that learning what his father had become would result in his permanent alienation from the two of us. Mitch reached over and stroked my thigh gently. "It'll be okay," he said, his voice a reassuring whisper. "He'll get used to the idea, sooner or later."

Before too long, the limousine pulled up to the back entrance of the Imperial, the restaurant that Victor owned. Below, were the offices and the living quarters of the Cadre. We took the elevator down and entered into the meeting hall where the organization had stood in judgment of me, for the murder of Max Hunter. The room was dark now, we moved through it quickly and proceeded down a dimly lit hallway. Victor stopped in front of one of the closed doors, removed a key from his pocket and handed it to Mitch. While Mitch unlocked the door, Victor explained, "This was Max's room. I hope you don't mind, it was the only vacant one currently available. His personal effects have been removed, of course, and put in storage for your use at a later date. But we have tried to ensure your every comfort during your stay here."

We started into the room and Victor continued, looking somehow embarrassed. "I hope you understand that you both are considered honored guests of the Cadre, so no payment for any of this is necessary. However, should you choose at some point to make this one of your permanent residences, and I sincerely hope that you will, arrangements will be made at that time."

"Thank you, Victor," I started, "but . . ."

"No, no, you don't need to decide anything now. You are most welcome here and your entrance into our community would be for the common good of us all. But we will not press you on the issue; you are free to stay or go. Make yourselves at home, please. And, if I don't see you before dawn, have a pleasant day's sleep."

He left us and I looked around the room that had been Max's. It was pleasant enough, but dark and sparsely furnished. The furniture was mostly antique, the bed an enormous four poster covered in a red brocade spread. But what caught my eye first was the heavy brass stand, holding a familiar artifact. Victor had indeed tried to see to my every comfort, for he had procured the coffin that Max had bought for me. Mitch was standing over it, shaking his head. Then he looked at me and laughed. "Don't I get one, too?"

"You can have that one, my love. You know I'll never use it." I smiled at him. Now that we were alone, I felt at ease again, as if my moments of fear and doubt had never occurred, as if his presence in my life was all I ever needed. The qualities of strength and integrity that I had admired in him had only intensified after his transformation. Victor was right; I had done well.

"But I want my own," his eyes danced mischievously, "I wouldn't want to break from the mysterious image of the vampire. We need to keep up with the others, you know, follow the crowd."

"You are so far above the others, Mitch, I do not think you need to worry." I walked over to him and put my arms around him.

He hugged me tightly to him. "Still, I wonder that Victor didn't take care of it, along with everything else."

"He didn't know about you, remember?"

"Oh, yeah. But it sure is nice to know he's not as omniscient as he thinks." He moved away from me, and sat down on the bed, testing the mattress. "I guess I was supposed to sleep in this big bed, all by myself, while you slept in your box." He stretched out on the surface, sighed, then lifted his head. "Well, aren't you going to get into that thing?"

"I'm not tired." I stared at him for a while and a slow smile grew on my lips. I unbuttoned my coat and tossed it on a chair next to me. Crossing to the bed, I straddled Mitch's hips with my legs and kissed him on the nose. "Besides," I said, my voice a hoarse whisper, "I want to try out the bed first."

His eyes shone with a familiar intensity. "Right here?" he asked, "with the entire Cadre surrounding us?"

"The Cadre be damned."

"My thoughts exactly, Mrs. Greer." He pulled me down on top of him and rolled us both over. His cool mouth brushed mine, then traveled to my neck, taking small playful nips. I shivered at the sensation and he laughed in delight. "I wonder," Mitch whispered against my neck and I could feel his sharpened teeth graze the skin, "how it would feel to drink from you while you drank from me as we made love?" He paused briefly and his breath was warm, enticing. "Shall we find out?"

I did not need to say anything; he could surely feel the response building in my body as I arched my back and pressed up against him. My gums tingled with the growth of my canines and although I had just fed, an overwhelming hunger washed over me. I had only one thought before the instincts took full grasp of me; I need never again struggle to hold back my passion. My hunger and appetite could no longer threaten the life of this man.

That he was technically not a man now, but a

different creature, a vampire, did not enter my mind. He was Mitch and I loved him. He eased himself from me slightly and his hands traveled down my body, touching and undressing me until I finally lay naked underneath him. The texture of his bulky sweater and the hard coarseness of the jeans he still wore pressed against my bare skin nearly driving me crazy with my need. I reached up and roughly grabbed fistfuls of his sweater, impatiently pulling it over his head and throwing it to the floor. I ran my nails up his back and he stared down at me, not moving, his eyes so blue and intense that I felt bathed in their light. Then their expression changed so suddenly and he jumped up from me so abruptly that I felt I had been dropped off a steep cliff.

"Cover yourself," he growled, "there's someone outside the door."

Four

Mitch did not bother to put his sweater back on; he bounded across the room and flung the door open with an incoherent snarl.

"Well, hello, you must be Mitchell Greer." I instantly recognized the voice, high-pitched, but with a slight lisp and a reverberating huskiness that almost caused the hair on the back of my neck to rise. Wrapping the red brocade spread around me, I slid off the bed and went to stand next to Mitch.

"Vivienne," I said, my tone wary and cautious, "it is good to see you again."

Her eyes raked over me, mocking, yet caressing and she pulled me to her briefly and kissed my cheek. "But of course, when I hear my sister has returned, I wanted to give her a welcome."

I introduced them. "Mitch, this is Vivienne; I don't believe you met her last time we were here."

"Sister?" Mitch questioned, not taking his eyes from her. "Deirdre is an only child."

Vivienne threw her head back and laughed her light metallic laugh. "I know that's how she would wish it, but sisters we are nevertheless.

And," her eyes focused on Mitch's bare torso, "I couldn't miss the opportunity to meet my new brother-in-law. But I have interrupted a *ménage à deux,* haven't I? I was so anxious to see you both, that I hadn't thought you might be otherwise involved. Please forgive me."

Vivienne headed for the door, then turned with her hand on the knob. "One other thing, *mon chers,* the days are long here and the corridors are completely safe from sunlight, so after your, ah, sleep, you may wander around as much as you like. And should you wish to join me for a glass of wine, I'd be happy to have you both. Good day." Opening the door, she walked out with a slow, sensuous stride. I reached over, closed and locked the door then looked at Mitch.

"You can stop drooling now, Mitch." I was only half-joking. Vivienne was equipped with more magnetism than should be permissible and even I, who knew her for what she was and could never trust her, felt the effect of the utter sensuality she exuded. Mitch hadn't any previous experience with another female of our kind and I feared his response to her.

His face lit up with a boyish smile as his eyes searched mine. "Why, Mrs. Greer," he drawled, enjoying the moment immensely, "I do believe you're jealous."

"Now, why would I be . . . ?" I started, then returned his grin with a smile of my own. "Yes, you're right. I am jealous."

"Good." His smile faded with that one word.

"Good?"

"Yeah, it almost makes up for all the other men in your life."

"Mitch, my love, there's never been anyone else since we met. You know that."

He frowned. "Except of course for all the men you had in England while I was institutionalized."

"Mitch, that's just plain cruel. I was not talking of food; I was talking of love. Surely you know the difference by now."

"I try, Deirdre."

I reached out and touched his cheek gently. "Yes, you do. And you are getting better. Now, speaking of love . . ." Dropping the spread I had wrapped around me, I grabbed the waistband of his jeans and pulled him to me.

"And food." His voice was warm and husky against my hair.

"And food," I agreed. "I believe you made quite an interesting proposition before we were interrupted."

"So I did," Mitch said and pulled me down to the floor with him. Rolling on top of me, he hesitated. "But I don't want to hurt you."

"As if you could."

Mitch's eyes lit with passion. He eased his jeans off and lay on top of me for a while, not moving. Then he began to nuzzle the side of my neck, gently at first with just his lips and tongue. His mouth traveled to my breasts, teasing each nipple with his front teeth, but not using his sharpening canines, not yet. I gasped when he reached between my legs, probing and stroking until I felt ready to melt. Time seemed suspended as he continued his ministrations, touching, licking, nipping.

Finally, not wanting to wait for him any longer, I reached down, guiding him inside me. And as he plunged deep within me, his mouth came down on my neck, his bite punctured my skin and I screamed, past caring about where I was and who might hear. He continued thrusting into me and I felt the blood rushing through my veins to answer his kiss. My own teeth sharpened and found his neck, pulling his blood into my mouth, savoring the rich and salty taste that was his alone.

The only sound in the room was our muffled sucking and the slapping of our sweaty bodies together. We continued for a long time, an eternity it seemed, making love and drinking from each other, constantly stoking our passion, continually renewing our strength. Then he withdrew his mouth from my neck and I did the same. He kissed me. The taste of my blood on his tongue was intriguing, enticing and I shuddered over and over as our bodies reached their endless climaxes.

When it was over, he rolled from me with a sigh. "You know," he said, finally, his voice low and breathless, "that has got to be against the law."

My laugh was shaky. "Yes, but we are, after all, consenting adults."

"Even so."

I snuggled into his side and he rested his hand lightly against my hip.

"I hope we didn't disturb the rest of the Cadre." He sounded smug and unconcerned.

"Like hell you do. You wouldn't have wanted Vivienne to miss out on what a great catch you are."

"Deirdre," he slapped me playfully on the thigh, "I like you like this."

"Like what? All sweaty and sticky?"

"No, jealous. It makes me feel wanted."

I gave him a little push, got up from the floor and stared down at him. "You should never have any doubt about that. But for now, I need a shower. Would you like to join me?"

"Hot water?"

I remembered the one shower we had taken while he was still human. The temperature of the water had been extremely uncomfortable for him. But it was not so now. I smiled at him, "Boiling, of course."

"Great."

We slept undisturbed until early the following evening. Mitch woke first and by the time I opened my eyes, he was already completely dressed, sitting on the side of the bed. "Good morning," he said and kissed the end of my nose, "did you sleep well?"

I stretched slightly and yawned. "Yes, actually, I did." I gave a little smug smile. "The plane trip really tired me out."

"Only the plane trip, huh? Well, if that's what it takes to get you a good day's sleep, I guess we'll have to fly every night."

"Fine by me."

He reached toward me, then over me, and picked up the phone from the bedside stand. I gave him a questioning look.

"I'm calling Chris," he said, his expression changing to worry, "I thought he'd want to know we were in town."

"That's a good idea, tell him I said hello." I got up from bed, went into the bathroom and closed the door behind me, allowing him as much privacy as was possible. I washed my face, brushed my teeth and hair, and inserted a pair of contact lenses. When I came back out, Mitch was unpacking his suitcase, hanging up what little he had brought with him in an ornate carved armoire. He stopped and looked over at me.

"Chris wasn't home. I left a message and this number. Do you think that'll be okay?"

I shrugged. "Who knows? But I'm sure if it's not, someone will let us know." I went to my own case, opened it, and pulling out some underwear, my black leather jeans and an ivory tunic sweater, began to get dressed.

"Personally, I wouldn't be surprised to find out that the entire setup here was wired, phones and all, with Victor being so extremely security conscious."

"That may be true, but you can't really blame him. He takes his responsibility for the Cadre very seriously." I glanced over at him while I

zipped up my pants. "The same way you would,
if the job were yours. The two of you are very
similar."

Mitch threw his head back and laughed.
"That'll be the day— Mitchell Greer, the grand-
exalted poobah of the Cadre."

"You never know, my love. Another couple of
centuries and the position might be open."

"I doubt it," Mitch said, "Victor's just too
damned pompous to die."

I shivered at his words. "Please don't talk about
it. I just barely survived the death of Max with
my sanity intact. God knows what would happen
if Victor . . ." Suddenly, I wanted to weep. I sat
down on the edge of the bed, curled my legs
underneath me and put my hands over my face. I
felt him move to me and stand by my side. Gently, he laid his hand on my shoulder.

"What's wrong, Deirdre?"

Shaking my head slightly, I moved my hands
down my face and clasped them together under
my chin, as if in prayer. Then I looked down at
them, flexed my fingers and dropped them in
my lap. "I don't know, Mitch. Maybe it's just the
atmosphere here— it's so confining, so old.
Maybe it's being called back here and being co-
erced into killing another vampire. Damn it all,
I don't want to do it. I don't want to see Larry
Martin ever again and, when I do, I have no real
desire to kill him." I jumped up from the bed
and paced around the room, searching for something, I didn't know what. "I need a window, I

need to see outside. I'd go crazy if I had to live here for long."

He stood, staring at me for a while. "Well, maybe you can't kill him, but I can."

"I don't want him dead." The desperation in my voice filled the room.

"How can you say that, Deirdre? I guess that after all he's done, you'd just like to invite him over for a drink. How could you have any sympathy for him at all? You should hate him. Have you forgotten what he did to Gwen, what he tried to do to you, what he did to me?" Anger crept into his voice, overlaying the concern for me and the confusion caused by my statement.

At the mention of her name, I was reluctantly swept back to the night that we had found Gwen dead, staked to my bed, her dying blood coating the room around her. I remembered the night Larry attempted to drive a stake through my heart at the Ballroom. I remembered Mitch after his last, almost fatal encounter with Larry; my fear of losing Mitch to death was what had forced me to perform his transformation. I had good reason to hate Larry and hate him I did, desperately, with a fervor beyond any comprehension. His death would be just and deserved. But, another part of me wailed, he was part of me, part of my life, and my blood flowed in his veins. We were bonded together like mother and child.

I gave a choked sob. "God, Mitch, don't you understand? When I killed Max, he didn't die—he stayed with me. That was bad enough and I loved *him*. But if I had to live with Larry inside me, I wouldn't be able to handle it. I'd rather walk out right now and wait for the sun."

"But if I were to kill him, he probably wouldn't . . ." his voice trailed off.

I walked over to him and put my hands on his shoulders. "The true fact of the matter is that no one knows what will happen. No one, not even Victor."

"But didn't Victor tell you that what happened between you and Max was a rarity, that his possession of you was unusual?"

"Now look who's taking Victor's side. I wouldn't like to trust my life and my sanity to his assumptions, thank you."

He ran his hands down my arms and pulled me to him. "Then what do we do?"

I looked up at him with a half-smile. "Damned if I know, my love. If we're lucky, we won't be able to find him at all. Hopefully, he's already left town."

"Larry, leave town?" Mitch gave a small snort. "I wouldn't bank on it— not when he's having such a good time."

"No," I said sadly, "neither would I."

We stared at each other for a long time, needing no words, then he kissed me, leisurely, passionately, as if our love was the only thing that mattered. And when our lips separated and he moved away from me, I sighed.

Mitch smiled. "So, shall we go?"

"Where?"

"Where else?" His mouth twisted into a grimace. "The only lead we have and I wish to hell it had burned to the ground years ago. The god-damned Ballroom of Romance, of course."

Five

The Ballroom had not changed. I am not sure why I had expected it would. The line to get in was probably shorter than in previous years, but from the noise of the crowd within, it was obvious that the place was still quite popular. Not recognizing the doorman, I gave him my name and asked to speak with Fred. Mitch studied the doorman intently, trying, I thought, to ascertain if he was one of our kind. I tilted my head slightly at him as we entered and Mitch responded with a slightly sheepish smile. There was no way of telling, it seemed.

"Miss Griffin," the doorman turned around and smiled at me, "Fred's expecting you. We have your regular table reserved."

I must have stared at him open-mouthed. This same event could have occurred last year or five years ago. How many times had I heard similar words from similar doormen? Had everything changed so little? It seemed my life was an endless coil, beginning and ending here. Sensing my confusion, Mitch took my arm and squeezed it reassuringly. "That'd be fine," he said, "thank you."

"Are you okay?" Mitch leaned over and whispered after we were seated. "You seem sort of disjointed."

"I want out of this, Mitch. The situation, the city, everything. How many times do I need to go through this?"

He nodded as if he understood. "But this time you have me around, and I won't let you down."

I touched his cheek. "I know you won't."

"Ah, so here's the happy couple." Fred's voice cut over the dance music as he sat down at the table. "It's nice to see you both again. Under better circumstances, I hope."

"That depends," Mitch's voice was cold, "on whether you still have your gun and whether you plan to strong-arm us again."

"I think we're on the same side this time, Greer. No hard feelings, huh? You didn't exactly do me any favors last time we met, either. I'd spent quite a lot of time worming my way into the Cadre's inner circle and it only took one look from Deirdre to drop me back down. I would have handled her a little differently had I known." As usual, his tone was nasty and malicious, but he shook his head a bit and managed to give us an almost friendly smile. "But, Victor tells me that if I help you it will give me a chance to gain back some ground. So, what exactly can I do for you?"

"Larry Martin." Mitch's voice was low, persuasive. "We need to find him. Fast."

Fred shrugged. "Yeah, he's been around. And all this time we thought he was dead." He gave me a shrewd look. "Can't quite figure that one out. Care to enlighten me?"

"Occupational hazard." Mitch's tone allowed no argument. "So, has he been here tonight?"

"No, not yet." Fred looked at his watch, "but it's still early. I expect he'll be hungry."

Mitch stood up and grabbed the lapels on Fred's jacket. "You knew he was coming here, picking up people and killing them, didn't you? Why didn't you try to stop him?"

Fred brushed at Mitch's hands, shrugging when he couldn't remove them. "I had no orders about him whatsoever. Why the hell should I get involved?"

Mitch gave an exasperated sigh and dropped his hands. "Why the hell, indeed." He sat back down at the table. "Get out of here," he muttered between his clenched teeth, "you make me sick."

Fred raised his eyebrows and gave a low laugh. "No problem, Greer." Then he looked at me. "Quiet tonight, aren't you, Deirdre? Shall I have a bottle of your favorite wine sent over while you wait?"

"That would be fine, thank you, Fred."

I watched him walk away from our table and surveyed the room, my eyes darting back and forth over the dancing forms. "I think I may sell this place, Mitch. Who needs it?"

"Good idea," he agreed, giving me a boyish grin, "or like I suggested earlier, burn it to the ground." He ran his fingers through his gray hair and grew instantly sober. "Maybe we can arrange for Fred to be inside at the time. And a few others I can think of . . ."

Mitch's voice trailed off when the waiter arrived at our table with the wine and glasses. After he left, I glanced around uneasily. "Mitch, you shouldn't say that here, or anywhere. Someone might take you seriously."

"I am serious, Deirdre. Unfortunately, I'm still too much of a cop to put my thoughts into action. But so help me God, if this situation puts you into any sort of danger, or hurts you in any way, I won't rest until the goddamn Cadre is ground into dust." His eyes flashed at me across the table. "And," he said, his voice full of determination, "I'm just the man to do it."

I reached over the table and cupped his cheek gently in my palm. "I know, my love, but it won't be necessary. I'm a big girl now and can take care of myself."

He pulled my hand to his mouth and kissed it. "I won't take the chance of losing you, Deirdre, not after it took me so long to get you."

"We'll do this together," I began, then stiffened as one of the dancers I had been idly watching turned and met my stare. His mouth twisted into a smile, a smile that at one time had seemed to me to be innocent and trusting. Now it was merely a grimace, an evil, tormented gesture from a damned soul. Through the darkness that hung over him, I could finally see him clearly. The smell of death coated him. Even the familiar scent of his cologne, one I once thought enticing and alluring, could not disguise the odor of decay and rotting flesh that engulfed him and the air surrounding him. And I, who thought I'd experienced every possibility in my unnatural lifetime, realized that I had never been faced with true evil until this moment. The dark sins that had haunted Max were nothing compared to the utter grotesqueness of the inhuman creature now boldly meeting my gaze and slowly crossing the room to the table where Mitch and I sat.

"Deirdre," Larry said when he came close enough to be heard over the band, "and Mitch." His eyes widened slightly, as if he were not expecting Mitch to be here. Of course, I thought quickly, Larry'd believed Mitch was dead. But he did not allow this surprise to interrupt his flow. "Mother and, ah, father, so to speak. I have so much to be grateful to the both of you for. Your bullet," he nodded at Mitch, "and your blood, Mother." He reached out and stroked my cheek, grinning at the shudder he caused. "The combination of those two things gave me everything I ever wanted. May I join you?"

Without waiting for our assent, Larry pulled a chair from the table, spun it around and straddled it, leaning himself toward me. "I wondered when you would get back in town, you might even say I was expecting you." He laughed, a low, sinister and mirthless sound. "I knew they'd send for you to clean up your dirty laundry."

I sat silently for a moment, staring at him, trying to determine exactly where his radiated evil dwelled. His physical looks were unchanged; he was still a blond, blue-eyed, broad-shouldered young man, handsome and innocent in his appearance. Even as he sat talking to us, I caught the interested glances some of the girls in the club directed his way.

The differences in him were subtle, but obvious when I looked closer. Now his mouth was drawn out, tightened in pain or anger. His eyes moved about nervously, betraying a manic attitude; his voice had acquired a malevolent edge. When he spoke, his tongue darted out of his mouth, like a reptile's scenting the air for prey. Underlying my repulsion and disgust, however, I could still feel the strength of the blood bond between us. And the realization that I had somehow given birth to this monster made my stomach wrench and the bile rise in my throat.

"So," Larry said, returning my look, "what exactly did the Cadre ask you to do with me?" His tone was one of amusement as if we were exchanging pleasantries or jokes.

"They told us we could kill you." Mitch's voice held no lightness, only a bitter hatred and Larry turned away from me and directed his gaze on Mitch.

"Did they?" Other than a quick intake of breath and a slight quaver in his voice, Larry's assurance never faltered. "Now that's an interesting development. I thought that the killing of another vampire was a definite no-no."

"Believe me, Martin, they'll make an exception in your case. As for me, I've already killed you once. I'd like nothing better than to do the job right this time." Mitch gave a little grunt and ran his fingers through his hair. "But Deirdre doesn't want you dead. God knows why."

"Why, Deirdre," Larry reached over and touched the top of my hand, "I didn't think you cared. I'm touched."

I pulled away from him abruptly, wiping my hand on the leather leg of my pants. "I don't care, Larry. I just don't want to be involved in your death."

"Whatever." He shrugged. "Either way works for me. So what do we do now?"

I was amazed at his compliance, almost as much as the calm assurance in my voice when I answered him. "If you agree, we go back to Cadre headquarters and arrange for a hearing."

"Just like that, huh? And who guarantees my safety when I get there?"

"I will, Larry." My eyes met his and I knew he could read the truth in them. "I will guarantee your safety, if you accept the Cadre's decision."

"Done. But let's finish the wine first, okay?" Larry called the waiter over, asked for another glass, then turned his chair slightly so that he could watch the dancers while he waited. "I guess," he said, his voice soft now, almost wistful, "that asking you to dance is out of the question."

I could feel Mitch tense, but caught his eye and shook my head slightly. I had a responsibility here, one that I had shirked before, one that was mine alone. For although it had been Mitch's bullet that allowed the blending of my blood with Larry's, it had been my presence and my life that originally set him out on the dark path he now walked. I had left town to pursue my own selfish interests, knowing full well of his twisted rebirth. I should have stayed to teach him, to comfort him. Perhaps if he would accept me now, it was still not too late for me to show him a better way.

"Larry," I said, standing up and taking his hand in mine, suppressing a shudder of distaste, "I would be happy to dance with you."

So I led him to the dance floor; he put his arms around me and we began to dance. The defiance and the cockiness that he had earlier displayed vanished; the evil air he exuded was still apparent, but was now subdued by a sadness, a solemnness. He held me almost reverently, as if I were delicate and breakable. Even though aware of Mitch's watchful stare, I finally relaxed in Larry's arms; he must have felt the easing of my tension, he tightened his hold on me and sighed.

Slowly we circled the dance floor, saying nothing, not even looking at each other. Every so often, I would catch Mitch's eye as we went around and I would nod to him and smile. Mostly my attention was centered on Larry and the conflicting emotions he was causing in me. The loathing and the disgust at his murderous actions still existed in me, but at war with them was the feeling that had been caused by his earlier greeting of me as "Mother." It was true— I was as much his mother as Max had been my father and

Larry had been as much betrayed, abandoned, and left to his own resources as I had been. But the biggest difference was that I had known of his existence and had chosen to do nothing to help him.

The band started another slow song and I felt Larry's grip on me change. I looked up at him and he gave me a small smile, but looked away from my direct gaze. "Deirdre," he said, and his mouth quivered, "I want to tell you what happened to me, how I have been fighting for survival. Will you listen, I mean, really listen? Will you try not to judge me too harshly?"

I swallowed hard. "I'll try, Larry, I really will."

"Can we go somewhere private, do you think?"

"Well," I hesitated, "I doubt that Mitch would stand for that. At least here he can see us."

Larry nodded. "Yeah, I understand. He should probably join us anyway, even though he hates me."

"You can't really blame him for hating you, you know." I smiled a bit to ease the tension. "You did try to kill him, after all."

"And he tried to kill me," Larry said, the madness seeming to return briefly to his voice. "But I guess," and he sighed again, deliberately controlling his temper, "that probably just makes us even. And here we both are, alive and well, no harm done."

Although I thought that point was extremely

debatable, I let it go. "Shall we see what kind of shape Fred's been keeping Max's office in?"

"Sure." He dropped his arms from me and stood back. "And thanks."

Six

The three of us entered Max's office, escorted by Fred, who sounded almost apologetic when he opened the door. "I hope you don't mind, Deirdre," he said, giving me a sidelong glance, "Victor thought it was time for a change in here. After you left town, he called me back to manage the place again. And my first job was to clear everything out of here, then redecorate the room. What do you think?"

Larry moved in quickly and settled in on one of the sofas; Mitch gave him a sharp hateful glare, then went to the bar and began to open a bottle of wine. I stood in the doorway, looking around me, a smile beginning to etch itself upon my face. Suddenly, Max's office wasn't Max's office anymore. It had been totally redone since the last time I'd seen it, over two months ago.

All traces of what had been here before were erased. Gone was the dark, brooding atmosphere that had been so prevalent; now everything was airy, light, and feminine, almost too feminine. The windows were covered with heavy beige tapestry curtains, patterns of gold, mauve, and pale green woven throughout, the carpet was a pale, plush ivory. The sofas were covered in a print damask to match the curtains, the chairs and desk were Queen Anne styling. Even the bar had been replaced, with a delicate-looking wicker one and the stools had been covered with fabric that matched the sofas. I was delighted, not so much by the decor, but by the fact that finally something had changed. The very thought that this office, a place that had remained static for close to ten years, was now a different place, no longer haunted by ghosts of the past, lightened my spirits.

When I started to laugh, Fred stated defensively, "Well, if you don't like it, we can have it changed, you know."

"I am not laughing about that, Fred. It's lovely, really." Knowing that I could not explain my sudden levity, I searched for an excuse. "I, well, I was just trying to visualize you with the decorator, choosing fabric swatches."

I was surprised to see him blush. "You thought that I did this, myself. No, actually Vivienne made all the arrangements."

"Oh," Mitch said, his voice filled with amusement, his eyes catching mine, "Vivienne."

Larry caught the look exchanged between Mitch and me, and gave a little snort. Mitch glared at him and the room suddenly seemed filled with tension.

No fool, Fred edged away to the door. "If there's nothing else, I'll leave the three of you alone. You want I should lock the door?"

"Yeah, do that." Mitch came around the bar

with a glass of wine for me and Larry, then, as the door closed and the latch clicked shut, went back for his drink, a scotch on the rocks. I wondered if Larry would recognize this as a sign of Mitch's bad temper, but with the icy blue stare directed at him, I realized that for Larry the clue was probably not necessary.

"So," Mitch sat down on one of the side chairs, and I sat down on the sofa facing Larry, "Deirdre says you have a story to tell us, something that might just keep me from killing you right here, right now. It'd better be good."

Larry gave him a glance out of the corner of his eyes, then looked over at me. I could almost tell what he was thinking: Mitch might be the judge, the one to pass sentence, but I was the jury. So he presented his case to me, completely ignoring Mitch. "You were right, you know."

"I? What was I right about, Larry?"

He gave a sigh. "That this life is not a gift, but a curse. That no one in their right mind would seek out this life." He shifted a bit uneasily on the sofa. "But then again, I was not completely sane at that time. I am now, you have to believe that, Deirdre."

I said nothing, but nodded. He certainly spoke with clarity, and his voice seemed calm, untroubled. But the glint of his eyes worried me. I could feel Mitch's body tense, heard ice clink as he took a drink, saw his stare fasten on Larry over the rim of his glass. "Go on, Larry," I urged softly.

"Looking back on it all, I think the worst part was waking up in the morgue." He drained his wine and looked down at the glass in confusion, as if wondering what it was doing in his hand. Then he shuddered and paused for a bit. When he finally continued, his voice was low and shaky. "Or maybe that was just the start of the nightmare . . . I probably don't need to tell you, Deirdre," and he began rolling the wine glass back and forth in his hands, "about the utter confusion of the senses I experienced when I woke up. The entire world I thought I'd known had changed: the sights, the smells, even the textures were all different— they were sharp and hurt me, physically. It was like I was a baby, who'd fought his way from the womb and burst screaming into his new environment. But not a baby, because I was born fully aware and functional. I knew instantly where I was and what I'd become. There was the coolness of the slab beneath my cold skin, the coarse weave of the sheet thrown over my body, the odors of death and disinfectant all around."

I grew increasingly fascinated with his account, his voice was emotionless, almost a drone now, and he was still rolling the bowl of the wine glass over and over between his palms.

"When I sat up, the sheet fell from my face. The bodies around me stunk of decay, and the lights stung my eyes. I glanced down at my chest and saw only a fading scar from where Mitch's bullet had exited. There was no sign of my skin having been cut open, so I assumed they had not gotten around to my autopsy yet." Larry stopped for a minute, looked away from his hands and into my eyes. "Would that have killed me, do you think?"

I answered him truthfully, "I have no idea."

Mitch's response was a short grunt, then he got up from the chair and refilled his glass at the bar. He lifted the bottle of wine and raised an eyebrow to me, but I shook my head. I did not want anything to break Larry's concentration.

I shouldn't have worried, he was too submersed in his past to let himself be distracted. The words flowed from him as if breaking down a dam. And perhaps they were; I remembered the utter loneliness of my earlier days. It would have been a joy and a release to have others of my kind to talk to.

"Well," Larry gave a small, mirthless grin, "I sure as hell didn't stay around long enough to find out. I found an extra set of lab whites in one of the open lockers, dressed myself and just walked out." His grin turned into a choked, almost furtive laugh. "I wondered how they'd explain the missing body. But, hell, from the looks of the place, they had so many of them and I figured that one less probably wouldn't be noticed for a long time. And they certainly wouldn't expect the corpse to be walking around."

Mitch settled back into his chair. "It was chalked up to paperwork error," he said curtly, "happens all the time."

"Oh, that's good then. No APB out on me."

"Well," Mitch gave him a grim look, "not per se."

Larry shrugged. "It hardly matters anyway. Now where was I?"

"Leaving the morgue."

Larry gave Mitch one last glance, then concentrated his efforts on me once again. "When I got out onto the street, into the night, it was like something exploded in my head, turning me completely inside out. The way the air smelled, the way the people smelled of blood and flesh and perfume . . ." He put his head back for a minute, resting it on the couch and sighed deeply, staring blankly at the ceiling. "Oh, now that part's probably worth everything else. You know, the way the city seems to touch your skin, the way the night seeps into you, filling you, completing you."

When Larry lifted his head, he looked first at me and then at Mitch; the air grew electric between the three of us. We were, for the first time since our lives intersected, in perfect concordance. "But I guess," he said with a shaky, passionate laugh, "I don't need to explain that to you, do I? You both know it as well as I do." He paused for a moment, collecting his thoughts, the wine glass still carefully grasped between his palms. "I walked the streets that first night, not caring where or even what I was. Just enjoying the feeling of being alive again, you know, being aware. I was so wrapped up in my senses I forgot about sunrise; so involved with the strength and immortality of my new body I almost blew it." His mouth twisted into a smile, mocking his newborn naiveté.

"Too bad you didn't." Mitch's harsh whisper carried clearly through the room.

But Larry either didn't hear Mitch's statement or chose to ignore it. "Fortunately I was near a subway stop when the sun came up. I ran down the steps and hid out the day there, far enough into the tunnel so that I would be safe. I curled into a ball with my back to the entrance and slept. When I awoke at sunset, the whole process began again: the sensory barrage, the fascination with the strength of my body, the scent of the night, but this time there was something else, a closer, more intimate sensation. I realized suddenly that a pair of arms were wrapped around me, that a warm, human body was pressed into my back. I pried the arms from me and rolled over.

"It was an old woman, a street dweller by the looks of her. She was dirty, smelly, her clothes were ragged and filthy; by her head was a large bag, stuffed with more rags, odds and ends that she must have valued. As I looked closer I realized that she was not so much old as used up, her face was dirt-streaked, but unwrinkled and her hair had only a little bit of gray mixed into the greasy brown. Her mouth was hanging open, she was snoring softly, and her breath stunk of alcohol. I figured she must have stumbled into the tunnel some time during the day, seen me and passed out beside me, taking comfort from the only sort of human contact she could have. Or," his eyes acquired a manic gleam, and he shrugged, grinning, "maybe she had the hots for my body. Who knows? Anyway, I reached over and shook her. She mumbled in her sleep, put an arm up around my neck and pulled my mouth down to hers.

"And then," Larry's voice began to shake, and I shuddered, "then, the hunger struck me. At first I thought it was a sexual thing, you know, her mouth was working on me, kissing me and I got hard, real hard. I started to undress her, strip her down through the many layers of dirty rags. By the time she was completely naked, she was half-awake, her eyes were open and she gave me a sort of sleepy smile. Her skin was almost clean where it'd been covered, and most of the bad odors had been removed, tossed away with her clothes. And I wanted her, or something, so very bad I couldn't control myself. Didn't care about anything but fulfilling the desire that was overcoming me with each moment."

Larry got up from the couch so quickly that I jumped, startled. I heard Mitch's soft intake of breath and watched Larry cross the room, pull aside the drapes and look out into the city night. He remained facing the window as he continued to tell his story. "So I screwed her, right there in the subway tunnel. Over and over again, I pounded into her. She enjoyed it at first, I think, she made all the right noises, but when I wouldn't stop— I couldn't stop, there was no satisfaction, no climax, just an uncontrollable hunger, an uncontrollable lust— she tried to push me away from her. She was whimpering softly and crying, and *she* tried to push *me* away from her." The pitch of Larry's voice rose, the tone was indignant, arrogant. "I think I laughed then, knowing that she was mine, however I wanted to use her. 'Can't take it, can you, bitch?' I said to her as I pulled her tightly to me again, still driving into her. And then," Larry stopped for a long second and a low-pitched growling noise emerged from his throat. A noise so inhuman, yet so in tune with how I felt, the hair on my arms began to rise.

"And then, my mouth found her neck."

He had still been holding the empty wine glass in his hands throughout the story. Now he brought his palms together, crushing the crystal, the tinkling of the shards was loud and compelling. More compelling was his deep intake of breath and the odor of blood that filled the room. I could remember the scent and even the taste of Larry's blood, but it seemed different now, tinged with an unfamiliar flavor. And I knew I was scenting, tasting the blood of the nameless woman in the subway, as easily as if the mouth on her neck was my own.

"And when her blood poured into my mouth, it was like every vein in my body exploded. I could feel the blood flowing through me, could tell that it was strengthening my body, my muscles, my bones. It was like a drug. No, it *is* a drug; I'd never been so high in my entire life. Never felt so alive or so vital. And the whole time that I sucked on her, I could taste her fear and her pain, feel her feeble attempts to pull away from me, from my mouth and my dick still thrust deep within her. And that only enhanced my enjoyment of the blood. The element of danger, the black chilled air of the tunnel, even her unwilling surrender spurred me on to continue to drink and drink and drink.''

Larry pulled in a long breath. "I drained her completely, still screwing her, drawing out her life. She was dead even before I had finished. And after I was through with her, I tossed her body onto the tracks. When they found her, she'd be just another homeless lush, passed out drunk and run over by a train. Any traces of me would be wiped out with the crushing of her body under the rails.''

There was a long, unbroken silence.

Somewhere outside this office the band played and people danced and laughed and drank; somewhere outside these doors people led normal lives, unaffected by dark hungers and thirsts and the desire for death. I realized then that the newly decorated office was a mockery and a sham. It made no difference. It was still Max's office, would always be. And the three creatures who occupied the room were just a continuation of his dark legacy.

I wanted to say something, wanted to cry out in protest, wanted to throw myself into Mitch's arms and take comfort there. But there was no comfort to be had. Larry was my creation, my child. And I was fully a part of the atrocities he had committed. I closed my eyes tightly against the tears that were forming and sat straight and rigid on the sofa.

When the voice spoke again, I wasn't entirely

sure that it wasn't mine. "And then I realized that this was what life truly is. It isn't the deceptive beauty of the night or the enhanced senses, it isn't the perfection of the body or the immortality of the soul. It is the taking, it's the seduction, it's the blood and the death." Larry laughed and broke the spell his story had cast. "And ever since then, I've been fulfilling that destiny. Living this life as it was meant to be lived. Although," he came away from the window and sat back down on the couch, pulling small pieces of glass out of his palms, "you know, sometimes I still wonder if what I am living is reality or fantasy."

Mitch cleared his throat slightly and his voice sounded hoarser than normal. "Well, it sure as hell isn't a fantasy for the people you murder."

Larry looked over at Mitch, a surprised expression on his face. "But it's not murder," he said confidently, "it's survival. And I think you're wrong, it is a fantasy, it's all really nothing but a dream." His expression changed suddenly. "But, you see, the hunger," he said, a hard, driving anger now coloring his words, "the hunger's not a dream, it's a nightmare. I could probably live this life forever and love it, if it weren't for the hunger. There are times when it's so deep and so cold, it's like falling into a dark pit or a grave. Times when the hunger is so strong, it tears me up inside, eating my guts, gnawing at my brain. And that's why I agreed to go along with you, and why I'll let you take me in for judgment. Maybe you can take away the nightmare and cure the hunger.''

Seven

Larry had put his face into his hands and slumped down on the couch. His shoulders trembled slightly and I sat staring at him, conflicting thoughts running through my mind. I desperately wanted a shower, with water hot enough to wash his evil from me. I also found myself wanting to comfort him, remembering when he was still human, remembering the time he'd made a declaration of eternal love for me. Had I offered him comfort at that point, would this entire situation have been averted? But I'd done nothing then, and I did nothing now, sitting silently on the couch, looking at him. Finally I felt in control of my emotions enough to raise my eyes to Mitch's face.

I had expected to find revulsion there and was not disappointed. But there seemed to be something else, sympathy perhaps, or even empathy. Maybe even agreement with Larry's summation of our life. I attempted a smile, managed only a trembling twist of my mouth, but Mitch seemed to understand and nodded at me.

"Let's get this damned thing over with." Larry jumped at the sound of Mitch's voice and removed his hands from his face. Small drops of blood tracked down his cheeks. Tears, I wondered, or just the tracings from his glass-splintered palms? His eyes held no clue as they fastened on Mitch.

"So," Larry said, his voice arrogant and assured once more, "what's it going to be, Greer? Kill me or turn me over?"

"I told you already," Mitch hissed at him, "I'd just as soon kill you dead as look at you. And your story certainly did nothing to convince me that you're anything other than scum, but Deirdre doesn't want you dead." He turned to me. "Unless you've changed your mind, love?"

I shook my head. "Let the Cadre deal with him, Mitch. I don't want his death or his spirit on my conscience."

Larry glanced at me. "But you'll still speak for me?"

"I promised I would, didn't I? I won't break that promise. Are you ready to go?"

Larry shrugged, got up from the couch and headed for the door. Mitch moved after him quickly. "Just a minute, Martin," he said in a stern voice, "if I have to hand you over to those bastards at the Cadre instead of killing you, I want to make damn sure you get there." Mitch reached into his coat pocket and pulled out a pair of handcuffs. Larry gave a smirk and held out his arms. Mitch snapped one of the cuffs on him, and put the other on his own wrist. "Now, I feel better. Let's go."

* * *

It was a silent cab ride back to Cadre headquarters. Larry sat, docile; Mitch was edgy and nervous; I looked out the window. And when we arrived, Victor was waiting for us at the lower elevator doors. I registered his presence there with shock, wondering how he knew we were coming. He seemed to read my mind.

"Fred called me, of course." Victor raked Larry with a scornful glance, then looked at Mitch and me angrily. "Funny," he said with a quirk of his eyebrow, "I don't remember the 'or alive' being an option in this case."

"And I don't give a damn what you remember, Lange. This is a Cadre matter, you wanted him, we got him for you. As far as I'm concerned he's your problem now."

"And mine," I reminded Mitch gently, then turned to face Victor's glare. "I have guaranteed his safety, Victor. And I count on you to uphold my word."

"Presumptuous of you, Deirdre, don't you think?" His lip curled up into a snarl. "You knew that we wanted him dead. However, in this case your word will be considered as good as mine." He stopped, his expression lightened and he gave me a slight bow. "Then again, you may have hit upon the best solution; there has been worry among some of our younger members that if we have this rogue killed, they might be next." Victor laughed. "Can't have dissension among the ranks now, can you?"

"I suppose not. Larry has agreed to stand trial and to accept the Cadre's disciplinary actions."

"And where in all the Cadre can I find some-one to stand for him?"

I met Victor square in the eyes and raised my voice to fill the empty hall behind me. "As a member of the House of Leupold, I will stand for him." Softening the formality of my voice, I continued. "Which is only right, considering he is my responsibility."

"Done and accepted," Victor agreed. "Now, Mitch, if you would kindly come with me and bring the prisoner with you." I moved to accompany them but Victor held out a hand. "You should go to your room, Deirdre. This does not concern you, yet."

His order angered me. "The hell it doesn't."

"Deirdre, please. I will explain this to you later, trust me." The sudden kindness in his voice decided me.

"Fine." My tone was still unhappy, but not defiant. I kissed Mitch lightly on the cheek. "Later, my love."

I could feel three pair of eyes on my back as I walked down the hall and entered the room.

The Cadre staff had been busy in our absence; the bed had been made, the bathroom cleaned and sitting next to my coffin was a larger but plainer one, obviously meant for Mitch. I shook my head, laughing only a little, hoping that he wouldn't want to live the experience and sleep in that crate tonight. Crossing the room, I sat on the edge of the bed and jumped when the phone rang right next to me.

"Hello?" I answered tentatively.

There was a pause on the end of the line. Then a familiar voice. "Deirdre, um, hi. It's Chris. Is my father around?"

"No, Chris, not right now. He'll be back in a little bit, though. How are you?"

"Fine," he said, but sounded unsure. "I, ah, wasn't expecting the two of you back for a while. I guess I'll move out as soon as I can find another place."

"Well, that's something you can discuss with Mitch, I suppose. But as far as I'm concerned, you're welcome to stay there as long as you like. We may not be in town that long."

"Oh, okay." He paused.

"Well, if there's nothing else . . ."

"Tell Dad I want to see him . . ."

We both laughed as we spoke simultaneously, breaking for a moment the uneasy tension between us.

"So," Chris said, "tell Dad I'd like to have lunch with him tomorrow, if that's okay."

Now the silence was on my end. I couldn't tell him that Mitch could never meet him anywhere for lunch, ever. And I sure as hell didn't want to be the one to break the news to Chris about what his father had become.

"Deirdre, you still there?"

"Yes, Chris, I'm sorry. Someone was outside the door, here, I thought it might be your father." I laughed nervously. "False alarm, I suppose. He should be back anytime now; do you want him to call you?"

"Yeah, that'd be good."

"Fine, and you take care. I hope we'll be able to see a lot of you while we're here in town."

"Yeah, that'd be nice." Chris's voice sounded reluctant, and I knew he didn't want to spend time with me. The realization of what I was, of what sort of creature his father had married must still be fresh and horrible in his mind. "Talk to you later, then."

He hung up before I had a chance to say good-bye. I put the receiver down gently and lay back on the bed, my fingers crossed under my head, staring at the ceiling, thinking about the convoluted ties that entangled us all. Chris, Larry, Mitch, even Victor to some extent, and myself—all bound to each other, inexplicably and eternally. I found myself wishing for the first time in many years that I had actually died in the accident that had transformed me. That I had been allowed to bleed out my life with my husband on that rain-soaked road. That I had been buried with him and the seven-month-old fetus who would have been our child.

I sighed and ran my fingers over my stomach, searching for a trace of that child, remembering its kicks and movement, and the feeling of total unity with it, the bond between mother and child that death could not erase.

When Mitch finally came back into the room, I was still lying on the bed, clutching at my barren stomach, blood-tinged tears streaking down my face and moistening the red brocade spread beneath me.

He did not notice me at first. "Hey," he began,

"look what the Cadre delivered while I was out. My very own coffin . . ." His voice trailed away as he looked at me and he quickly shut the door behind him. "Deirdre, what's wrong? Why are you crying?"

I choked out the words between sobs. "Chris called."

"He made you cry?" Mitch came over to me, sat down on the bed and stroked my hair. "What the hell did that little bastard say to make you cry?"

"Nothing," I sat up and wiped at my eyes, giving him a little smile. "He started me thinking, that's all."

"Thinking about what?"

"The baby I lost." Getting up from the bed, I shrugged. "It doesn't matter, really, it was a long time ago."

He gave me a curious look. "Obviously it must matter some, for you to still cry over it."

"No, really it doesn't," I assured him. "It's just that this trip back here has been rather depressing for me. Having to deal with Larry and everything."

"Speaking of that, it's a fascinating setup the Cadre has here. Have you seen the cells, or as Victor called them, the retention rooms?"

"No, I wasn't permitted there, remember?" I went into the bathroom and splashed cold water on my face. Picking up a towel, I walked back into the room, drying myself, glad that he had been sidetracked from the previous issue. "What was so interesting?"

Mitch may have taken personal retirement from police work, but I could tell that he had lost none of his enthusiasm; of course he would find the Cadre judicial system fascinating, especially now that it no longer threatened me. "Well, there are all kinds of problems in retention, apparently, given vampiric existence and individual experience."

I wandered aimlessly around the room, clutching the towel in my hands. "So?" From my tone of voice I knew he could tell that I had no idea what he was talking about.

"Well, think about it for a minute. Older vampires have more powers than the younger ones, you know. But the security system has to be beefed up, to a level that can hold the ones who transform." He shook his head. "Although from what I can tell, the older ones generally don't need to be incarcerated. I gather that Max was an exception to that rule. You would have been too, I suppose, but you haven't yet realized your powers."

I gave a small forced laugh. "And I don't intend to do so, anytime soon."

Mitch shrugged.

"And," I continued, wanting to avoid that topic also, "I do not see how any kind of room could hold a creature who can transform himself into a mist." I walked into the bathroom and hung the towel back up.

"Airtight," he said simply.

I stood in the doorway and stared at him for

a time in shock. "Airtight? Then how do you breathe?"

Mitch gave me a broad grin. "That's the beauty of it, Deirdre, we don't need to breathe."

"But," I protested, "I breathe, you breathe. I don't understand."

"Victor was kind enough to explain it to me, although he was rather horrified that I didn't know to begin with. We actually only breathe for two reasons. One of them is force of habit, the other is so that we can speak. But our bodies don't need the oxygen to survive, all we really need is blood."

Somehow, being sealed inside a room with no air struck me as more hideous than the starvation that would accompany it, and the very thoughts of it made me shudder. "You know, Mitch," I said, changing the subject yet again, feeling the walls of this room close in around me. "You should probably call Chris now. I told him you wouldn't be too long and he'll be expecting you."

He went for the phone and began to dial.

"And by the way, my love," Mitch stopped when I spoke and looked over at me, "he wants to meet you for lunch. You'd better either tell him why you can't straight out or have a good excuse ready."

"Damn," he said quietly and hung up the receiver. "What the hell can I say?"

"You could tell him the truth, I suppose."

He snorted. "Yeah, I can hear it now. 'I'd love to meet you for lunch, son, but unfortunately I can't go out in the sun anymore, because your stepmother has turned me into an evil creature of the night.' That'd go over real well."

His words struck me hard. "Jesus, Mitch," I walked to the door and put my hand on the knob, "that was a low blow."

Our eyes locked across the room. "Deirdre, I didn't mean it like that . . ."

"I know you didn't. Why don't you stay here and talk to Chris in privacy?" I struggled to give him a smile. "You could even try out your new coffin or get someone to teach you how to transform into a mist. I need to get out of here for a while, need to be alone in an open space. I'll be back soon, I promise."

I was sure he could hear the urgency in my voice, the desperation I felt locked away in this windowless tomb. He smiled reassuringly and nodded to me. "Walk softly this night," he said, his tone husky and sincere.

The traditional greeting of the Cadre from his mouth unnerved me and I fled down the corridor, rode up in the elevator, and burst through the back entrance into the comfort of the night.

Eight

After walking several blocks, my claustrophobia faded somewhat and I felt sufficiently recovered to hail a taxi. Even at that, when I climbed into the back seat, I rolled down the window and breathed in the night air appreciatively.

Managing to make the cab driver understand my destination, I finally arrived at the dreary brick building with barred windows. I paid the driver, watched him drive away and walked up the steps to the outer door. Pausing to take a deep breath, I sighed and opened the doors to the institution that had held a crazed Mitch not so long ago. The nurse at the reception desk greeted me with a warm smile, and I laughed inwardly at the difference between her and Jean, Mitch's favorite nurse, who, we discovered later, was also a member of the Cadre. I wondered how Jean would take the news that we were back in town, and together; how she would react to the fact that Mitch had been transformed.

The current nurse interrupted my thoughts. "May I help you?"

"Yes, I'd like to speak with Dr. Samuels if he's in."

"He is." She picked up the phone. "May I give him your name?"

I nodded. "Deirdre Greer."

There was no recognition of the name in her eyes, she merely smiled again and buzzed Sam.

"Yes?" Sam's voice sounded tired and slightly depressed.

"There's a," she stopped and glanced at my left hand, seeing my wedding ring, "Mrs. Greer here to see you, Dr. Samuels. Shall I show her back?"

"Mrs. Greer?" he questioned, paused and then laughed. "Oh, yeah, of course, Mrs. Greer. Certainly, Susan, bring her back right away."

The nurse got up from her desk and motioned me to follow her down the hallway.

Sam stood waiting for me just inside his office door. "Deirdre," he said, all traces of weariness vanished from his voice, "when did you get back? Is Mitch with you?" He leaned over and kissed me on the cheek, then took my arm and guided me into his office, closing the door behind him.

"Hello, Sam," I said, settling into the chair facing his desk, wondering why I had felt the need to come here. "Mitch is in town, but didn't come with me tonight."

Sam sat down behind his desk and his eyes raked my face. "Then I guess this isn't just a social call, is it?"

"Well, no," I started, "I don't quite know why I'm here, except for the fact that I needed to talk to someone. And you seem to be the only person that I know and trust in this city that's not dead and not a . . ."

He gave me a quick glance, reached into his top drawer for his ashtray and lighter, opened a new pack of cigarettes, and offered me one. It was a ritual we'd instated while Mitch was a patient here and signaled the switch from social pleasantries to serious discussion. I accepted the cigarette and he lit mine, then lit one for himself. He inhaled deeply then blew the smoke out before speaking again.

"Not a what, Deirdre?"

"Not a vampire," I said in a small voice.

"You have trouble saying that word, don't you? A problem admitting to anyone, even yourself, what you are?" His manner became at once professional. "Would you like to talk about why this is?" He took another drag on his cigarette, paused, then choked a bit as the ultimate meaning of my words seemed to hit him. "But you said Mitch is here with you. You can trust him, for God's sake, and he's not a . . ."

I laughed a bit at his hesitation. "You see, Sam, I'm not the only one that seems to have a problem with the concept. But unfortunately, Mitch is a vampire, now."

"Jesus." He stubbed out his cigarette, only half-smoked. "How did that happen? I wouldn't have thought that you could do that to him, knowing the way you feel about your life."

"It's a long story, Sam." I took a drag on my own cigarette and flicked the growing ash into the ashtray. "And," I had a sudden thought of

Victor's security measures for the Cadre, and how he would react to my revealing its secrets to a stranger, "most of it, I should probably not tell you. I'm not at liberty to reveal certain details to you."

"Tell me what you can," he said, sharply. "I'm pretty good at piecing puzzles together."

Skipping the preliminaries, I started right in. "I transformed Mitch because I had no choice, he would have died had I not. To this day, I still wonder if that was a mistake."

"He's having trouble adjusting to the life?"

"Mitch?" I gave a low laugh and crushed my cigarette out. "Actually, he's adjusted quite well, perhaps all too well."

"Too well?"

"There are times, when I hardly recognize him," a note of panic entered my voice, "when I feel like I don't know him at all. I've never had the company of my own kind before. And Mitch is undoubtedly that." I sighed. "To be perfectly honest, Sam, he frightens me. It wasn't too bad, when we were in England and alone, but now that we're back here and surrounded by . . ." I broke off, realizing that I was saying too much, "well, surrounded by memories and the like, the reality of his, or our, existence, hits me hard."

Sam gave a noncommittal grunt and cleared his throat. I looked away from him and reached across the desk to help myself to another cigarette. As I lit it, our eyes met, locked together and I felt myself blushing under his close scrutiny.

"That wasn't what you were going to say, Deirdre. You're a terrible liar."

"Only with you, Sam. I never seem to have this problem with anyone else."

"Including yourself?"

"Especially myself. I'm very good at lying to myself." I grinned slightly and he grinned back briefly before growing serious again.

"Surrounded by what, Deirdre?"

I gave him a long, calculating look, took another drag on the cigarette and exhaled slowly. "You must promise to keep whatever I tell you in the strictest confidence. To do otherwise might have dire circumstances for you."

"Of course," Sam nodded, his voice pained. "I'll treat everything you say as patient confidentiality. I would've anyway, you should know that you can trust me."

"Well," I leaned back in the chair, "trust, as you should know by now, is an extremely rare commodity for me." But I proceeded to relate the story of the Cadre, how they had been wrongly persecuting Mitch for the murder of Max Hunter, how, when they had discovered that I had actually been the one to kill Max, I was put on trial and escaped their sentence only through Max's ghostly intervention. By the time I reached the end of my story, involving Larry's attack on Mitch and my frantic attempt to transform him before he died, we had smoked at least half of the pack of cigarettes; the room was filled with a cloudy, gray haze. Sam's eyes were red and teary, perhaps some of that was due to the smoke.

"And now?" I jumped a little at the sound of a voice other than mine.

"And now we have been brought back to New York to kill Larry Martin."

"How does that make you feel?"

"How the hell do you think it makes me feel?" I glared over at Sam from where I sat. "I don't want to kill him, or anyone. But," I shrugged away the thought, "it's out of my hands now, anyway. Mitch and I found him tonight and delivered him to the Cadre; other than speaking for him at his trial, I need never see him again."

"You're speaking for him? Why?"

"I must. He's my child."

"I see."

"Do you really?" I got up from my chair and walked around his desk to the window. Pulling aside the venetian blinds, I studied the night streets. "If you do, then you'll be the only one so far. Even Mitch wants him dead."

Sam rose from his desk and came to stand next to me. He put an arm around my shoulders and I leaned into him. Just the warmth of his human body and the fact that he showed no fear of me was comforting. I sighed, thinking that maybe it was this human contact that I missed in Mitch. Even as it crossed my mind, the disloyalty and the inherent betrayal in the thought distressed me. I loved Mitch, he was my mate, my lover, my husband. And if now he was something other than he used to be, I knew fully where the blame rested. "Damn."

"Deirdre," Sam moved away from me, seeming embarrassed by our physical contact, "I'd like to help you. I really would. But I don't quite know what to say, what to do." He gave a small laugh. "All of this is just a little out of my area of expertise."

"Yes, Sam, I know. Like I said, I'm not sure why I came here tonight."

"You already answered that question yourself, you know. You needed someone to talk to, needed a friend."

Friend? the bitter thought jumped to mind, *this man is not a friend. I have no friends. This man is prey, nothing but blood for the taking.* "Yes, well," my voice trembled with the desperate strength of that thought and I felt a tingling in my jaws. "I must go. I'll call you later, maybe we can all get together sometime, before Mitch and I leave." I moved away from the window and quickly went to the door.

"But you can't be leaving so soon. You just got here."

"Our work here is practically done, Sam, now that Larry is in Cadre custody. I need only stand for his trial. And there are too many painful memories in this city for me now, too much death, too much guilt."

"But none of that is your doing, you should know that."

I gave him a hard look as I opened the door.

"I only wish that were true, Sam." Then I hurried down the hall and moved out into the streets.

I couldn't return to Cadre headquarters, not while it was still night; couldn't lock myself into the tomblike room Mitch and I had been assigned. Just the thought of it made me shudder, made me want to run screaming down the streets. I felt confined, pent-up, suffocated. Hungry. The human scent of Sam still lingered in my nostrils. Oh, God, I was so hungry. I wanted to live the word, wanted to glut myself on blood, any blood. And as that thought took hold, so did the hunger, a blinding, burning-red wall that loomed before me, cutting me off from the rest of the world. There was, at that moment, no one who loved me and no one whom I loved. Nothing existed but a raging hunger, gnawing my stomach, and the hot wild visions of teeth tearing flesh.

I stopped dead in the middle of the sidewalk, forcing the crowd of evening pedestrians to swear and part around me. My eyes were closed, fists clenched so tightly that my nails dug deeply into the flesh of my palm. I centered on the pain, smelled the rich warm scent of blood dripping onto the concrete under my feet.

Concrete, I thought scornfully, what business did I have here, in this city, surrounded by concrete and glass and steel? A hunter was what I was: predator and creature of the night. I craved clear night skies and wide forests to run, with wild, swift and velvet-skinned prey to pursue through the evening shadows. Not puny humans with their pitiful limbs and tamed blood.

Deep shudders shook my body and I seemed to close in around myself, sinking to the sidewalk, flames of pain shooting through me. The calls for help that rose in my throat became guttural growls on the way and I felt the startled shock of the pedestrians surrounding me, scented their fear and their flesh, heard the tearing of cloth as it ripped away from my limbs. A small human voice cried out in the back of my skull. "No!"

But my body was no longer my own, and this one rejoiced in a freedom denied it for over a century. I sprang to all fours, the feel of the pavement foreign and rough beneath my paws, kicking away the last of my restrictive clothing. Glancing around, tail whipping with anger in the air, I narrowed my eyes. My sensitive ears ached with the screams of terrified humans, and I opened my mouth and roared. And then roared again, leaping forward, running for refuge in a city where none was to be had.

How long I ran, I did not know. Neither did I know if I caused harm or death. I do know that it was a futile escape; the city was endless, the forests that I craved much too far away for me to reach them. It was close to dawn when I found an alley in which to hide. For I knew I must hide, instinctively knowing the danger of the sunrise, as well as the danger from an unidentified pursuit. And although I had managed to evade capture, I was still uncannily aware of the presence of my stalker. But as I settled in, I scented the air and judged it safe for now. Curling into a corner, I licked the blood from pads of my feet, ripped into shreds by the rough concrete.

They took me completely by surprise, a man and a woman, with no fear of me in their minds as they approached. He held his hand out to me; immediately I lashed out with my claws and opened his arm from elbow to wrist. The smell of his blood filled my senses and I knew him. Our eyes met, his so intensely blue and full of love that his name came back to me. "Mitch." I could not say the word, but I know he heard, as I heard and understood my name on his lips.

The woman came over and stroked my head, teasing and caressing the soft tufts of hair around my ears. Her soft lisping voice and metallic laughter echoed off the brick walls surrounding us. "Come, sister, we must try to get you back," Vivienne laughed again, "in more ways than one, I fear."

Nine

When I finally woke, I found myself naked, covered only with the heavy red brocade spread, lying on the carpet of our room in Cadre headquarters. My arms and legs twitched as I tried to remember what had happened to me. It would have seemed a dream, except that I knew I was no longer capable of dreams. And the stale taste of blood that remained in my mouth, the undeniable ache of the loss of a freedom now beyond my reach told me that what I remembered was all too real. I sat up and looked around me, my eyes narrowed, attempting to adjust to the limitations of this different sight.

"Deirdre?" Mitch rose from where he had been stretched out in one of the chairs. He was wearing only a pair of jeans and it looked like he'd been holding vigil over me for a while. "How do you feel? Are you okay?"

I shook my aching head. "I don't know. What time is it? And what happened?"

"It's just a bit before sundown. As far as what happened, well, you changed, transformed." He smiled at me and held out a hand to pull me up to him. "Damn, it was incredible. You were beautiful."

The spread dropped from my body. I shivered and he wrapped his arms around me. "Why am I naked?"

Mitch shrugged. "When you transformed, your clothes were destroyed. They're probably lying in a heap on the street where you lost them. Vivienne says that most vampires prefer to be nude before they begin the change."

"I'll try to remember that next time." My voice was dry and I moved away from him to the dresser, finding clothes to replace those that were gone. "If there ever is a next time. I don't really remember much about it. What was I?"

"A lynx."

"A lynx?" I stepped into a pair of jeans and zipped them up. "But why?"

"Vivienne says that each individual has a different form, some even have two, one with wings and one without." His eyes met mine and his excitement at these new revelations was completely apparent. This situation was a game to him, and one that he very much wanted to play.

"No, that's not what I mean. I don't give a damn what kind animal I turned into or why I chose that particular form. The question is: why did I change at all? I had no intention to. I certainly never wanted to." I pulled on a black sweater and hugged my familiar human-shaped arms to myself, "And I never want to do so again." Even as I said it, though, I caught the faint growl of disagreement in the back of my mind. Mitch was right, it was beautiful, it was wonderful.

He ignored my denials, concentrating instead on the specifics of the change. "Vivienne says that inadvertent change can be caused by extreme emotions: fright, hunger, hate. Or by the transformation of another vampire, either nearby or linked to the other."

I sat down on the end of the bed and gave him a long calculating glance. "Then what exactly is my dear sister's assessment of the change?" My voice sounded brittle.

Mitch laughed a little. "You really are jealous of her, aren't you?"

"No, but the two of you seem to be getting very friendly. Considering you've just met."

"You *are* jealous." He smiled at me. "She's only trying to help."

"Is there any reason why we need her help? I don't trust her. Quite honestly, I don't trust any of them. And neither should you."

"Vivienne is harmless. The others, yes, you know how I feel about them. I hate them. For what they tried to do to you, for what they did to me. And yet . . ." Mitch's voice trailed off.

I could finish his thought for him. Had none of that ever happened, he wouldn't be what he was right now. And Mitch liked what he was— with almost as much fervor as I hated what he was, both for him and for me.

I sighed. There were reasons not to trust Vivienne; she had so very conveniently detained me the night of Larry's attack on Mitch. She may even have been involved in that attack. But it would do me no good to attempt an explanation right now. He was too excited with the prospect of his potential powers to listen.

"Besides," he continued, "Vivienne's okay. She had nothing to do with the threats to me or to you. And she was one of the Cadre members who decided for you during the trial. So she's on our side."

"You and me and Vivienne against the rest of them? How very cozy." I rubbed my hand over my eyes and leaned my head against the bedpost, realizing that my anger was not really meant for him. "I'm sorry, Mitch," I said, my voice softer now, "I don't mean to be so difficult. But my head aches, my body aches. And I'm very hungry."

"Yeah," he agreed, a predatory light gleaming from his eyes, "we should hunt tonight. Soon I should think. But before we do, I'd like to get reacquainted with your human form." With a low laugh he crossed the room and sat down behind me on the bed. His hands began kneading my shoulders and I leaned back into him. "How's that feel?"

I didn't answer, just gave a long, low sigh. He pushed aside my hair and nuzzled the nape of my neck. I shivered slightly and he laughed again. "You made one hell of a wild cat, you know. You practically ripped my arm open to the bone."

"Which one?"

He held out his arm and I lightly traced my

nails down his naked skin. "No scars." I sighed.
"I miss your scars. Did it hurt?"

"Just for a minute. I was so relieved to find
you before dawn that it hardly mattered. When
you didn't come back in an hour or so, I started
to worry. And then I felt you almost like you had
climbed inside me. Felt your rage, your confusion, your hunger. I thought I'd go crazy, until
suddenly there was a blankness, as if you'd been
snuffed out of existence. That was even worse."
He wrapped his arms around my neck, rocking
me slightly back and forth. I could feel the muscles of his chest play against my back. "I practically knocked down Vivienne's door trying to get
an explanation of what was happening to me and
to you. She was not pleased," Mitch chuckled and
continued, "and neither was the guy she'd been
playing with."

I laughed with him. "Well, fair is fair, after all.
It serves her right. Anyone we know?"

"No one I've ever seen before. He was very
young, very blond and very human." The last
word sounded scornful, demeaning.

"But, Mitch, it hasn't been that long since you
were human, too."

"Yeah, I know, but I'm better now."

I pulled away from him only slightly, but he
noticed immediately. "Deirdre, I was only joking.
I know how remaining human has always been
important to you. It's just that this whole thing
is so exciting for me. You should remember how
it was."

I thought for a minute before answering. I remembered all too well my initial brush with what I had become and it was anything but exciting. I'd had no one to counsel me, to support me; I had managed to survive by my wits alone, and through the intercession of a bloody and mindless war providing me with an endless supply of dying bodies on which to feed. It had been an initiation only into death and decay and the despair of unending life. For me, there had been no excitement, no joy, no hope.

"Yes, I do indeed remember how it was." I moved out of his embrace, got up from the bed, went to the door and opened it. "I have to see Larry."

It took some time to locate the administrative offices of the Cadre. The entire area below the Imperial was like a maze, endless corridors of closed doors through which I padded, barefoot, guided only by an inner sense of where I would place such offices. The halls were empty and as I walked I imagined scores of Cadre vampires prowling the streets of the city in search of prey. The thought first made me shudder then drew a grim smile to my face. For ten years I had lived in this city believing I was alone, the only one of my kind. Had I only known then, would it have made a difference to my life? Would it have made a difference to the choices I had made?

"Choices?" I muttered to myself, following the

faint noise of activity and voices I'd finally picked up. "When was I ever given choices?"

"Deirdre?"

I looked up and saw Ron, standing in an open doorway. "I want to see Larry."

He looked at me and shook his head. "Well, you sure won't find him here."

I paused for a moment, collecting my anger, centering it and met his eyes with a cold, direct stare. "Look, Ron, I've had enough of all of this bureaucratic secrecy. I have a right to speak with him, I need to speak to him. If you won't tell me where he is, I'll pull this goddamned place down around us. So help me God, I will."

"Deirdre." Victor's smooth calm voice preceded his entrance. "No need for violence, my dear. If you want to see Larry, then by all means you shall. Ron would be happy to take you, wouldn't you, Ron?" The nuances of his tone merely infuriated me further. Humor her, they said, give the little lady what she wants so that she'll go away and leave us to our important business.

Ron laughed, the sound a combination of nervousness and eagerness. "I'd take Deirdre anywhere. She should know that by now." Then he looked down at my feet. "Where are your shoes? It'll be cold where we're going."

"Gone," I said simply, "and it's cold everywhere, Ron."

"Deirdre." Victor nodded a dismissal and turned to retreat into his office, then spun around. "Oh, and sometime after you are done speaking to Larry, you and I will need to talk about the trial. At your convenience, of course, but we should make it soon."

"Fine," I agreed, "I'll come back afterwards, if that's all right."

"Watch yourself, my dear." His face twisted into a grimace, "I understand Larry's been highly agitated these past few hours."

"I can take care of myself, Victor."

He laughed. "Yes, so I've heard. Until later then."

Ron touched me lightly on the elbow after Victor went into his office and closed the door. "Are you sure you don't want to put on a pair of shoes, Deirdre?"

I shrugged and gave him a small smile. "Cold feet are the least of my worries, Ron. Besides, my favorite pair got lost on the streets last night." At his questioning look, I shook my head. "It's a long story. And one I'm sure others will be happy to tell you. For now, let's go. I don't really know why I feel compelled to talk to Larry, but I would like to get it over with as quickly as possible."

Ron nodded. "Yeah, I hear you. Larry's one real strange guy. Gives me the creeps."

I said nothing, but allowed Ron to lead me back through the corridors and to the elevators. Once inside with the doors shut, he opened the control panel and, taking a key from his pocket, inserted it and dialed in a code on a computerized key pad. The elevator started down with a bit of a jolt, throwing me off balance and into

Ron's steadying arms. We stood for a second, his hands on my shoulders and I blushed, remembering shared intimacies with this man.

I hadn't known what he was at the time; had no idea of who he really was and why he'd befriended me. He was, I thought, just another man, a source of blood and comfort, one more in an ever-expanding list. And he'd made himself available during a time when I had desperately needed someone. Finding out that Ron was working for the Cadre was a betrayal, but no more of one than his finding out that I was married to a then mortal man. I thought that the scores between us had been evened.

"Deirdre," his voice caught on my name as his hands reluctantly let go of my shoulders. I stepped back from him, and our eyes met. In a brief flash I felt my mind laid open in front of him; my recent fears and insecurities about what Mitch had become, my uncertainty about our future together, underneath all of which flowed a strong undercurrent of love. In Ron's mind there lay a submerged anger and a passion that he feared would forever go unsatisfied.

"Ron," I reached up, gently touched his cheek and the moment's intuition faded, leaving only a wash of sadness in its wake. Of all beings, I knew what it was like to be unloved, to contemplate centuries of aloneness; I had lost Mitch once and upon finding him again, had made a conscious decision to accept losing him eternally in his death. It was true that circumstances and an impetuous act had taken that decision out of my hands. Somehow, to contemplate loving him for all eternity, to have him in front of me, visible and live, and not be able to act on that love, was truly horrible.

"Oh, Ron, I'm so sorry." My voice was soft and I brushed away the forming tears as the elevator doors opened on our final destination: the holding pens of the Cadre.

Ten

Ron was right; I should have worn my shoes. The floor was made of rough concrete and my feet were still tender from the abuse I had inadvertently put them through the previous night. And with one step off the elevator I felt a bone-chilling coldness sweep up my legs.

I followed him through dimly lit, winding corridors, totally different from the ones found on the upper levels. This area was almost like a cave, with no doorways, no windows, and the concrete block walls painted gray. I tried very hard not to imagine how far underground we were, but failed and the claustrophobic feeling that I'd felt earlier returned, stronger than before, overwhelming in its intensity. By the time we arrived at the end of the maze and Ron was unlocking the door, my pulse had quickened and my breath was coming in shallow gasps.

"Not very pleasant down here, is it?" He smiled at me, his one hand on the knob of the heavy metal door, his other brushed my shoulder in a gesture meant to reassure.

"No," I said, as he pushed open the door. "But

then jails aren't supposed to be pleasant, are they?"

A flood of light spilled into the hallway from the room. I squinted and shook my head. "Why is it so bright in there?"

"Sun lamps," Ron said, reaching his hand around the doorjamb, finding the switch and turning them completely off. The sudden absence of brightness seemed like a blessing. I rubbed my hands over my eyes and I noticed that Ron did the same. "There's something about the particular intensity of the light that acts as a deterrent."

"Deterrent?" My voice rose slightly and echoed down the hallway. "Deterrent? Hell, it seems close to torture." I began to have second and even third thoughts on the benign nature of the Cadre's justice system. "Is this where I would have been held had I been found guilty?"

Ron gave me a curious glance and nodded.

"Jesus," the word escaped my lips almost unconsciously. "Hundreds of years locked away down here in an air-tight cell, no food, no escape, and sun lamps? Sun lamps?" I started to laugh, "No wonder everyone in the Cadre is so obedient to Victor's every whim. No wonder many people choose suicide over detention."

"Well, I admit it seems rather bleak, but vampires have survived it. . . ."

"Bleak, Ron? Bleak doesn't even come close." I shuddered violently, still hesitating in the doorway. If this was the Cadre's version of "humane" punishment, I hated to contemplate the other alternatives. "At least a stake through the heart is quick and clean. And kinder."

Ron shrugged. "This is the way it is, Deirdre. The way it's always been."

"Well, that doesn't mean I have to like it."

"And whether you like it or not doesn't matter. Do you want to go in, or not?"

I nodded. "Yes, let's go in." And we entered.

Even had I not known what this area of the Cadre's quarters was meant for, I could have surmised its purpose from the furnishings. A metal desk and a few uncomfortable chairs were scattered around what looked like a reception area. The desk held only an empty in-out basket, a calendar blotter, and a telephone. With the sun lamps off, the lighting consisted of a few overhead fluorescent fixtures. Everything was utilitarian and nondescript, unlike the flush luxury of the personal living quarters. It was a waiting area.

So were the glass booths I glimpsed beyond a partial wall. We entered the actual cell area and once again my feeling of pent-up anxiety returned. Not for me this time, but in sympathy for the hunched over figure occupying the very last booth.

Larry sat on the edge of a narrow bunk, his elbows on his knees, his head resting on his hands, his shoulders shaking. I rubbed my hands nervously over my pant legs. Why did I feel I had to see him? Wouldn't I have been better off not knowing his condition?

"No," I said aloud and Ron looked at me in

confusion. "Sorry, just a little argument with myself. Can I talk to him?"

"Sure," Ron said, walking over to the wall and throwing a switch. Suddenly the room was filled with the whistling sound of air being forced into the chamber. Starting low, then growing louder and louder as the air filled his lungs, we could hear Larry sobbing. I gasped. The sound system obviously worked both ways because he heard me and raised his head. Our eyes met and some of the despair in his demeanor lifted, to be replaced with a glimmer of hope. He jumped up from the bed and flung himself at the wall, fingers splayed on its surface, his face so close that his features were distorted in the thick glass.

"Deirdre." There was no mistaking the relief in his voice. "Shit, I'm so happy to see you. Hell, I'd be happy to see anyone right now. Even Mitch's ugly face. How long have I been here? And what took you so long?"

"I'm sorry, Larry. I wasn't sure they'd let me see you. . . ." The lie was apparent, even to him.

A twisted smirk replaced the pleased smile that had been on his face. "I know, and you didn't exactly rush to find out, right?" Larry shrugged and laughed. "No, it's okay, really, why should you? I mean, what am I to you that you should care?"

I sighed. This wasn't going to be easy. "Larry, you are my responsibility. One that I have neglected, I confess. And I apologize for that. But I'm here now and I want to help if I can. We can talk; you can communicate with me, tell me your needs, your fears."

"You're here now? Actually, you're there and I'm stuck in here. How can we communicate through this wall? I mean really communicate? And shouldn't I have gotten bail or something? I haven't been convicted of anything yet. What happened to innocent until proven guilty?"

Ron laughed. "That's not a Cadre rule, Martin. Don't push your luck."

Larry struck at the glass wall with his fist. The noise was amplified through the microphone and I jumped. He continued punching to emphasize his words. "Oh, that Ronny is a brave one." Thump. "It's fucking easy to laugh when you're on the other side, isn't it, buddy?" Thump. "Let's trade places and see how much you like it."

"No thanks." Ron made a grimace of distaste and turned to me. "Deirdre, are you sure you want to talk to this creature?"

"Yes, I do, Ron. I want to. I have to." I gave Larry a quelling glance which seemed to calm him then looked back to Ron. "And I'd like to see him inside the room, if I may."

"Jesus, Deirdre, I'm not sure you should do that."

"Are there rules against it?"

"Well, no, not really. But he's a strange one. He might hurt you."

I threw my head back and laughed. "Ron, what on earth could he possibly do to me? He has no weapons, and no defenses. I think I can reach him, make a difference to the way he is, but I can't do it through a wall of glass." I reached out and touched Ron's arm gently, looking up into his face, studying his eyes. "We've been friends, good friends, all things considered. You may stay and watch if you need to, but let me go in. And turn off the microphone. This should be a private discussion. Please."

It was the last word that settled him, I think. And although I could tell he was not happy about the situation, he agreed. "Stand back, Martin," he said in a sharp voice. Larry moved quickly to the end of his cot. "Okay, Deirdre," Ron said, his hand resting on another switch on the wall, "the door will open for just a few seconds. Once you're inside, you'll be sealed in with him. And when I turn the microphone off, the air goes, too. Although there should be enough in there for at least a half an hour of conversation." He looked over at Larry and back at me. "Are you really sure you want to do this?"

"It's the only way, Ron."

"Okay," he said reluctantly, then grinned at me, "you always do this to me. Talk me into doing things I don't want to do. It's not fair, you know. And Victor will have my ass for this if anything goes wrong. But you know I've never been able to resist the pleas of a lady in distress, especially yours."

I smiled back at him. "Yes, I know, Ron. Don't worry; I'll take full responsibility for any consequences." I stretched up and kissed his cheek. "Thank you."

He motioned me to the corner of the cell and

I stood there waiting, until the glass slid aside, leaving a very thin opening the height of the cell. I squeezed through quickly and heard the panel thump closed behind me with a finality that echoed through the room.

Larry still stood placidly at the end of his bunk. "Nice place, huh? I bet the room they gave you and the hubby is just a little bit better furnished, but I suppose they figured this is good enough for the poor relatives." Then he held out his arms in a welcoming gesture. "But I'm forgetting my manners, please, sit down."

I settled in on the edge of the bed and Larry walked over to the outermost cell wall. He knocked on it. "Okay, Ron, you can turn off the mike now." Ron's eyes met mine across the room, I nodded and the switch was turned. The whistling sound dwindled then stopped; other than my low breathing we were surrounded by total silence.

"So," Larry moved over and sat next to me. "To what do I owe the honor of your visit?" His voice was sad without any trace of anger or vindictiveness.

"I've been doing a lot of thinking, Larry. And I've come to the conclusion that what you have become is my fault. I shouldn't have left town knowing you were here, knowing what you were. Of all of the Cadre, I'm the only one who can understand the total solitude you've been experiencing, the confusion, and the fear, because I have done to you what Max did to me."

"Oh."

I don't know what kind of explanation he'd expected to hear, but from his reaction this hadn't been it. Still, I continued. "I am truly sorry, Larry. I should have stayed. I should have helped you, taught you, led you the way you needed to go."

He brushed off my words. "None of that shit matters now. But do you think," his voice wavered and I was afraid he would begin to cry again, "I mean, can you get me out of here? Please, Deirdre," he reached over and touched my hand, then grasped it in his. "This is horrible. You can't imagine how awful it is, to be locked away in this stinking place." He dropped my hand and jumped up, pacing the room. "You should have let Mitch kill me. It would have been better. Anything would be better than this."

"Larry, I'm sorry, I thought this would be, well, more bearable. I really had no idea."

"You promised me it would be okay." Larry's voice grew petulant, whining. "You said that it would be okay if I came with you. That you would help me, take care of me. And then you calmly let them take me away and lock me up. Down here where there's no sound, no air, no food. Just the damn lights and eternity ticking away a second at a time."

I lowered my head and opened my mouth to speak. "Larry, I . . ."

"Oh, I know," he interrupted, spinning around to snarl at me, "you're sorry, so very sorry. Fat lot of good that does me. You say you're responsible for what I've done, but hell, you go scot-free and I'm the prisoner. How long, Deirdre? How long do you think you could handle this situation?"

"Not very long, Larry. Probably for less time than you have already. But what can I do now? Until the trial, you have to stay here. I've no control over it anymore."

"Oh, but you do." He came over and knelt before me, taking my hands into his again.

"What can I do now?" I repeated. "I can't fight the Cadre. Jesus," my voice rose, sounding strangely dead in the static air, "I couldn't even fight them for myself. The only reason I'm not occupying the cell next door," I shuddered, "is because Max's ghost spoke for me."

"Well, I don't imagine I'll be that lucky. But there is something you can do." Larry's voice lowered to a whisper and he glanced over his shoulder to see if Ron was watching. He was, but not intently. He was confident that both Larry and I were under his complete control and his relaxed stance confirmed it.

Larry shrugged and looked back up at me. "You could kill me. Kill me and put me out of my misery. This is hell, Deirdre, a hell you sent me to. Kill me, now. Please. I won't even try to stop you. I'd do it myself if I could."

"Oh, God, Larry." I pulled my hands away from his and covered my face, pressing in on my eyes, trying to prevent the tears. "I don't think I can. Not in cold blood. Not even if you beg me to."

"You're too soft, Deirdre. But you could have

Mitch do it. He'd do it if you asked him to. Hell, he'd be overjoyed to kill me, he already said so. The only thing that stopped him from killing me was you."

I shook my head and gave a humorless laugh, dropping my hands back to my lap. "Yes, you're probably right. But I don't know, Larry. I just don't know."

"Deirdre," he grasped my wrists and brought my hands down to his face. "You have to help me. You just do. Here, feel how it is, see how it feels to be me."

I tried to pull away from him, but he was strong. I made the mistake of raising my head and meeting his eyes. And I fell deep into his madness.

Fell deep into his hunger. *This* was the hunger of last night, the blinding red hunger that allowed no other feeling. It took hold of me and I began to shake. Larry's anger and pain were mine. We were one. I screamed and as if from far away, I heard an odd rasping noise, heard a voice from outside calling a name I should have known. But the voices inside were stronger, the roar of the creature that lived within me, the roar of the creature that sought to control my soul. I cried out again, a half-human, half-feline call of distress and despair.

Larry's hands slipped from mine and he seemed to fold in on himself, collapsing into a misshapen lump on the floor. I roared again and felt the air pressure in the room change. Ron had opened the door.

Before I could even react, I felt a wisp of air pass me, heard the high-screeching call of victory, saw a winged body fly past a startled Ron and out the door. I felt the elation and expectation wash over him as he disappeared from sight. "Death, " he sang. "I fly to find death and freedom."

Eleven

With Larry's influence gone, I was able to force my body back from the partial transformation it had already made. When my mind cleared and I was myself again I discovered that I was alone and trapped inside the cell. The door had snapped closed before I could escape. Ron, I assumed, had gone in pursuit of Larry.

Grateful for the time alone, I sat back down on the cot and tried to calm my shaking and collect my thoughts. The first one that ran through my head was: Victor would not be pleased. I laughed grimly at that monumental understatement.

Looking to the doorway, I spoke out loud. "Victor is going to have us both for dinner, Ron. And we'll deserve it." But how could anyone have known that Larry had achieved the power of transformation so quickly? He'd only been a vampire for a little over two years. And he'd have had no training.

Or, and my distrust of Vivienne surfaced anew, maybe he had. What if she'd been working with Larry for the past two years? Teaching him the tricks of the trade? She seemed secure in the knowledge that she could instruct Mitch in the mysteries and he was only a few months into his existence. "Damn."

I turned on the cot, pulled my legs up, and wrapped my arms around them, hugging them close to my body, noticing as I did so that my jeans were ripped in a few places. A totally irrelevant thought made me laugh. "I had better get the hang of this changing pretty soon, or it's going to cost me a fortune in clothing." I flexed my toes a bit, easing the stiffness from them. At least this time I hadn't lost a pair of shoes, too.

"Clothing should be the least of your worries right now, Deirdre."

Victor stood in the doorway, by the control panel on the wall. I resisted the impulse to jump to attention at his presence and just swiveled my head to meet his angry gaze. "Can you give me one good reason why I shouldn't just leave you in there?" he asked, his long aristocratic fingers playing with the controls. "I could flip on the sunlights and close the door. A year or so locked up in here might teach you caution. Or at least respect for authority."

I sighed. "Actually, Victor, I have no reasons and no excuses. Do what you want. I'm hardly in any position to prevent you."

"But I am." Mitch appeared behind Victor. "Let her out, Lange, or so help me, I'll bring you down. Right here, right now."

Victor did not turn to meet him; instead he shook his head slowly and a smile played on his lips. "It was my idea to enlist your help, you know." He spoke to me as if Mitch was not present. "Not all of the Cadre was in favor of asking a rogue to come in and meddle in our internal affairs. You are an unknown quantity to them and hence, a danger. I argued that I needed you here for those same qualities and I still feel that way. When it turned out that we had not just one rogue to work with, but two, they were not happy. Fortunately," and the smile on his face broadened, "I have the final say in matters such as this, but," he turned the switch on the wall and the glass panel slid open, "before you pull a stunt like this again, promise me you'll think long and hard."

I squeezed myself through the opening, took a large breath of fresh air as I did so, and exhaled in relief. Mitch came to me and put an arm around my waist, hugging me close to him. I returned Mitch's hug, then moved away from him and started toward the doorway, anxious to put the place and the event behind me.

"To say I'm sorry, Victor, wouldn't be exactly true. This set-up has got to be one of the cruelest forms of torture ever imagined. And I'm not sure if anyone kept here deserves this particular punishment, regardless of their crimes. But you must believe that I didn't come down here with the intention of setting Larry free."

"Of course you didn't, my dear, it's just that unexpected things happen when you're around. And for what it's worth," Victor looked back over his shoulder and locked the main door before following us into the hallway, "I've always felt the same way about this place. This was never my idea, you know; it's one of Max's little brainstorms. I always felt that death was far preferable to incarceration."

"Interestingly enough," I observed, "so does Larry, at least now."

"Good," Mitch said as we reached the elevator, "then when we catch him again we can just kill him without having to worry about consulting him first."

"Indeed," Victor agreed with a low laugh. "Mitch, there are times when you and I are in complete agreement; there are other times when I understand why you never progressed past the level of detective in your mortal life."

Mitch bristled and Victor laughed again. "It's not a bad quality, you understand, this questioning of authority and the determination to go against it in the face of your conscience. It just rarely endears one to superior officers." The elevator door opened and the three of us got on. Victor pushed the floor for the Cadre's living quarters; I noticed that no key was needed for the upward trip. So did Mitch.

"I see that your security on the way up is slack. How many people have you actually had escape from down there?"

Victor cleared his throat, nervously. "Larry was the first one. But then he was also the first rogue to ever be incarcerated. Dammit, I can hardly believe he was capable of escape. His powers should never have been that fully developed. For one as young as he, he had an abnormally strong will. With Cadre members, it usually only takes twenty-four hours in the cell and a full barrage of the sun lamps to bleed away all resistance. This event will surprise some people, shock others, and confirm old beliefs . . ."

"Those old beliefs being?" I knew what they were, I had heard enough of them spoken and implied during my trial by the Cadre. But I wanted Victor to admit the facts. And I wanted Mitch to hear what these vampires, of whom he was so enamored, thought of beings like him and me.

Victor dropped his eyes and studied the floor. "The only good rogue is a dead rogue."

"Does that include us?" Mitch took a defensive stance, positioning himself between me and Victor.

"Actually, Mitch, your status is questionable. You are, after all, being trained by another vampire. And your reactions and sentiments seem to closely resemble ours."

The elevator stopped. "You know, Victor," Mitch said, "I'm not so sure that's a compliment."

Victor snorted. "No, from your point of view, I suppose it's not."

"How about Deirdre? What is the official Cadre decision on her status?"

The three of us stood in the hallway and Victor gave me a calculating glance. "Had she accepted our offer of her own house last year, we would have welcomed her as one of us. But her disdain of the organization was then and is now apparent in her every move. She is a rogue in our eyes. I doubt after this event she will ever be viewed as anything else. And ultimately, we know that your true sentiment lies with her, Mitch."

He started down the hallway then turned back. "Tomorrow evening the Cadre will be meeting to discuss plans for the recapture and disposal of Larry Martin. If I were you, I'd make definite plans to be there. And I'd also watch my back. Have a good evening."

Once back in our room, I collapsed on the bed. Mitch sat next to me and stroked my hair. "Still hungry?" he asked. "Do you feel up for a hunt tonight?"

"No, but we need to do something. I want to be out of this place for a while. And I am sure I can work myself into the proper mood."

He smoothed my cheek with the back of his hand and gave the low throaty laugh that always set my pulse racing. "Well, I know it's been a tough night already for you," he glanced at the clock on the night stand, "but it's still pretty early to go out. And I think you need something to occupy your mind other than the bloody Cadre and Larry Martin. Do you think you could work yourself into the proper mood for anything else?" I caught the gleam in his eyes and smiled up at him, reaching my arms around his neck, pulling his mouth down to mine.

When we kissed, his lips were cool, like the coolness of his skin against mine as he removed first my sweater and then my bra. His one hand cupped my right breast, teasing the nipple, rolling it between his fingers. It was like the touch of marble against marble, but it was Mitch's touch and it never failed. I moaned and his kisses grew fiercer while his other hand unzipped my jeans and reached inside to stroke me.

I bucked up into his caress and he laughed again, then slid my torn jeans and my panties from my body. Removing his mouth from mine he kissed my neck and then my breasts, pausing to suckle each of them in turn. He continued to trace his way down my stomach and further, until his kiss grew warmer, and I caught fire. His mouth teased and encouraged me, his hands stretched up over my body, molding my breasts. And when his tongue stabbed inside me, I could feel the hint of growing sharpness around his teeth.

I gasped and thrashed about on the surface of the bed. The sensations he was causing with fangs and tongue were almost too much to bear. He raised his head from me for one brief second, enough so that I could see the passion in his face and his eyes. Then he bared his fangs and quickly brought his mouth back down on me, penetrating the delicate skin.

I screamed as the flooding orgasms shook my body. And he held on to me, his hands grasping my hips now, keeping my writhing body tightly pressed against his mouth. Mitch pushed me over the brink uncountable times and just when I thought I could stand no more, he took his mouth away, looked up my body at me and smiled. A crimson blotch of blood smeared his lower lip.

He rose from the bed and stood over me. "Still hungry, Deirdre?"

I laughed and began to unfasten his pants. "The blood can wait, my love. Right now I just want you."

"I was hoping you'd feel that way." He eased himself out of his clothing and covered my body with his. This time I did not notice the absence of heat in his skin as he entered me, gently at first as if he were afraid to hurt me. But his thrusts grew more frantic as he was rewarded with my shudders and calls of passion. Wrapping my legs around him, digging my nails into the flesh of his back, I tasted the salty flesh of his neck with my tongue and whispered mad words of encouragement into his ear. In a time that seemed an eternity and a mere second, we spiraled down into the deep waves of our passion, holding each other's spasming body and mind closer than ever before.

He finally rolled from me and I realized that I was crying. And when I looked at him where he lay next to me, I discovered to my surprise that he, too, had been crying. Blood-tinged tracks streaked his face; I touched them with my fingertips in wonder.

He leaned over and kissed me lightly. "Oh, Deirdre, I love you."

I giggled.

"What? Is something funny?"

"No, I was just thinking that poor Vivienne will never know what she's missing."

"You mean you aren't jealous anymore?"

"After that performance, my love, how could I ever be jealous of anyone?"

"Too bad," he tried to sound disappointed, but I could hear relief in his voice, "it was sort of fun to get you worked up about it."

"More enjoyable than this?" I ran my nails along his chest and laughed when he shivered.

"Never."

We lay for a while, side by side. Barely touching each other, but together and calmed, at peace. There was no need for words between us. Eventually, though, Mitch pushed himself up on one elbow and leaned over to kiss the tip of my nose. "Let's get dressed and go out. It's early and there's lots of night left to enjoy. And I'm hungry."

"Fine by me." I got up from bed and went to the armoire that held my clothes. I dragged the hangers back and forth, then opened the drawers one by one. "Damn."

"What's wrong, sweetheart?"

"What was I wearing last night?"

Mitch chuckled. "Fur and then skin."

"Very funny. No, I mean before that."

He thought for a while. "Your black leather pants, I think."

"Damn. That's what I thought, too. And now

they're lying on the sidewalk somewhere in shreds."

"And let me guess," he said, rising from the bed himself and putting his clothes back on, "you have nothing to wear?"

"Well, nothing I really want to wear. I think I'll give Betsy a call tomorrow and see what she has on her racks this season."

He gave me a pained glance. "While you're with her, I think I'll stop over at the old place and see how Chris is doing."

"Chicken," I teased him. The last time he'd seen Betsy was at our wedding where she'd put the moves on every other man there. The first time they met, the night I'd sold my fashion business to her, she had attempted to seduce him while I was in the ladies' room. She was brisk and abrasive, but we had become friends of a sort. I always felt that she would make a better vampire than I ever did.

"No," he spoke quickly, "I really should see Chris. I called him while you were downstairs and got the machine again. Didn't leave a message this time."

"Fine." Still looking through the clothes, I finally pulled out a short black skirt, a pair of pantyhose and a red silk blouse, with a deep v-neck, full sleeves and yards of ruffles. "These will do."

I dressed and as I went into the bathroom to put on my makeup, the phone rang.

"Should I answer it?"

I stepped into the doorway. "Well, yes, Mitch, why on earth wouldn't you?"

He shrugged. "Lots of reasons, probably. It might be Victor summoning us into his presence. It might be Vivienne trying to arrange for our lessons. It might be Larry Martin wanting to gloat about his escape."

"I suspect Victor is done with us for the evening. And Larry wouldn't call, not this soon. And if it's Vivienne," I grinned at him, all the bad feelings I'd had about her had been loved out of me, "tell her you can't come out and play right now."

He smiled back. "Yeah, I am sort of played out right now." He picked up the phone and I went back into the bathroom, to finish the attempt to bring a normal color into my complexion. "Hi, Chris," I heard him say, "I tried to call you about an hour ago." He paused a minute. "Well, we were on our way out, but we could probably meet you in an hour or so. Hold on a second, okay?"

I heard Mitch set the receiver down on the wooden nightstand. "Deirdre," he called and I came back into the bedroom, "Chris would like to meet us at the pool hall a little later on. Think we can make it?"

I nodded. "That would be nice, Mitch." Then I looked down at my short skirt. "But I'll need to change my clothes again."

"Why?"

"Can you imagine me bending over the pool table in this?"

His eyes flashed at me. "Yeah, I can." I felt myself blush at his look of arousal and his knowing smile. "And yeah, you'll definitely need to change your clothes again."

Twelve

I put on my last pair of jeans, pulled on a pair of calf-high boots and we left the room. Mitch gave me a questioning look. "Should we lock it?"

"From creatures who can change into winged beasts or wild cats or a puff of smoke? It seems sort of useless."

"Yeah, well, if you put it that way, I guess you're right."

We left through the back entrance to the Imperial. Mitch stood on the sidewalk and sniffed the night air. "Garlic sauce," he said, with a strong note of regret in his voice, "steak and potatoes. Damn, I'm hungry. And I miss food, I miss the process of eating. I'd give everything I have for a plate of fettucine."

I sighed, an expression of relief rather than sadness. This was the first time Mitch had ever sounded sorry for what I'd made him into. His lack of regret had bothered me more than I cared to admit.

"I'm sorry, Deirdre, I didn't mean that to sound resentful."

"No, that's not it, Mitch. I miss food too, even now after all these years. I can remember a cake my mother used to bake. It's one of my earliest memories."

"That's interesting. You hardly ever talk about your life before." He put an arm around my shoulders and we started to walk down the street. "Is there a reason for that?"

"Not really, Mitch, only that there's no use in it. Those days are gone, the people I loved then have been dust for decades. And talking about them won't change matters, won't bring them back. So when I remember, I try to forget."

"I see." We walked about a block before he spoke again. "So tell me, if I had died after Larry attacked me, is that what you would have said about me?"

I stopped, reached up and touched his cheek. "Mitch, my love, had you died I would have mourned you for all eternity."

"Good."

I linked my arm in his and we started walking again, slowly and in the general direction of the pool hall, but with no particular destination in mind. I imagined that we looked like nothing more than two ordinary lovers, enjoying each other's company, taking a stroll in the crisp night air. It was a sweet illusion and one that I knew was more useless than old memories. I could feel tension build up in the arm I clasped, could sense Mitch's eyes sweeping the nearby streets and alleys for likely prey. As I myself was doing.

We found what we were looking for about three blocks away. A couple of kids in their mid-twenties, lounging in an alley entrance, passing around a bottle of cheap wine. They were dressed almost identically, in black leather and chains with the same spiked-up hair, dyed in streaks of various colors. At first I thought they were both boys, but as we got closer and heard their voices, I realized that one was a girl. They were discussing in loud tones a movie they'd seen.

"He wasn't whining, Danny," the girl said, taking a swig of the foul-smelling drink, "he was sensitive. He didn't know what he was getting into at first, and then afterwards when he decided he didn't like it, it was just way too late." She sighed, took another sip and passed the bottle to her friend. "But he's a hunk, anyway."

Danny took a drink and belched loudly. "Nah, he was a fuckin' whiner. But, that other one, man, Judy, was he ever cool."

Mitch laughed as we walked up to them. "Hey, kids, seen any good movies lately? And how would you like to find out what that all is like for real?"

I was startled by his open statement; it was unlike him to talk to his victims first. It seemed cruel, somehow. But I bit back my reprimand when I thought of the way I used to feed before we began to hunt together. I was hardly in any position to criticize his methods.

He looked down at the girl and leaned over to take her chin into his hand, bringing her face up so that she could look into his eyes. Her body followed and she stood, staring at him in admiration and awe.

"Hey, old man," the boy said, jumping up and

pulling a switchblade from his pocket, "quit screwin' with my babe. Jude, you don' wanna mess with this old shit."

But Judy wasn't listening, she'd been caught in the tantalizing quality of Mitch's gaze. He led her down the alley and into the darkness.

"Hey," the boy said again and tried to follow them. I grasped his wrist and held him there.

"Judy will be fine, Danny, there's no need to get upset." I twisted his hand slightly and the knife dropped to the sidewalk. "And," I said, staring into his eyes, "there is no need for your weapon. Is there?"

"No," I felt his resistance fall away. "I— I guess not."

I smiled at him, exposing my sharpening canines. "Then let's join them, shall we?"

"Ok." He allowed me to take him to where Mitch and the girl stood. Mitch's mouth was on her neck and she grasped his arms tightly. Her eyes were closed and she was smiling, almost humming her pleasure.

"You're for real, aren't you?" Danny's eyes widened as he watched Mitch feed upon his girlfriend. When he swung his head back to me, I nodded.

"Yes, we're real. It's a shame that you won't be able to remember after we leave."

"Because I'll be dead?" Surprisingly, his voice held no fear of this circumstance. Perhaps, the wine he'd consumed affected his judgment, I thought, or perhaps it was just his age speaking. Whatever the reason, I regarded him almost in the same light as he did me, as if we were two alien creatures meeting on common ground.

As indeed we are, I thought and laughed, reaching over to touch my palm to the top of his hair; it felt exactly the way it looked. "No, you won't be dead. Trust me."

His eyes worshipped me. "I do. I love you."

"Thank you, Danny." I pulled him to me and pierced his neck. His blood tasted clean and young and he pressed himself up against me as I drank, wrapping his arms around my waist and holding me close. I could feel the heat of his skin through the leather, feel him grow erect, feel him tremble.

I drew on him slowly, enjoying the warmth of the blood entering my mouth, flowing down my throat and through my body. He shuddered, his grasp on me weakened and I sighed, knowing that I should stop. Still I drank, one more mouthful, one more swallow. When I finally took my mouth away and licked the wound on his neck, I stepped away, and held him out at arm's length.

He opened his eyes. "That was way cool," he muttered in a shaky voice.

"I am glad you liked it." Truly an alien species, I thought with an inner laugh. "Now, Danny, look at me and forget. Forget that this happened. You were drinking wine and you passed out on the steps."

"Yeah," he agreed, "that was some pretty nasty swill we was drinkin'. Thanks for waking me up, lady. This ain't such a good place to fall asleep in."

Mitch came over to where we stood, his arm wrapped around Judy's shoulders. "You two should go home, now," he said forcefully, letting go of Judy and giving her a small push in Danny's direction, "it's late and the streets can be dangerous. Stay out of trouble."

"Yeah, come on, Jude, let's get home." They twined their arms around each other and stumbled down the alley and onto the street, without even stopping to turn around and look back. We had been completely forgotten, or had merged somehow in their minds with the movie they had been discussing before our arrival.

Mitch and I watched them leave and exchanged a quick contented smile. "That was almost too easy," he said, taking my arm again, "if this trend continues we could get fat and lazy."

We walked slowly for another few blocks without speaking again; both of us still so wrapped up in our after-feeding euphoria, that there seemed to be nothing to say. I could feel new life and vitality spreading through my veins and when he smiled I could tell that it was the same for him. At one point he stopped and took me into his arms, kissing me hard and insistently, the taste of the girl's blood still strong on his tongue.

"There are times," I said softly, echoing Larry's earlier sentiments, "times like these, when this existence is worth all of the pain, all of the hunger. And being able to share it with you, my love, is a pleasure beyond anything I ever thought possible."

"Yeah." He kissed the curve of my jaw and

held me up against him, as if he were afraid I would disappear. Then he checked his watch and whistled. "Do you know we've been out here for two hours?"

"Has it been that long?"

Mitch shook his wrist, held the watch up to his ear and brought it back down again, looking at the dial in disbelief. "Yes, it really has. And we're very late to meet Chris. You want to take a cab?"

I laughed. "Sure. I guess that's the end of romance for tonight."

"Oh, I don't know," he said, as he stepped to the curb and flagged down a taxi. "The night is still young and I think we've done pretty well in that department so far."

Chris was waiting for us in the near-deserted pool hall bar with three empty beer bottles lined up in front of him, and a fourth, half-drunk in his hand. He slipped off his barstool unsteadily as we entered, returned Mitch's hug enthusiastically and shook my hand.

"Hitting it a little hard tonight, aren't you, son?" Mitch looked at the bottles pointedly.

"Yeah," Chris's voice sounded sulky. "Maybe I am. What of it?"

"Nothing." Mitch shrugged and stepped up to the bar, motioning the bartender. "You're of legal age. And it's your life, not mine." Chris gave him a startled look, expecting, I supposed, more of a lecture from his father. Mitch grinned at the man behind the bar. "Two more beers, please, George. And run a tab for me, if you wouldn't mind."

George clapped him on the shoulder. "Sure thing, Detective. Long time, no see. Where've you been? Chris here was telling me you got married." He gestured with his thumb at me. "This the lucky lady?"

I walked over to him and shook his hand. "Nice to meet you. I'm Deirdre."

"You look kind of familiar," George said, squinting slightly through the dimness of the bar. "You been here before?"

"Once or twice," I replied, taking the bottle he offered me. "Thank you."

"My pleasure." He gave me an admiring glance and turned to Chris. "You know, buddy, as far as stepmothers go, I'd say you made out okay. She doesn't seem all that bad to me. Quite the contrary, actually. Your dad's one lucky bastard." He laughed, loud and boisterously. I was instantly reminded of Pete back in England, realizing with a sudden rush of homesickness that I missed him, and that I'd promised to call him when we arrived.

"Got any tables free, George?" Mitch picked up his beer and took a long draught.

The bartender shrugged. "Take your pick, the joint ain't exactly jumping tonight."

"Well, then," Mitch slapped me lightly on my backside, "let's get going, woman. Seems to me I have a score to even up with you, a reputation to uphold. Last time we were here you managed to beat me by a close margin."

"Close margin, my ass, Dad," Chris laughed, "she skunked you. Royally. And you know it." He shook his head. "And I'll bet you she does it again."

"Oh, I don't know about that, Chris. Maybe I've gotten better since I've been away."

"Wouldn't count on it," Chris said.

I winked at Chris. "I'm afraid, Mitch, that you are going to have to prove that. And be prepared to put your money where your mouth is."

I was rewarded with a genuine smile from Chris, and the three of us left the bar to play pool.

Ten games and two hours later, Mitch conceded defeat with a laugh and placed his cue back on the wall rack. "You'll at least admit that I've improved, won't you? I almost won that last game."

"Another century or two, Mitch, and you might even stand a chance of winning. But yes, you have improved. Your reflexes are much faster than they were."

"Yeah, it's a nice side effect. Like being able to drink as much as you want without that happening." He gestured to where Chris was slumped over a table, sound asleep. "I guess we'd better get him home," he looked at the clock on the wall, "and then get back ourselves. It's getting late."

"Yes." Putting away my pool cue, I dusted the chalk from my hands. "The nights are getting shorter. And time seems to pass so quickly that the seasons blur into one another." I stretched my arms over my head, arched my back and yawned. "I think I'm getting old. I tire so quickly these days."

"Well, it's been a rough two days, you know."

I laughed a bit, then grew serious. "And there seems to be no relief in sight. I wish we'd never come back."

"I know what you mean," Mitch went to Chris and shook him. "Up and at 'em, sonny boy. Time to go home."

"What?" Chris lifted his head and looked around. "What happened? Who won?"

"Don't ask." Mitch took hold of his arm and helped him to his feet. "Let's get you in a cab and home to bed."

"Skunked you again, huh, Dad?" We moved him out of the pool room and into the bar. "That's what you get for playing with a vampire."

"Shut up, Chris."

"Night," George called from the bar. "See you later."

"Hey, George," Chris called, "you didn't know that my stepmother was a vampire, did you?"

"Yeah, Chris, I think you told me that after your third beer. Go home and sleep it off."

Thirteen

Chris muttered about vampires most of the way home. We didn't try to quiet him; his drunken condition was fairly apparent. The cab driver snickered every so often when Chris's voice grew loud, but for the most part he was concentrating on the road and not on his passengers. I had always been amused by the protection of people's disbeliefs even when I'd thought I was close to the only one of my kind. And now that I knew the city was the headquarters for an international society of vampires, it amused me even more. If they only knew.

Yes, I thought and sobered slightly, if they only knew, they'd be after the Cadre in no time at all, armed with stakes, holy water, garlic, and crosses. Not that anything but the first would do any good, the rest were common superstition. Or possibly not, for with the revelation of new powers, almost anything could be true.

Chris wasn't talking when we finally arrived at Mitch's old apartment building. Instead, he was sleeping soundly, his head lolled on the back of the seat, his mouth hanging open slightly.

I caught Mitch's eye. "Maybe I'll just wait here with the cab while you take him in."

"Fine," he agreed. He opened the back door and half-dragged, half-carried Chris out, up the front stairs and into the building.

The cab driver turned around and winked at me. "Your friend's got a real snootfull. I wouldn't want to be living inside his head tomorrow morning."

"No," I smiled and settled back into the seat to wait for Mitch's return, "I wouldn't either."

"What's his problem, anyway? All this talk about vampires?"

I shrugged when I saw Mitch coming back down the stairs. "You wouldn't believe me if I told you."

"No," the driver said as Mitch got back into the cab, "I probably wouldn't. Where to now, folks?"

Almost without thinking, I told the driver my old address. "Righto," he said and we started off.

Mitch gave me a questioning look. "I don't want to go back to the Imperial, my love, I've had enough of that place for one night. But you may go back if you like."

"Why would I want to go back without you, Deirdre? There's nothing there for me."

"Nothing?" My voice was sharp, distant.

He laughed. "I thought you weren't jealous anymore."

I shook my head. "I'm not jealous of her so much as of the entire situation. You love the life, the environment, and the possibilities. Sometimes I feel like I'm holding you back."

He thought for a long time, staring out the cab window. As we were nearing the hotel, he spoke. "It's not love, Deirdre, not really. It's pretty close to a morbid fascination and a desire to push everything to the limits. Quite frankly, I don't understand it myself."

The taxi pulled up to the front door. I touched his arm lightly. "I think I do, Mitch, but we can talk about it later. Just for fun, why don't we see if my old room is free?"

The driver turned around and accepted his fare. "Lady, nothing in this city is free."

"So true," I said to him as I got out of the cab. "Everything has its price."

Mitch put his arm around me and we went through the revolving door and over to the desk. "May I help you?" I didn't know the clerk at the desk, he was young and awkward.

"Well, yes, I hope so. Can you tell me if room 2154 is available?"

The clerk seemed to be startled by the request and looked uneasily around him. "I just got here so I don't know for sure. Let me check, okay?"

I nodded and he turned. "Hey, Frank," he called toward the half-open door behind him, "there's someone here asking whether 2154 is open."

"What?" He came out of the door and saw me, his face turned pale for a second and then he smiled. "Miss Griffin?" He came around the front desk toward us. "Miss Griffin, oh, my God, it is you. This is really strange that you should come back tonight." His arms came up as if to hug me and then dropped as he seemed to remember his place. "Sorry," he said sheepishly, "it's just that it's been so long and it's so good to see you."

I laughed. "It's nice to see you, too, Frank." I reached up and gave him a light kiss on the cheek. "But why should it be strange? I lived here for almost ten years, it's only natural that I come back to visit if I'm in the city, isn't it?"

"Well, yeah, I guess so, but that's not what's strange." He looked over at Mitch for the first time.

"Frank, this is my husband. Mitchell Greer."

"Pleased to meet you," Frank shook his hand. "Say, I remember you. So you two got married, huh? Congratulations."

"Thanks," Mitch said. "You have a good memory. I wasn't here all that often."

"Often enough," Frank started, "I mean before you showed up Miss Griffin never had any visitors . . ."

"Thank you, Frank," I interrupted him after taking a glance over my shoulder at the outside sky. I'd lost track of the time, but knew that dawn was close. "We're tired, and we'd like to check in immediately if you don't mind. We'll have time to get reacquainted later."

Instantly his years of subservience resurfaced. He was no longer an old friend, but an old servant. "Oh, yes, of course. Sorry to keep you waiting." He motioned to the young man behind the desk. "Get the keys for 2154, Eddie, and let Mr. and Mrs. Greer sign in."

Eddie reached under the counter and came up with two sets of keys, laid them on the counter next to the register and handed Mitch a pen. While he was completing the needed information, Frank turned to me. "I'll see you up to the room. Where's your luggage?"

"We don't have any luggage," Mitch said, turning around and walking with us to the elevator. "We left it at, um, a friend's house."

"Fine," Frank said, "that makes it easier then, doesn't it? But I'll still take you upstairs, if you don't mind. Personal service is what we're known for here."

After we'd gotten on the elevator and the doors closed, he reached into his pocket, extracting a small white envelope. "This," he said, holding it out to me, "is why it was strange to see you tonight. Someone left this on the front desk earlier this evening; no one saw him come in and no one saw him leave. All of a sudden there was this envelope with your name and number, like it had appeared out of nowhere." He laughed nervously. "It spooked the hell out of Eddie and I was having quite a time trying to figure out how I was going to get it to you."

"I'm sure you were." I accepted the envelope and stared down at it, barely controlling the impulse to crumple it in my hand and throw it to the floor. I knew the handwriting and could sense the hurried desperation that drove the pen, but the recognition did nothing to quell my nervousness. How could he have known I'd planned to come here? "I'm sure you were. Thank you, Frank."

"No problem, but it was real fortunate that you decided to show up tonight. What a coincidence, huh?"

Mitch snorted. I caught his eye and gave him a smile, remembering his theory on the subject, remembering with amusement the moments when his human mind had struggled with the inhuman and came up frustrated and confused.

"Coincidence?" he said with a catch of laughter in his throat, "there's no such thing."

"No?" Frank said as the elevator stopped, holding the doors open for us to pass through. "Maybe just luck then?"

I looked at the black writing one more time and slapped the damn thing up against my thigh. "Luck?" Shaking my head, I watched Mitch open the door to my old suite of rooms. "I wouldn't count on it, Frank, but thank you for thinking it."

Dropping the envelope on an end table in the sitting area of the suite, I looked around me. The furnishings were the same, but had grown shabbier over the years that I'd been gone. It made me feel old. But Mitch seemed very much at home and moved to the bar, slowly, idly checking inside the refrigerator. Frank came in after us and made a move to open the curtains. "Leave them closed, please," I stopped him, my voice harsh. "I suspect we'll want some rest."

"Whatever you say, Miss Griffin. You're the boss."

"Thanks, Frank," Mitch walked over to him, and handed him a tip. "We'll be fine now."

"Thank you, and sleep well. I'll be going off duty soon," he said, checking his watch, "but Charlie, he's the day guy now, will be on. Call him if you need anything."

When we were finally alone in the room, I sighed.

"Glad to be home again, Deirdre?"

"This is not my home, anymore. I have no home." I stared at the end table holding the envelope.

"Well, aren't you curious about who sent that? Aren't you going to open it?"

"It can't be good news."

"No, but the sooner we know, the sooner we can deal with whatever it is. You never used to be so cautious, Deirdre."

"I've always been cautious, Mitch." Then I met his eyes and smiled. "Except where you were involved. I do love you."

"I know you do." He walked across the room and picked up the envelope. Some of my wariness must have influenced him, he acted as if the thing could bite him. "Want me to open it?"

"If you'd like."

"Well, I'm sure not going to go to sleep with it unopened. It'll make me crazy."

"We don't want that to happen now, do we? Yes, open it. Besides, I already know who sent it.

Which," I laughed humorlessly, "is why I know it can't be good news."

He slid his finger under the flap, pulling out the single sheet of paper. He unfolded it, read it once, twice, then held it out to me. "It's from Larry Martin."

"Of course." I took the page from him.

"It's odd."

I laughed for real this time. "What else would you expect, my love?"

"Read it." His voice was stern. I gave him a curious glance and began to read aloud:

"Deirdre, I can't go back to that place. I know you understand. And you have to know that my only response to all of this is death. I don't really have any other choice, and I'm sorry, but I won't forget you."

I folded it back up and handed it to Mitch. "Not quite what I expected, but it will do, I suppose."

"Will do for what?"

"A declaration of intent." I turned away and walked into the bedroom, sitting on the bed, taking a quick glance to verify that the curtains were safely drawn in this room also. Mitch followed me and stood in the doorway.

Dawn was close, so close I could see the rising sun as if it were in front of my eyes, feel the scorching heat and the agony of seared flesh, the burning away of skin and muscle and blood and bone.

"Intent to do what?" Mitch's voice came to me as if over a great distance, his words made meaningless by the vision that was forcing itself into my mind: *There is a sadness that calls to me and ties me to the soul within— the strange and familiar sadness of life lived too long. There is an ache for the denied fire of the sun, an urge to hold my face up to the sky and feel its rays caress my skin with burning fingers, an overwhelming wish to fall deep into oblivion and live no more.*

"Sleep," *a voice says,* "sleep."

The voice is calm and the eyes in the vision close in peace, a peace unlike any I have ever known. Sins and the guilt of sins fall away before it, hunger has no hold and the self is no more.

All that exists is the peace, the oblivion and the cleansing fire of a rising sun.

Mitch was grasping my hands tightly when my eyes opened and he shook me roughly. I noticed with shock that I was no longer sitting on the bed, but instead stood in front of the bedroom window. "Deirdre?" His voice was harsh. "What the hell is happening?"

I blinked my eyes and shook my head, squirming slightly against his tight hold on me. "How did I get here?"

"You got up from the bed, walked over here, and started to open the curtains. You would have been fried to a crisp if I hadn't stopped you. What happened?"

"I don't know."

He loosened his grip on my wrists, but still controlled my movements. "Do you feel better?"

"I don't want to open the curtains now, if that's what you mean. Why on earth would I want to do that?"

Mitch let go of my hands, but stayed close to me, poised and watchful. "Beats me. You muttered something about sleep and smiled, then came over here. I only managed to stop you a second before you reached the window. What do you remember?"

"The sun." I shivered. "I remember the sun. I wanted to sleep in the sun."

"But that would have killed you."

I shivered again and hugged my arms to myself. "That, if I remember correctly," I gave him a rueful smile, "was the whole point."

"But why would you want to kill yourself? I thought you were happy with me; thought you loved me." Shock and hurt showed in his eyes and I reached a hand up to touch his cheek.

"Oh, I am happy, Mitch, and I do love you. But it wasn't me, you see, who wanted to sleep in the sun. It was someone else."

"Someone else?" Mitch's voice rose in anger now, not at me, I knew, but in frustration and fear. "It would damn well've been you anyway, if I hadn't been here."

"That could be." I fell silent for a while, staring at the closed drapes, remembering the purifying pain of the vision with both dread and desire. "Thank you."

Stripping off my clothes, I walked over to the

bed and pulled the covers down. "I'm tired, let's sleep."

"You sleep." He walked out of the bedroom and came back with one of the chairs from the sitting area. He placed it square in front of the window then sat himself in it emphatically. "I'll watch."

"There's no need, my love, everything is over now."

"I'll watch anyway."

I stripped off my clothes and crawled between the coolness of the sheets. Just as I was drifting off, I heard his soft question.

"Who was it, Deirdre?"

"I don't know," I mumbled, falling into a blissfully dreamless state. "I don't know."

Fourteen

Sometime during the day, I became aware that Mitch finally lay sleeping next to me. I woke and looked over at him, pulling the covers down to study his transformed body, something that I had been avoiding since his change. I remembered standing in front of the mirror with him in this room, comparing the difference between his mortal body and my supposedly perfected one. Then his skin had color and texture and scars. I'd lain in bed with him, tracing the welts and tracks of past injuries, listening to his brief descriptions of how they'd occurred. I'd loved his scars, loved the stories they'd told about the truth of him. I'd loved his humanity.

Now his skin glowed with the same translucency as my own and our glorious contrasts were gone, wiped away. I had single-handedly destroyed his past. A tear rolled down my cheek, but I ignored it and closed my eyes, placing my hand softly on his chest, imagining the feel of him as he was before. He stirred in his sleep and I moved away, got up from the bed, and picked up the shirt he'd left draped over the chair. I put it on and quietly closing the door behind me, left the room.

I walked over to the bar and pulled out a bottle of red wine— not as good a vintage as I'd stocked when I lived here, but it would do. I opened it, poured myself a glass, and carried both glass and bottle to the couch where I curled up, my legs tucked underneath me. As the afternoon waned, I drank and I thought.

Mostly I thought about Mitch. I had expected to feel guilt at his transformation. I'd introduced him to a life I'd always loathed. But what I hadn't expected was his ready adaptation to the life. It was not that I loved him less, I reasoned, but that he had changed. I longed for someone in whom I could confide and realized with a flash of lone-liness that I had few friends, that my closest ties were to Mitch. And he was a vampire.

Draining my glass, I poured another. There lay the problem— as much as I'd like to deny the fact, Mitch *was* a vampire. And, ridiculous as it was, in my mind, vampires were to be held at a distance; they should be feared and hated, not loved. "Damn," I said softly to myself, "this is getting me nowhere. I don't even know where I want to go."

The note from Larry was lying on the end table where Mitch must have left it. I stretched over the couch and picked it up, opened the envelope and read it again. When I'd first seen it, I'd as-sumed it was a death threat. Vague and deceptive like its writer, the ominous words that finished it were chosen with care to impart a certain meaning. And yet, with the vision I'd had, I wondered now if it wasn't a suicide note, if the soul I had witnessed in the sun hadn't been him. Had I been the one to be confined to that hell-hole in the Cadre depths, I knew I would do almost anything to avoid being caught and reimprisoned. Even up to causing my own death.

So was Larry dead? I tried to reach out into the city and touch his mind. We are tied together, I thought, I should be able to find him. But I felt nothing except my own sadness, my own weariness with life. I put the letter away and held the envelope up to my cheek as if this touch would give me some answers.

I was trapped, here in this city, where I had never intended to be again. I longed for the years and months I had spent in England. Even the time I'd been without Mitch now seemed idyllic, when my only worries were what sort of profit the pub was pulling in and when my next meal would walk in the door. I laughed briefly and wondered if I should call Pete. Maybe the sound of his voice, cheerful and normal, would dispel the clouds that seemed to be gathering around us.

Mentally, I added the extra hours to the clock; the pub would be full now, the dart players would be arguing and the pints of ale flowing steadily. If I closed my eyes I could almost hear them, Pete's thick accent cutting through the other voices, calling greetings to regulars and strangers alike. With a smile, I picked up the phone and dialed the number of the pub.

I let the phone ring twenty times before I hung up, shaking my head. It was too early for them to have closed, especially on a Friday evening, unless Pete had somewhere to go and no one to cover for him. It hadn't been that long since we'd left; he would hardly have had time to arrange for a replacement for me by now.

I put my hand to the receiver and jumped when it rang. "Hello?"

"Deirdre, it's Victor. I thought when you didn't return to your rooms that you might be there. Is Mitch with you?" His voice sounded cold and distant, angry.

"Yes, he's here. Is there a problem?"

"I need to see you, both of you, as soon as you can get here."

I looked at the clock again. "We'll be there in two hours. What's happening?"

"Larry Martin. All of the Cadre house members received odd letters from him, all different, revealing facts about them that he should not have known. But all similar in that they were death threats. He must be stopped."

"Yes. I received one, too. But what if he is already dead?" My words were tentative, testing the waters of this theory. "Suicide."

"Dead?" Victor seemed lightened by the words. "Suicide? Can you verify this?"

"No." And because I wasn't sure myself, my voice quavered just a bit.

"Then how can you say he may be dead?"

"I felt something."

Victor laughed, a cold, hard-sounding laugh.

"You felt something? Deirdre, I have all of the house leaders incensed, calling for blood, in some cases your blood, and I'm supposed to tell them you felt something? He has threatened our very existence. You must understand this is serious business. You and Mitch were brought here to do a job. If that job is not done, there will be serious repercussions."

"Victor," I began, but he cut me off.

"No, I will not listen to your persuasions or your excuses any longer. You were to have killed Larry Martin and you brought him back for judgment instead. That was acceptable in a way and would have been workable, but then you got involved where you should not have. And you released him—accidentally, or so you say." His sarcastic emphasis on those last words caused me to shiver and his distrust of me echoed from every word he spoke. "He is your creation, Deirdre, and your responsibility. And you will be held liable for his crimes should you not be able to stop him. This is not a game we play here. I advise you not to rely on blood ties and sympathies to extricate yourself from this situation. You miraculously avoided punishment for Max's death, but I assure you the Cadre will not be as lenient this time. And we will not be toyed with."

Had Victor not been so angry, I would have laughed at his pompousness. As it was, I began to shake, feeling the full impact of his words. If Larry were not found and brought to justice, I would pay for his sins, trapped for centuries in the airless glass booths of the Cadre. I drew in a deep breath in anticipation of that incarceration. And knew then that Larry was not dead, he could not be dead. He had engineered this situation, deliberately and with malice, with the very personal intent to make me suffer. I could almost hear his laughter.

"Deirdre? Do you understand? If any member of the Cadre is harmed by Larry Martin and you do not bring him to justice, you alone will be held responsible. The ghost of Max Hunter will not save you now. And neither will I."

"I understand, Victor. Believe me, I understand." I hung up the phone and turned around to see Mitch standing in the doorway of the bedroom.

He came over to me and wrapped his arms around me. "I heard everything," he said, "you don't need to repeat a word."

"Mitch," I said, "I won't let them put me in their cage."

"I know, Deirdre, I know," he smoothed my hair in a gentle gesture. "They won't put you in any cage. I won't allow it. We'll find that bastard and we'll kill him. Or we'll tear the whole Cadre down and scatter their fucking ashes over the city."

"But," my voice got softer, sadder, "you're one of them now."

He held me out at arm's length and stared at me for a long time, speaking my name softly. His eyes, which had always held a compelling intensity, now shone unnaturally; their effect seemed to be multiplied ten-fold by his new vampiric nature. And the emotions of which they spoke were so strong they would have been terrifying, except that the strongest of these was love for me. Mitch pulled me deep into himself as if our souls had been merged.

Our souls *were* merged. I felt my body flow into nothingness, all physical sensations faded, and there was nothing left in the world but Mitch, his eyes and his love. And they held me as my grasp on the material world faltered and drifted, dissipating into a mist. A momentary panic flooded my mind and my disembodied voice called his name.

His answer to my distress flowed around me, flowed into me. He came to me and we were one; one in a nothingness that was everything, drifting and entwining, folding into one another. It was a union beyond anything I had ever experienced, beyond the enraptured bond of feeding, beyond the imperfect unity of sex, beyond even the compelling call of a dead soul. It simply was. And in its existence it was perfect.

I became Mitch and he became me and *we were one*. There was no other way to describe the feeling. We had become a hybrid creature, a blending of all that we both were. The inner doubts and fears that we each hid were revealed and channeled back and forth between us— they were swallowed and digested and fed back in almost incomprehensible forms of reassurance and love. I found strengths within him barely untapped. I found insecurities that I would never have expected to have existed. And they were also mine.

"You fear me?" It was not a vocal comment and it did not come solely from my mind.

"No longer, my love."

Then there was laughter and joy, flowing through the particles that had once been our bodies. And love so strong it threatened to be overwhelming in its intensity. But the threat did not matter; we would never be alone again. Unless we should die.

"Then we must not die," came the united thought. "We will not die."

"But we must still go back. We must make it all right."

It was the sadness of that thought, the cruelness of having to leave this perfected unity that brought us both back down to earth, trapping us once more within imperfect bodies. I felt an indescribable coldness wrap around my being and I was torn apart from him, thrown back into the shell of skin and bones and blood.

I was the first to solidify back into material flesh. I watched as he began to materialize, the mist that contained his soul sluggishly reforming, gelling. His eyes glowed as if from nothingness, then his face grew apparent, his hawklike nose, his strong mouth and chin. His torso came next, and his legs. Until finally Mitch stood in front of me again. He reached out to me and I fell into his familiar arms. We both shivered then moved apart.

We stood, facing one another, not touching.

After a while we found the strength to meet each other's eyes and smile.

Then I began to laugh and so did he. Shaking our heads at all of the misconceptions we'd held between the two of us.

"I only tried so hard to be the perfect vampire to make you proud of me," he said, his voice raspy and low.

"I know, my love." I faltered slightly. Words were so difficult to form. "I know. But I don't want you to be the perfect vampire, I just want you to be Mitch."

He nodded, "I know that now. And I'll not let you down."

"You could never let me down, Mitch."

He reached over and rubbed my shoulders. "I won't. Now, let's go get the bastards."

Fifteen

I realized with a shock that hours must have gone by. The sun had been at least two hours from setting when Victor had called. Now it was fully dark outside.

"Damn." Unbuttoning Mitch's shirt, I slipped out of it and handed it to him as I passed.

"What's wrong?"

"We're late." I turned in the doorway and smiled at him. "Victor will probably have his bloodhounds out after us if we don't get there soon. Why don't you call down to the desk and ask them to call a cab while I get dressed."

"Fine." He held his shirt up to his nose, sniffed, then smiled. "Smells good," he said, as he went for the phone.

I retrieved the jeans and sweater I had worn the previous evening and dressed hurriedly. Before he was off the phone, I stepped out of the bedroom, fully clothed, running my fingers through my tangled hair. "I'm ready. Shall we go?"

When we got on the elevator, I met Mitch's eyes, and to my surprise I found myself blushing. He gave me a sheepish smile and I knew he must

be feeling the same as I. Our newfound unity
was wonderful, but embarrassing. We were like
lovers opening our eyes to each other after making love for the first time. All of our virginal
inexperience and clumsiness had been exposed,
not during the passion of the act itself, but afterwards, as we fumbled for something to clothe
our nakedness.

I reached over and took his arm, rubbing my
head on his sleeve.

"That whole thing will take some getting used
to," he said. "And I don't think it's an experience
we'll want to do very often." He whistled. "It's
way too hard coming back."

"Yes."

The elevator doors opened on the lobby and
after stopping at the desk to keep the room reserved for our use later, we went on to the street
and into the waiting cab.

The Imperial was crowded, a line forming up
outside, so we instructed the driver to take us to
the back entrance. After we paid him and he
drove away, Mitch touched my arm.

"Call me cautious," and I smiled, because he
always was, "but I don't think we should confide
in Victor what just happened to us."

I looked at him questioningly. "Why not?"

"I have the feeling that what we experienced
is not a common occurrence."

"Oh, how would you know?"

"Well, for one thing, other than us, have you seen any others keeping constant company?"

"Well," I hesitated, thinking, "now that you mention it, no. But I can't say that I ever noticed or even considered it."

"I have." Mitch's voice was quiet but emphatic. "I've been studying them all and have spent more time with them than you have. They're solitary and distrustful of each other. If they were bonding into pairs, I would've noticed. I haven't. And they aren't."

He stopped, running his fingers through his hair. I prompted him to continue. "And?"

"And on top of all that, they fear us. I can smell it on them. We are an unknown quantity and they'll admit that. Have admitted that. It's the reason why they are normally so polite. Because they can't gauge us and have no idea of the depth of our powers. And I'd sort of like to keep it that way. Shield yourself from their thoughts if you can."

"I'll try."

Mitch opened the door and we descended again into Cadre headquarters.

As before, Victor was waiting for us at the elevators. But this time he wore a broad smile and his manner was completely at ease. "Deirdre," he took my hand and kissed it, "and Mitch. I'm so glad to see you."

The change in his manner was amazing. I could only shake my head and stare at him in disbelief. "Victor?"

"Ah, my dear, you are confused. Please accept

my apologies for my recent unpleasantness towards you. Perhaps we can put it all behind us. You see, I have received good news. Larry Martin has been found dead."

"Dead?" I thought back to my vision. "How?"

Victor laughed, "Just the way he deserved, burnt to a crisp on a park bench. Nothing much left of him but charred bone and teeth."

"Then," said Mitch, his voice suspicious, "how do you know it's him?"

"His watch." Victor reached into his pocket and brought out a heavy gold wristwatch. "Nice piece, too. I wouldn't have thought he'd have such good taste." He turned it over to show the name engraved on the back. "We have this," he playfully tossed the watch into the air, caught it and put it back into his suit coat, "We have the dead body, we have Deirdre's feelings, and," he paused, seeming pleased with himself, "we have a witness."

Mitch's attention snapped in on the last word. "A witness? That's good," he said, barely hiding the scorn in his words, "because everything else you have is nothing. The body could be anyone's, the watch could have been planted and Deirdre's feelings, while I have more trust in her than anyone else, are still just feelings. Can I talk to this witness?"

"Mitch, your diligence does you justice. But the entire experience was so traumatic for her that she's requested to be left alone. She is fairly new and very unsettled. It cannot have been a pleasant experience to witness the death of another."

"I'll bet." Mitch remained unconvinced. And on the strength of his skepticism, I began to doubt myself. Remembering my vision, I shuddered. That it *had* happened, I felt sure. But to whom?

Victor gave me a curious glance. "Trust me. The dead body belongs to Larry Martin. Our witness gave testimony to the house leaders and they all agreed on her testimony. In fact, after we'd gotten together and compared the letters we received, we realized that they could just as easily be considered suicide notes as death threats."

"So I thought, too, Victor," I said, unsure, "but now I don't know. Maybe Mitch should speak to her anyway."

He looked at me, "Deirdre, I should think that you of all people would be happy about this. Why would you want this any other way? And why wish up circumstances that are not true? Larry Martin is dead. You are freed of responsibility for him."

"I don't feel free."

"Give it time, my dear, and you will. This whole thing has been hard on you, I'm sure." He put his arm about my shoulders for a second and gave me a brief hug, before pushing the elevator button. "In fact, as far as I'm concerned your duties are done here. You are free. You and Mitch may leave at any time you wish."

I opened my mouth to protest and caught Mitch's warning glance, deliberately forced myself to relax and to smile. "Thank you, Victor."

"Until then, you are still our honored guests. Now if you will excuse me, I have a full house upstairs."

We watched as he got on, then linked arms and walked down the hallway to our room. It wasn't until we closed and locked the door that we turned to each other to speak.

"So, what do you think?"

I shook my head with a grim smile. "I have absolutely no idea, Mitch. None whatsoever. The vision I had was true. We know that now. One of us died this morning in the rising sun. But I can't know who it was. Or even why it happened. What do *you* think?"

He laughed. "Me? I think the whole thing stinks of a setup. By whom and for what reason, I don't have a clue, either. It doesn't matter; it still seems like a setup to me. And even if it's just a gut reaction on my part, they tend to be correct more often than not. Then again, if the Cadre has a witness they trust . . ." His voice trailed off in thought, then resumed. "It's their lives that seem to be endangered. I guess, if they're satisfied, I should be, too."

"Yes."

"But you're not sure either, are you?"

"No." I sat down on the edge of the bed, then lay down, my feet dangling over the side, locking my fingers together and pillowing my head on them. "I'm not at all sure."

"Do you think it might possibly have been Larry?"

"I felt a bond with the soul involved. That's all I can say."

He sighed. "Personally, I think what I've always thought: Larry is crazy. But much too crazy and egotistical to reach the somewhat sane decision to suicide." He paced the room briefly. "I won't rest until I'm satisfied he's dead. He's too much of a danger, not just to them, but to you. And that's what matters. I really need to talk to this witness."

"But Victor won't let you. He won't even tell us who she is."

Mitch sat down next to me and smiled, a mischievous glint in his eyes. "Fortunately, Victor is not the only vampire in the Cadre. And I know how I can find out. For now, at least, I want you to trust me. We'll stay here and bide our time. If within a week there has been no sign of the illustrious Mr. Martin, I think I can start nosing around without arousing too many suspicions. And," he began to unbutton his shirt, "if there has been no sign of Larry in a week, I might even believe he was dead. I doubt that if he's alive he'll be able to hold out any longer than that without causing trouble."

"I want to leave now." I shrugged and smiled, watching the play of the light on Mitch's chest muscles. "But I've felt that way all along, from our first night here, and I haven't changed my mind. But because you ask it, I'm willing to wait your week, and see what happens."

"Thanks." His eyes were alert, sharp, and I thought to myself that this, finally, was the old

Mitch. The man with whom I had fallen in love, the man with whom I would share my never-ending life.

My body tingled where his came into contact with mine. Suddenly, worries and thoughts about Larry Martin were buried deep beneath the urgency of my need for him. I longed to see where our newfound unity could lead us.

Slowly, sensuously my hand snaked up around his neck and pulled his mouth down to mine. "After all, my love," I whispered, in a voice hoarse with passion, "we have all the time in the world. And we're still supposed to be on our honeymoon."

"Mrs. Greer," Mitch said, his eyes glowing, his hands slowly traveling down my body, "have I ever told you that I love the way you think?"

I laughed. "And have I ever told you that I love the way you love?"

What a strange lovemaking that was, I thought, as I lay back in his arms, coming down slowly from the waves of orgasms. Yes, it had been completely satisfying, intimate, and passionate, like every other time Mitch and I made love. Yet I felt more alien and more distant from him than I ever had before. The fault, if fault it was, did not seem to lie in the comparison of the earlier blending of our souls with this physical merging. It lay instead with our subsequent division into ourselves again.

Mitch kissed the top of my head. "That was

wonderful, Deirdre. But," I heard the confusion in his voice, it mirrored my thoughts, "it hurt me."

"Hurt you? I'm not sure I know what you mean."

"And I'm not really sure I can explain." He stroked my hair lightly and I shivered, then grabbed his hand and put it to my mouth, kissing each finger separately.

"Try."

Mitch thought for a while longer. "I don't mean it hurt physically, far from it." He chuckled slightly. "It felt wonderful, physically. Maybe our best ever. But somewhere, deep inside, it hurt. As if, by pulling away from each other this afternoon, we left behind some sort of psychic wound, one that'll ache until we're fully together again. But as aches go, it wasn't bad."

I laughed at him, then sobered. "I think I understand. I'm not sure it can be described, but I think I understand."

"I knew you would."

We lay quiet for a while, separate physically and mentally, each of us trapped inside thoughts and feelings for which we could find no words. I got up from the bed and began to get dressed.

"Where are you going?" Mitch pushed himself up on one elbow and watched me solemnly.

"I know we agreed to wait for a week, but I want to look for him anyway. In my own way."

"Would you like some company?"

"Absolutely, my love. We can look together. But

be warned, I plan on starting my search where it all began.''

Mitch groaned slightly and shook his head. "Well, I don't like it much, but it makes sense. Perfect sense. Criminals usually return to the scene of the crime, and while the Ballroom may not be that specifically, we can't deny that there is something that keeps leading us back there. It's the ideal place to start our search."

He got up from the bed and started to dress. "But I still say we should burn the damn place down.''

Sixteen

I was already settled into the back seat of the cab and Mitch was just about to get in when a familiar figure burst from the front doors of the Imperial, waving frantically in the attempt to get our attention. "Deirdre, Mitch, wait." Vivienne's voice was earnest and warm. "Where are you going? I want to speak with you."

Tensing slightly, I caught back a sound of annoyance. One thing we most certainly didn't need or want tonight was the presence of another Cadre member. But Mitch shook his head while motioning for me to stay inside. He straightened back up, smiled at her and she ran over to him, holding out her hands in greeting, laughing the odd, metallic laugh that never failed to make a shiver run up my back.

I studied the two of them from the back seat. For once Vivienne was not dressed provocatively, but instead was wearing faded denim jeans, a powder blue sweatshirt, and a pair of running shoes. Her long blond hair was pulled back into a ponytail and she wore very little makeup. She looked pale and delicate, impossibly young and beautiful, her tiny hands enfolded in his.

Mitch had put on black jeans, with a black t-shirt that was tight enough to reveal a lean and muscled torso. His gray hair was tousled by the wind and I noticed for the first time that he was wearing it longer. I'd never seen him look less like a cop. Or more desirable. Together, I couldn't help but admit, they made a nice-looking couple.

"We're just going out for a bit, Vivienne," I heard him saying, "but maybe you'd like to join us?"

"Well, yes, I would." She rolled her eyes at him. "But only if I'm not interfering. I don't want to be the unwanted third."

"Vivienne," Mitch's voice caressed the name, "how could a lovely woman like you ever be unwanted? Please join us."

With his second impassioned invitation I realized what he was attempting, understood his motivation as plainly as if he had spoken his intentions out loud. He was going to get the information he required from her.

Understanding didn't necessarily mean I had to like his methods. Suddenly I had a flash of how he must have felt while he was still mortal; how he must have suffered to know that I had need to seek out the embrace of another. Even though the need had always been for sustenance and not for love, it was still a kind of betrayal and it hurt.

"Deirdre, sister?" Vivienne leaned into the cab. "If you are sure you have no objections?"

I forced back my petty jealousy and gave her

my brightest smile. "Mitch is right, you should join us."

With another laugh, she got into the cab next to me, giving me a small hug as she settled in. "I can't tell you how happy I am to have you here," she whispered into my ear. "I have been so wanting a sister, and a friend, for so long."

Mitch crawled in after her and draped his arm over the back of the seat, lightly caressing the tip of my shoulder. "This is nice, isn't it? One big happy family."

Vivienne leaned her head back into him and giggled again. "Yes, it's very nice, Mitch. So where are we going? And what are we going to do once we get there?"

"Good point, lady." The driver turned around. "Where to?"

Mitch and I said in unison and with about the same amount of enthusiasm, "The Ballroom, please."

"Oh," she purred, sounding as young and innocent as she looked, "I love the Ballroom. What fun. Such a marvelous idea."

We were a block away when she turned to me. "I was very angry, you know, when I'd found out that Max left the place to you. I always thought that it would be mine someday. I even had plans for it."

"Really?" I shook my head, the club had never been anything other than a burden to me. And although I'd never admitted it to him, Mitch's idea of burning it to the ground appealed to me. "What sort of plans?"

To my surprise, Vivienne took a sidelong glance at Mitch, then blushed. "It's silly, you know, but I hate to say, actually. It's a difficult thing to explain without sounding, oh," and she waved her tiny hand in the air, "rather indelicate. Let us just say I had planned to close it, redecorate it and open up an entirely different type of club."

Mitch leaned forward and met my eyes, nodding. "Seems like a good idea to me, no matter what type of club Vivienne wants to open. What do you think, Deirdre?"

I shrugged. "It sounds like a wonderful opportunity for all of us. I never wanted any part of the damn place." I looked out the window and sighed. "And it always seemed a vindictive joke on Max's part to will it to me anyway."

"Max." His name on her lips seemed to drip with venom. "Please don't get me started on Max. We should be having a good time and not be raking up the past tonight." Her childish manner had instantly vanished and her eyes narrowed, studying my reaction, "But, in the matter of the Ballroom, you would perhaps consider selling it to me?"

"Perhaps. What sort of price did you have in mind?"

The price she quoted made Mitch and the cab driver whistle in disbelief. There was probably a time in my life when I would have been impressed also, but that was before I had amassed a small fortune through the sale of my fashion business and a large one through the death of

Max. "That seems satisfactory. Let's draw up the papers as soon as possible."

Vivienne clasped her hands together, in an appealing gesture. "Oh, my sister," she cooed, "my sweet, sweet sister, thank you."

"Don't mention it," I said, embarrassed by her enthusiasm. "It's my pleasure."

The doorman recognized Vivienne and let us in with no questions and no hassles. We pushed our way across the crowded dance floor and up to the bar.

"What'll it be, folks?"

I glanced at the bartender with no recognition. He was young and good looking, with no characteristics to make him different from every other normal man here, as if he had been assembled half-hazardly from available parts.

"We'll have a scotch on the rocks, a glass of red wine," Mitch looked down at Vivienne, "and?"

"Oh," she laughed, "Marky knows what I want, don't you?"

The bartender winked at her. "I most certainly do, Miss Courbet."

He mixed the drinks and handed them over to us one by one, "Scotch on the rocks, red wine, and my special formula Bloody Mary. On the house, of course, and with your permission, Ms. Griffin."

At my look of shock he grinned at me. "Fred

told us that first night who you were. And he said you were always to be greeted by name."

"Thank you." I motioned to Mitch and Vivienne. "Why don't you two get us a table someplace? I'll be right over."

After they left, I looked around. "I'd like to speak with Fred. Is he in tonight?"

"Nope, nobody here but us chickens," Mark laughed. "He mentioned last night that he was going to take a few days off. Said he figured since you'd probably be in town for a while, that you'd be in every now and then to keep an eye on the place. The place pretty much runs itself anyway. No problems, the customers drink and dance and get into just a little bit of, well," and he winked at me this time, causing me to laugh in spite of my dismay at his familiarity, "hanky-panky every now and then to keep things interesting."

"I see." I picked up my wine glass and took a sip. Then another. It was from the special stock that Max always saved for me.

"How's the wine?" Mark asked, making an idle sweep over the surface of the bar with a dish rag.

"Wonderful, thank you. Just like old times."

"But better I'll bet." His eyes glinted at me through the dim, smoky air.

"Yes," I admitted with a smile, relaxing with surprise into his warm, friendly manner. "Infinitely better."

"Good," Mark said, "we aim to please."

* * *

Mitch and Vivienne were deep in conversation when I arrived at the table. He glanced up at me for a minute then turned back to her. "The doorman?"

"No, not the doorman." She took a long sip of her drink, then pulled out the celery stick and sucked on it briefly, before smiling at me. "Mitch and I are playing a game of questions. He is most delightful, but I don't suppose I have to tell you that."

"How wonderful." I sat down and took a pull on my wine. "Who's winning?"

Mitch shot me a hard look for intervening. I could feel his frustration. Vivienne was proving to be harder to manipulate than he thought. It was a good lesson for him to learn, I thought, and I turned my chair slightly and watched the dance floor.

"So, what about the bartender Mark, then?"

Vivienne put her head back and laughed. "That is an interesting one, Mitch. And one that I cannot answer. It's not that easy, you see, telling one of us from one of them. I think that Marky, if not a vampire now, will be one soon. He's only here two maybe three months and he's already a favorite of Fred's." She waved her hand in the air again, seeming to dismiss the situation. "And you should know, *mon chou,* that I am, in any event, the wrong person to ask. Now Victor, he is a different story. Victor knows everyone, poor man, that's his job. He knows the new ones and the old ones and the ones that only appear every century or so." She picked up her drink and stared at him over the rim of the glass. "Why do you need to know all this, anyway?"

Mitch smiled. "Curiosity, mainly. I'm so very new and Deirdre is unfamiliar with the turf, so to speak. I still find it hard to believe that the city could contain so many vampires and no one would notice."

"Ah," Vivienne said with a tilt of her head, "curiosity. I understand that quite well. And there are really not so very many of us, Mitch, as you seem to think. Most of the house leaders had been called here when Deirdre was under scrutiny and on trial. And they seemed to have lingered longer than usual. Even I have stayed much longer than I planned. It was fortunate in a way, that the Larry Martin situation turned up so quickly after your departure. We would all have been in very unpleasant moods if we'd left, then had to be called back after such a short time."

I gave a half laugh. "If the house leaders' recent moods can pass as pleasant, then it really was fortunate."

Vivienne reached over and laid her hand on my arm. "Poor Deirdre, we have not been very nice to you, have we? Myself, I think that Victor put you in an impossible situation, one which looked like you could never win. But," her face brightened a bit and she drained her drink, "you did win. I am very relieved, for many reasons, that things turned out as they did."

She waved her hand and the waiter almost instantaneously appeared with another round of drinks.

"Good service," Mitch observed with a grin, "even better service than Deirdre usually gets. She often has to wait for a minute or two." He eyed Vivienne's glass. "So what exactly is in Mark's special blend Bloody Mary?"

"A little bit of this," she admitted, "and a little bit of that. But," she gave Mitch a serious glance, "certainly not what you're thinking. I much prefer that drink unadulterated."

The band stopped playing and the dance floor began to thin out. I couldn't stop myself from studying the dancers intently, although I knew that catching Larry a second time would not be as easy. If he was even around and alive to be caught. The whole endeavor seemed futile to me. If he were dead, we were wasting our time. And if he were not, he most certainly would not come here.

Mitch followed my gaze out on the dance floor and suddenly tensed. "What?" I whispered to him over the table, completely ignoring Vivienne's presence. "Is it him?"

"No," Mitch said, rising from his chair and waving, "it's Chris. What the bloody hell is he doing here?"

"Hi, Dad." Chris sat down at the table and nodded to me. "Deirdre." He was drunk again; he'd barely had time to sleep off last night's alcohol. Mitch frowned in his direction and Chris looked away from both of us, focusing instead on Vivienne with growing interest. "And friend."

"Mitch," she said, her voice light, "aren't you going to introduce me?"

"Vivienne, this is my son, Chris. Chris, this is our new friend Vivienne Courbet."

"Very nice to meet you, Miss Courbet." Chris was teasing her with his formality, to his eyes she would appear younger than he.

"And you, Chris." Her words were as soft as velvet. Velvet covering cold hard iron, I thought and stole a glance at Mitch. His expression of distrust seemed to agree. "I see that you are as charming and handsome as your father. But younger," she laughed at Chris and winked at Mitch, "and far better looking. Would you like to dance?"

"Well, yeah." Chris was completely enchanted with her, "I'd like that very much, but the music's stopped."

Vivienne's voice deepened. "Ah, *mon petit chou,* when one is young and in love the music never stops. Besides, I have monopolized your father's attentions for way too long. We wouldn't want Deirdre to get jealous, now would we?"

"No, 'course not." Chris's voice cracked slightly. She rose, took his hand, and led him to the empty dance floor.

Mitch stared intently as the two of them began to dance. "I don't think he knows what she is, do you?" I asked him. "Do you want me to stop them?"

"No," Mitch shook his head and flicked a

glance to me, before returning his attention to the dance floor. "I think this might be a good thing for him. Maybe he'll be able to understand our relationship better as a result. And maybe he'll be able to accept the fact when he learns what I have become."

"Maybe," I agreed half-heartedly. "Or meeting her might just prove to be the worst mistake of his young life."

We watched them dance for a while; he towered over her and the top of her head barely reached his shoulder. To any outsider they would look like a young couple in the first flush of love.

At first they held each other apart while Vivienne chattered up into his face. She smiled, she flirted, and he responded, warming to her more, rewarding her efforts with a smile so much like Mitch's that it made my heart twist. As they continued swaying to their own personal music, they drew each other in closer, their bodies touching, not even a hair's breadth separating them. Chris put his head down closer to hers and she stretched up on her toes, her lips straining to reach his ears.

"I hope she's not hungry," I said to myself, feeling somewhat uncomfortable and very much a voyeur.

Mitch groaned a bit. "I suspect watching this is not such a good idea. Excuse me for a minute." He got up from the table and disappeared into the men's room. I continued to watch Vivienne and Chris, fascinated at how she managed to hypnotize him, there, in full view of everyone in the club. Was this how I looked in the process of the hunt? Was I as good as she?

"She's really something, isn't she?"

Mark's unexpected arrival made me jump and I knocked over my wine glass, not breaking it, but spilling the dregs on the table. "Yes, she certainly is." I mopped up the wine with the loose napkins on the table and when I was done he set three more drinks in front of me, removing the empty ones to a tray set on the table behind him.

"Fred says you were the best." He placed both hands on the heart-shaped table top and leaned into me, an undisguised admiration reflected on his face. "He says you could capture them with just a look, just a movement of your hand."

"I was the best?" I saw no need to hide my nature from this young man and I was too weary for denials. "Why the past tense?"

Mark looked away, blushing. "Fred says that when vampires," his voice lowered on the word, "fall in love, they lose their touch. They become soft; their instincts get dull."

"Ah, I see. I suppose Fred is an expert."

"He's usually right."

The laugh I tried to give came out more of a growl; it was a threatening sound and he backed away. "And Fred probably is right," I continued. "I don't know. But I have never gone hungry. Please tell him that for me next time you see him."

"Oh, God, I— I mean, I meant no offense, Miss Griffin. Really. I was just sort of talking off the cuff. That happens when I get nervous."

"No offense taken, Mark. At least not from you. But from Fred?" I shrugged. "Our Fred should remember not to sit in judgment over his elders and his betters. I've won with him before and I have no doubt I can do so again."

Mark gulped. "I'm sorry I said anything at all. Shit, Fred will be really mad at me now." His hangdog attitude did not calm me down, but merely annoyed me further. Who the hell was Fred to inspire such devotion in a man? But I kept my thoughts to myself and pulled my eyes away from him, fastening them again upon the couple on the dance floor.

"Please, don't say anything to him about this, Deirdre."

"Fred and I are not close. Not by any stretch of the imagination, Mark. Should we never come into contact with each other again, I would not spend even one minute of my endless time seeking him out. So your secrets are safe with me. And you're free to think whatever you like." I turned my direction back to Chris and Vivienne on the dance floor. His hands had reached lower on her body and had pulled her in against him. Her mouth was still on the level of his ear and I could see her lips moving. She was not biting him, I realized with a sigh of relief, she was only talking to him. And what kind of harm could that do?

Mark snuck off when he discovered that I was

paying him no attention and Mitch returned. "Are they still at it?" he asked, a tone of disgust appearing. "Maybe we should just leave."

The band, now, had returned to the stage and they started to tune their instruments, laughing and joking with each other, some of it apparently focused on the two on the dance floor. It seemed good natured though and I assumed that they were well acquainted with Vivienne's presence at the club.

Without warning, Chris abruptly pulled away from her; his sudden separation and withdrawal of support caused her to stagger. They stared at each other, their breath coming in short gasps. Finally, Chris looked over at our table, then back to her. All the blood had rushed out of his face, as if she had indeed been feeding off of him. And in a sense, that was only too accurate.

"That can't be true . . ." His voice carried even over the discord of the instruments. "My father is not a vampire. And he will never be one."

Seventeen

Chris took one last look at our table, catching my eyes and holding them for a time. Then he pushed Vivienne away from him and ran out the door. The three of us watched him leave without making a move to stop him, without saying a word. There was nothing that could be done or said.

Vivienne slowly approached the table, her hands pressing firmly against her mouth. When she lowered them, her lips were almost white. "I'm so sorry, Mitch. I thought he knew."

Mitch stared off in the direction of the street as if he were able to see through the walls and watch Chris's retreat. His face was expressionless. "Maybe it's better this way; I'm not sure I could have found the right words. He'll go away for a while, sleep off the beer, and things will be okay."

"*Oui.*" She stretched up on her toes and kissed Mitch's cheek with a gentleness that surprised me. "Perhaps you are right. I pray that you are."

I said nothing. I had seen the expression on Chris's face. Had read the hatred in his eyes.

There would be no forgiveness, no understanding and it would tear Mitch to pieces. I sighed.

"We are doing no good here, Mitch," I said to him. "Let's go home. Vivienne, are you coming?"

"No, I think I'll stay here for a while, if you don't mind. I'm sure you wish to be alone and I've caused enough trouble for one evening. Please know that I did not mean to." She shrugged her shoulders. "Trouble seems to follow me wherever I go."

She seemed so sincere in her upset that I almost believed her. I could see from Mitch's face that he did. Perhaps that was most important right now.

He straightened his shoulders and ran his fingers through his hair. "Don't worry about it, Vivienne. It was inevitable that Chris find out sooner or later." He gave a humorless laugh. "It's not as if I could've been able to hide what I am from him indefinitely. I was deliberately avoiding the issue, knowing that there was no way he would take it well. We should have told him immediately, even before we left for England."

"But," I reached over, took Mitch's hand and squeezed it, giving the only comfort I could, "now at least he knows."

"Yeah," he agreed, "and strangely enough, that's a big relief. Let's go."

We said brief goodbyes to Vivienne, waved to Mark as we walked through the club and stood on the street for a few minutes. Mitch looked intently at the crowd of pedestrians for Chris's familiar figure, but he was nowhere in sight.

"You want to go after him, don't you?" It wasn't really a question on my part. It is what I would have wanted to do.

"Yeah, do you mind?"

"Even if I did, my love, what else would I have to do?"

We started walking down the street in the direction of Mitch's old brownstone apartment building. "Chris was always such a good kid. Never gave us any trouble, not even during his teenage years. Most kids go crazy at a certain point; turn rebellious and hate their parents, you know the phase. But not Chris. He always followed my advice, was always around to talk to after a particularly bad day at the department. And even if he never said that he was proud of me, I knew that he was."

"He's your son, Mitch, and he loves you. He'll come around."

"And what if he doesn't?"

We stopped under a streetlight and I squinted up into the light reflecting from his face. "You want the truth?" I waited for his nod, then continued. "If he doesn't come around, you'll both still survive. You'll both go on with your own lives. Isn't that the way it should be?"

"Yeah, I suppose it is."

We searched until the sun was almost up. Chris was nowhere Mitch thought he might have gone.

We made a final check back at the apartment, let ourselves in the front door, and listened. His place was empty.

"We'll have to go somewhere soon, Mitch. It's almost dawn."

"I know. But I'm worried about him, where could he be?"

"It's a big city, my love, and Chris is a big boy. I'm sure he'll be okay. Could he have gone to his mother?"

Mitch always teased me that I had no past because I chose not to speak of it. I thought he had told me most of the intimate details of his life, but I realized that there were things he held back on also. His previous marriage was one of them; I didn't know his ex-wife's name.

"Barbara's?" He thought about the idea and rejected it. "No, I don't think so, the two of them have never really gotten along that well since the divorce. And he absolutely hates her new husband."

"Sort of like he hates your new wife?"

Walking to the curb and signaling for a cab, he laughed and looked back over his shoulder at me. "Much worse than you."

"Worse than me? Is that possible? Who is this guy, Jack the Ripper?"

He gave me a quick look. "I've never told you the story of my divorce, have I?"

"No, other than the fact that your wife, Barbara, was tired of being a policeman's wife. So she remarried? Who was the lucky man?"

"My ex-partner." His voice held no emotion and I couldn't read his eyes.

But I couldn't help stifling a quick laugh as I got into the cab and gave the driver the address of the Imperial. Mitch slid over next to me and put his arm around my shoulders. "I can understand why you don't want to talk about it, Mitch. That must have been a pretty humiliating experience for you."

"Actually," he spread the word out, trying to maintain a serious expression, but failing, "it was the funniest situation I've ever been involved in. You'd be amazed at the machinations these two put into the affair, when all either one of them needed to do was tell me, honestly and up-front, what was going on. I knew for years before Martin got up the nerve to confess."

"But you still don't like to talk about it."

"I don't talk about it, Deirdre, because it's unimportant to us. Unimportant to almost everything in my life. And I never loved her the way I love you." He touched his hand to my upper thigh, rubbed down to my knee and up again. "You're all that matters to me. And I don't ever want you to forget that."

The Imperial was deserted when we arrived and the pre-dawn streets surrounding the restaurant were practically empty, giving the area an almost surrealistic quality. We let ourselves into the back entrance with our key and made our way through the corridors to our rooms.

I smelled the roses before we were halfway into the room. I stopped, inhaled deeply, and turned to Mitch, who was turning on the light by the bed. "They're lovely, Mitch. Thank you so much."

"Huh?"

I pointed to the bouquet sitting atop of the dresser; a dozen blood red roses and one black bud. Walking over to them I buried my nose in the blooms and pulled in their rich scent.

"I didn't send them."

I spun around and he was smiling a rather sheepish smile. "I've been a little busy and haven't really had time to think of flowers. They must be from Victor, or maybe the whole Cadre; you know, as a sort of thank you for a job well-done."

"Well, maybe." I turned back to the dresser and looked around for a card. "But I didn't really do anything. If Larry is truly dead, he did that on his own. They should have sent these to the cemetery in that case."

"Maybe they're just standard Cadre decorating, then. Pretty though, I wonder why there's one black rose with the rest."

"Max used to do that. Do you remember when we first met and my office was filled with flowers?"

"Yeah." He smiled at the memory. "I wanted to know who died. I'm afraid that's as close to romantic behavior as I ever get, Deirdre. You've tied yourself down to a very practical man."

"You don't hear me complaining. I don't need roses, my love."

"Well, if this is a Max-type tradition," he walked over to the dressers and looked at the roses, fingering one of the velvety blooms, "I would expect that these came from Victor. Maybe as an apology for his 'unpleasantness.' "

I smiled at his impersonation. "You do that so very well, my love. But I keep telling you to watch your step; Victor might just resign and they'll elect you to the job."

I stepped out of my clothes and kicked them over into the corner of the room. "I really have to call Betsy this afternoon; I can't go on wearing the same things over and over again. But first, I want a shower and some sleep. Interested?"

His eyes lit up and ran appreciatively over my naked body. "You're perfection, you know."

I gave a low chuckle as I went into the bathroom. "You aren't so bad yourself, Detective, or have you failed to notice? Come here."

He stood in front of me and I pulled the t-shirt from his body. "Now," I reached up and took hold of his shoulders, turning him around to face the mirror over the sink. "Look at yourself."

I stood behind him, one arm stretched around his neck and the other resting on his upper arm. We both stared at our reflection and our eyes met. Our skin glowed, his a slightly darker hue than mine. His gray hair flowed back from his forehead, ending just a bit above his shoulders. He might be mistaken for an old man at first glance until he opened his eyes; electric blue as always, they glowed with an inner heat that hinted of stronger flames within. We were both strong and conditioned predators. "See," I said with a twisted smile, "perfection."

Then I slapped him lightly on his backside and ducked away from him, pulling open the shower curtain and turning on the water. "I get first dibs on the hot water."

Mitch skinned out of his jeans and his underwear. "The hell you do." He stepped into the shower and lifted me up by the waist, twisting me around and setting me down behind him. We played the game for a while with the hot water splashing over our bodies, warming our skin to a near human temperature. It had been a difficult night and we had more than our share of problems to solve, but together we were one. In that unity, all else in the world seemed to pale.

After all the soaping and the teasing, the nipping, the gentle and the not so gentle love play, we dried each other off and got into bed. Mitch gave a great yawn, exposing slightly sharpened canines that had grown during our play and I laughed at him, softly.

"What's so funny?"

"You're like a great big dog, sometimes. Especially when you yawn like that."

"Oh, yeah?" he said, baring his teeth to me in a fake snarl. "I prefer to think of myself as a wolf, hunting the wilds in search of warm, rich blood."

He growled at me and just for a second his face seemed to twist into another shape; I saw what he could be. I gasped; he was frightening but beautiful. Then he yawned again and the illusion disappeared.

"Damn, I'm beat," he said, reaching over and giving me a light kiss. "Sleep well, Deirdre."

He was out almost instantly, sleeping the way I used to, effortlessly and deeply, almost boneless in his utter relaxation. I lay sleeplessly next to him for a while, disturbed by the sounds of daily life outside the room, sounds that urged me to find a window somewhere in this crypt and look upon daylight one final time. I stayed in bed and resisted the whispered seduction, but the seeds of yesterday's dawn vision had been planted.

This time the picture seemed clearer, sharper; a lone figure in the pre-dawn mist, sitting quietly, unmoving. The sky lightened, the sun rose, and the figure glowed, echoing the colors of dawn, before bursting into flame.

I turned my face to the ceiling of the darkened room as if to feel the cleansing heat of my vision. Ah, to see the sun once more, I thought and sighed. But Mitch stirred next to me, and murmured my name, reminding me that I had reason yet to live. Closing my eyes, I nestled into the cool skin of his shoulder and slept.

Eighteen

I woke in the late afternoon with a start, shivering in the draft from the open door. Open door? I sat up in bed and elbowed Mitch.

"What?" His eyes opened and he stared around the room hazily until they focused in.

"Mitch, we did close the door this morning, didn't we?"

"Of course, closed and locked."

"It's open now."

"What the hell?" Mitch jumped from the bed and crossed the room, slamming the door shut and turning the dead bolt. "That's strange. Really strange." He started back across the room and yelped as he stepped down on something. He bent down and picked up the stem of a rose. It was missing its bloom completely. "Damn," he said and then, "stupid thorns." Hopping over to the bed, he sat back down, laid the stem on top of my covers and inspected the sole of his foot. "I suspect I'll live." He pulled a thorn from his skin and tossed it into the corner of the room. "This is why I never send a lady roses, she just finds a way to hurt me with them." He smiled to soften his words. "What the hell were you doing while I was sleeping, Deirdre, dancing the tango with Max?"

I looked at him, puzzled. I remembered the vision before I fell asleep, but afterwards there were no memories. It had been an exhausting week so far and my sleep must have been deeper than normal. I shook my head, and the covers were scattered with the petals from the missing rose.

"Tell me," he said, the expression in his eyes betraying the fact that he knew that I could not, "that you got up from bed, opened the door, and got that rose, tossing the stem to where I would step on it and sprinkling your head with the petals."

"Mitch," I started, swallowing hard to overcome the rush of panic I felt, "I didn't do that. Someone else was in this room today."

"Yeah," his eyes flashed angrily, "I was just sort of hoping that you'd developed a taste for stupid practical jokes in your old age. I wonder who it was. Vivienne, maybe? She seems like the type somehow, to perpetrate a little playful fun, nothing serious."

"Vivienne would be more likely to crawl into bed between us than to pull a prank with a flower."

He laughed. "I suppose you're right."

"Chris?"

Mitch thought about that for a minute, went to the dresser and pulled on a pair of jeans. Then we went back to the door and inspected the knob. "I know I locked this; I do every time we're in here. In order for anyone to get in they would have had to either break the lock or have a key. The lock isn't broken that I can see, and it's not been tampered with. Even had it been, I don't think Chris has the skills for breaking and entering. But as far as the key situation goes, we only have Victor's assurance that ours are the only ones." He walked back to the bed, his gaze falling on the two coffins held on the ornate stand. "Although, wasn't this box delivered for me when we were out? So it's possible that a staff member might have access, like in a hotel."

"We never bother locking the door when we leave, Mitch. You always says what good does a lock do against a creature who can dissolve into a mist."

"Exactly."

Our eyes met. "And of course," he said with a scornful laugh, "if you want to narrow a suspect list down to only one creature like that, this place sure as hell is the wrong bloody place to start."

"Well," I tucked the covers under my arms, checked the clock and picked up the phone. "We'll mention it to Victor. Maybe it was just a staff person after all. No harm was done, really. And although I don't much like the thought of people coming and going without my knowing about it, they can't have meant to hurt us. We'd both be dead, if they had." I dialed my old office. "I'm going to give Betsy a call. I still need some clothes to wear. I hope she'll deliver."

It was a comfort to hear Betsy's brusque voice answer the call. And there could be no question in my mind that she was delighted to hear from me.

"Deirdre," her voice boomed from the receiver and I laughed softly, seeing Mitch's fake wince, "how've you been? And what have you and that handsome husband of yours been up to?" She laughed so loudly that I had to hold the phone out away from my ear. "As if I didn't have a good idea of what I'd be doing in your place."

"Betsy," I said, always tickled by her no-nonsense approach to everything, "you'd be surprised."

"Try me." Her voice was sly and devious. "You might be surprised instead. Now, what can I do for you?"

"I need some clothes; we ended up staying in town longer than we'd intended to and I under packed."

"What kind of clothes?"

"Like the last time you rode to my rescue, an assortment, mostly casual, but some dressy. You remember the sizes and colors, don't you?"

"Yes. You're in a rut, you know. And you're fortunate that I have some here that will suit you. But is there any reason why you just can't go shopping like everyone else in the world?"

I laughed. "It's just so much fun making you do this, Betsy. Meet me at the Imperial in about an hour or so and I'll buy you dinner."

"Damn straight you will, Deirdre. And you'll pay my outrageous prices, too." I could visualize her, writing up the invoice while we were still talking, tacking on a huge percentage for the inconvenience of my wanting to do business this way. I didn't mind, the money meant nothing. I needed the clothes and I would get the pleasure of her company for the evening on top of everything. It was a fair exchange.

"I don't suppose you'll be staying in town for too long this time either, will you?"

"No, Betsy. We have some unfinished business to complete and then we'll be gone again. I'd say no more than two or three weeks at the most."

She sighed. "Too bad. I could still use you as a consultant. Maybe next time." Then her voice brightened. "I'll meet you in the Imperial bar in two hours. And bring your detective with you if you can."

I hung up the phone and looked at Mitch. "Betsy says . . ."

He grinned. "You don't have to repeat it, I suspect the entire Cadre knows what Betsy says. But you'll have to count me out on this one, babe. I am not going to dinner with that particular predatory female." He sighed and pulled a shirt out of the closet. "I suspect I'm going to have to spend the entire evening convincing Victor that he's got a security problem here in his little kingdom. Then I need to track down Chris and see if we can talk about this. I'll meet you back here sometime later tonight, okay?"

He came over and wrapped his arms around me, kissing me not too gently on the lips. Then he ran his fingers through my hair; a few rose petals floated down. He studied them and shivered. I knew what he was feeling. Against the backdrop of the pure white sheets they looked like many drops of blood. If our daytime visitor'd had murderous intent they could very easily have been. He pulled me close to him again, and kissed me for a very long time; his mouth working on mine, his tongue running over my lips, my teeth. His eyes were opened and we locked gazes.

When we finally separated, I sighed. "I love you, Deirdre. Be careful tonight. I'm going to convince Victor that he's got a problem here if it kills me. And until he manages to set up some sort of security system, we'll have to maintain a watch ourselves."

"You be careful, too. Go softly with Victor; he's not as placid as you'd think. And probably too powerful to annoy."

He laughed. "I don't give a flying fuck for Victor's power. He's put you in danger and he'll solve that problem or pay for it."

He kissed me one more time, just a brushing of his lips against mine. He was halfway to the door when he turned around and spoke again. "Do me a favor?"

"Anything, love."

"Ask around, if you can, and see if anyone else received either roses or a visitor today. If this is happening to everyone, it's not quite the same as if it is just happening to us."

I nodded. "I shouldn't be too late, Mitch. Expect me around eleven o'clock or so." I blew him a small kiss and he chuckled and went out the door. After he closed it, I could hear the jingle of keys outside and saw the dead bolt turn. He was locking me in, to keep me safe. I smiled softly to myself, stretched and got up, brushing the rose petals from the sheets on to the floor.

Betsy was waiting in the bar for me when I arrived. I'd found a black mini-skirt and a lacy blouse in my luggage and wore them with a pair of plain high-heeled pumps and flesh tone hose. The skirt and blouse were left-overs from my years alone in England, where my provocative dress had been designed to entice my victims. She looked me up and down and made a clicking noise with her tongue. "You should be paying me double, you know. God, that outfit is horrible."

I shrugged and looked down at myself. "I didn't have much else that would be suitable at this point. This is good enough."

She threw her head back and laughed loud and long. "Yeah, good enough, but only if you're planning on picking up a few bucks on the street afterwards. Here," she shoved a bag in my direction, "I knew somehow that you wouldn't have anything appropriate. Go to the ladies' room and change into this."

"But, this is fine . . ."

"The hell you say. I will not eat dinner with someone who looks like she's a twenty-dollar hooker. At least what's in the bag raises your price a bit. Put it on and I'll order you a drink."

I leaned over the table and gave her a kiss on the cheek. "You haven't changed a bit, Betsy McCain. And it's nice to see you, too. I'll have a cabernet or a merlot or something similar." I took the bag and went into the ladies' room.

It was a simple dress, elegant and understated, made of dark green velvet in a princess style that fit tightly through the bust and the waist and flared out through the hips. I slipped it on over my head after removing my skirt and blouse and smoothed it down. The material felt soft and rich under my touch, the skirt fell only about two inches above my knees.

But the color, although flattering, made me nervous. The only times in the past years when I'd deviated from my normal black, white or red pattern, I'd worn this color. And each time it had been a disastrous evening. I didn't need any more of those. But it was a pretty dress and Betsy would be disappointed if I didn't wear it. I shrugged off my superstitions as best I could and smiled at myself in the mirror before I left the room.

As I walked into the bar area, I heard her voice in heated tones. "She only went to the ladies' room for a minute, for Christ's sake. And hell no, I'm not going to go get her; whatever you have to say can't be all that important. If it is you can get her yourself."

Betsy was very petite, shorter than me. Her brown hair was worn slightly longer than last time I'd seen her, but otherwise her appearance hadn't changed. She was brassy, inside and out.

At this moment she was standing at the table, hands on her hips, feet firmly planted on the floor, staring a very agitated Victor fully in the face. And winning, I observed, with a wry grin, a fact established by the fact that Victor's answer to her was soft and placating.

"Is there some sort of problem, Victor?"

He jumped as I came up behind him; he'd been so preoccupied with Betsy that he hadn't heard my approach.

"Deirdre." He spun around and grabbed my arm. "I need to speak with you, now."

"Fine, Victor," I pulled away from him with a quick gesture, "I take it this is a private discussion."

"Yes."

"Then let's go somewhere else and keep it so. Betsy, why don't you get them to seat you in the dining room now? I'll join you as soon as I can. But there's no reason you should miss dinner on my account."

"Okay," she agreed. "I've left the box of clothes with the coat-check girl and I'll leave the bill for you if you don't return."

"Ms. McCain," Victor made a slight bow in her direction, "I apologize for interrupting your evening, but rest assured I would not have done so unless it was very important. Dinner tonight will be on the house." He waved his arm and the maitre d' came over to us. "Give Ms. McCain our best table, a bottle of our best champagne, and the best steak she's ever had. Give the check to me."

Betsy eyed the young host admiringly. "I'm not really in any hurry, Deirdre, take your time."

Victor took my arm and led me away hurriedly. "Green," I muttered under my breath.

"What?"

"Nothing. Just that sometimes superstitions have very good basis in fact."

He escorted me to his restaurant office without another word and closed the door once we were safely inside.

"So, what seems to be the problem, Victor?"

"We have another body. We think it's the body of yet another vampire, but we don't know right now."

"And how did this one die?"

"Same way, an apparent suicide. He was sitting on a bench in Central Park when the sun came up."

"Do you know who it was?"

"No, we don't."

"When will you know who it is?"

"Soon, I hope. But identification in these cases is often next to impossible. The police cooperate as much as possible, but when all you have to work with is a pile of charred bones and teeth, it's difficult."

"I take it there's no witness this time."

He cleared his throat. "None have come forward at this time."

"And are you sure this is another suicide?"

"Dammit, Deirdre, it's hard to tell. But there are very few other ways that a vampire can be forced to witness a sunrise, short of shackles and chains, and there is no evidence of that in this case."

"Are you positive? It just seems to be too much of a coincidence, two suicides right in a row."

"Yes. That is what I thought. I was hoping you might know something."

"I? I know nothing at all."

"Ah." He fell silent for a while, brushing slightly at the sleeve of his impeccable suit coat. Then he looked up and met my eyes. "We do have one theory. Tell me, my dear, have you ever been caught in the sun?"

"Well, yes, of course."

"And what was your first reaction?"

"Truthfully, Victor? My very first reaction?"

He nodded.

"I wanted to stay, regardless of the danger. I miss the sun. But then the pain would grow unbearable and I'd remove myself."

He nodded again. "That seems to be the way we all feel. There is the longing for the sunlight at the same time there is the fear. So when a vampire suicides, this method is the one normally chosen. Having two right in a row is unusual, I'll admit, but not totally unheard of. It might be possible for one of us to take that desire in another and twist it, so that it is acted upon. We are connected to each other in strange ways and the actions of one, as you well know, can carry unimaginable consequences for another."

I shook my head in agreement and remembered my recent visions. "Yes, I can see how that might happen. But what I don't understand is why you needed to tell me about it."

"Where's Mitch?"

"What?" My confusion must have been very apparent. "Mitch? He was going to talk to you about your sloppy security and then go to find his son. You must have seen him."

"I did see him, about an hour or so before sunset. He stormed into my office, talking all sorts of nonsense about how someone had broken into your room overnight and scattered rose petals. When I told him I had better things to worry about than flower petals, he stormed away, blustering about how we would pay if anything ever happened to you."

"You think he had something to do with this?" My voice rose in anger for the first time. "Mitch?"

"Well, we haven't ruled out the possibility. He hated Larry Martin. And he's not exactly on good terms with anyone in this organization. And while Mitch may have perfectly good reasons for his reaction, the fact still remains that he's been overheard calling for the downfall of the Cadre on many separate occasions."

"Jesus, Victor," I shook my head in disbelief, "that's all just talk. You can't really think that."

"Well, we would like to speak with him as soon as possible. He's with his son, you say?"

"He's looking for his son. Last night Chris found out from Vivienne that Mitch had been transformed. He's more than just a little upset about it."

"Um, hmm."

"What?"

"One more reason for him to be angry."

"Victor," I went to the door and opened it, "if you can believe that Mitch is twisting the minds of other vampires so that they'll sit out in the sun and burn themselves to a crisp, then you are just as crazy as whoever is doing it. If anyone is."

"Could be. But when you see Mitch, please tell him we need to talk."

"You're wasting your time, Victor. If there is a killer loose, it's not Mitch. I'd put my money on Larry Martin if I were you."

"Larry Martin is dead."

"Well, then, almost anyone else other than Mitch. And I wouldn't write Larry off completely. Theoretically, Victor, we're all dead. You, me, Mitch, Vivienne, the whole damn Cadre. We're just a bunch of animated corpses walking around preying on the lives of others."

"And just maybe," I said softly to myself as I closed the door, thinking about my strange visions, wondering if perhaps these thoughts traveled and were intercepted and acted upon by the others, "maybe I'm the one doing it."

Nineteen

Betsy was halfway through her salad when I arrived at the table and sat down. She smiled at me, then frowned, seeing the expression on my face. "Something wrong, Deirdre?"

"Damn green dress for one thing."

"Oh, come on, the dress looks wonderful on you; I meant to tell you so before that Victor person waylaid you. What did he want, anyway?"

I picked up the almost empty bottle of champagne and poured myself a glass, draining it in one draught. Then tipped the bottle again to get the last few drops.

"Deirdre?" she repeated, "what's wrong?"

"Nothing of importance, Betsy. Politics, suspicions, murders—just business as usual." I gave her a light smile. "Victor has an overactive imagination, I'm afraid."

"So do I." She pushed her salad bowl away and leaned over the table toward me. "You can tell me, sweetie, I can keep a secret. And if you don't tell me, I'll just have to let my imagination fill in the details."

I sighed and signaled the waiter to the table. "Another bottle of champagne, please." When he left I looked her dead in the eyes. "Don't ask me for confidences, Betsy, and don't try too hard to be my friend. Do you know what happened to the last female friend I had?"

Betsy only hesitated a minute. "Sure, she was murdered—brutally, as a matter of fact, and in the apartment behind my office." She raised an eyebrow at the surprise that must have shown in my face. "Of course I know about the incident; it was in all the papers. And even if it hadn't been, I would have made it my business to find out. Hell, it *was* my business to find out. I needed to know why you were so anxious to sell me Griffin Designs for such a low price."

She looked around her cautiously, exercising a discretion I would never have suspected she possessed, especially after drinking almost an entire bottle of champagne by herself. "I know quite a bit about you, Deirdre. More than you'd think."

"Even so, Betsy, a friendship with me is a dangerous commodity. I imagine that Gwen died cursing me."

"I think, Deirdre, that you were cursed long before Gwen was killed. And that you carry the curse within your veins."

I stared at her for a moment, growing uncomfortable with the closeness of her words to the truth of my existence. "Yes," I finally said, getting up from the table, "I think you may be right."

She reached over and placed her hand on top

of mine. "You're not leaving so soon, are you? You can't— we haven't eaten yet."

"I'm sorry, but I really need to go. I've lost what little appetite I had, anyway. It's nothing personal, Betsy. Just that the little unfinished business I told you about keeps growing and if I don't get started on it soon, it may go completely out of control."

"Okay, then, go if you have to. Take care of yourself, Deirdre. And if you need a friend, I'll be here for you."

"Thank you, Betsy. Enjoy your meal, and thank you again for the clothes. You're a lifesaver, truly. I'll call before I leave town and we'll reschedule dinner."

"And I'll hold you to that." She gave me a knowing smile and a wink.

"Good night, Betsy. And thanks again."

"Anytime," she replied and I started to walk away. "Oh, and Deirdre?"

I turned, "Yes?"

She held her glass of champagne up in a toast. "Good hunting."

I didn't stop to ask her what she meant, just turned again and walked away, not looking back. But I did remember to stop at the coat-check counter. The young girl looked up at me when I approached. "Can I help you?"

"Yes, I think you have a package here for me."

"Your name?"

"Oh. Deirdre Griffin or maybe Greer?"

The girl nodded and smiled at me. "Victor had

it sent to your rooms, Ms. Griffin. I hope that's all right."

"That's fine."

Once again I navigated the elevator and the corridors, and went back in the room, I checked the clock. It was only a little after nine, plenty of time before Mitch would return and more than enough to sort through the clothes that Betsy had provided, maybe even time to take a walk alone afterwards. I realized with a small rush of surprise that I missed the solitude I had grown accustomed to over the years, missed the feeling of unity with the night and nature.

The box of clothes had been placed on top of the coffins. I shook my head as I walked over to it, thinking that I really should get Victor to remove them. Neither Mitch nor I had the desire to try them out. Slitting the top of the box open with my nails I pulled out several pairs of black jeans and heavy black sweatshirts.

"Bless you, Betsy," I said as I delved further into the box. She'd also included a red sweater tunic almost identical to one I once owned and had to discard, some oversized t-shirts, a dressy black and white lightweight suit and three dresses identical to the one I now wore only in different colors, a red one, a black one and a white.

I shook out the dresses and the suit and hung them in the armoire. The rest I folded and put away in the dresser drawers, keeping out a pair of jeans and a sweatshirt. When I shut the drawer, the dresser shook and some of the rose petals fell away.

Picking up the vase, I carried it into the bathroom to freshen the water and to find an aspirin. The medicine cabinet actually held a bottle to my surprise, and as I dropped a tablet into the water I realized that I'd forgotten to ask Victor if he'd sent the flowers. "Well, it had to be Victor," I said aloud, contemplating the black rose bud surrounded by the sea of red, "Who else would know?" It made sense that Victor would remember Max's methods; even made sense that he would attempt to copy them.

I placed them back on top of the dresser, turning the vase slightly to show them off to their best advantage. As the vase twisted I noticed a corner of white underneath it, almost invisible against the white dresser scarf.

The card that came with the flowers had been taped to the bottom of the vase, almost as if the sender had not wanted me to find it right away. The envelope was not written on, but when I pulled the card out, I recognized the handwriting and wished Mitch were here for many reasons.

The least of which was to vindicate his theory that Larry Martin was still alive. Larry's card read: *"Deirdre, I hope these flowers find you happy and well. Unfortunately, by the time you read this note, some will be missing, torn away in violence from their kindred."* I glanced away from the note and counted the flowers. Ten red and one black were remaining. There had been twelve red ones last night, I was sure. *"I told you I wouldn't forget you,"* the note continued, *"and as I'm sure you remember, the black rose is you."*

It was easy to connect the two missing roses and the two dead vampires. Larry was once again displaying his flair for the melodramatic. I would have laughed out loud had I not been so convinced that this time he would succeed in his plans and I would be dead.

I dropped the note on the floor and walked over to the bed. Pulling off the green velvet dress, I vowed with a grim smile never to wear the color again, no matter how long I lived, put on the jeans and sweatshirt, pulled on my boots and left the room.

When I hit the street and the outside air I let the breath I'd been holding escape in a sigh of relief. My heart was racing, but I walked slowly, in an attempt to calm my panic. Fleeing Cadre headquarters seemed a good first step. That sanctuary, if it ever had been one, was no longer safe for me. Larry had been there at least two times that I knew of, once to deliver the roses and then just this morning or afternoon while Mitch and I lay unaware. I shivered in the warm spring air, imagining him standing over me, watching the rise and fall of my chest in sleep, showering me with blood red petals.

How could he do all these things? He was a relatively new transformation and a rogue at that with no one to teach or to guide him. I had to find the answer to that question. If I didn't, ten other Cadre members would die. And then it would be my turn.

I thought back over my unnaturally long life. There was a time when I would have welcomed Larry's attention, when I would have given him all I owned to have him provide for me the release of death. "But not now. Please, not now," I whispered to myself. "Now I have Mitch."

I continued walking, my pace picking up now. Without conscious thought of where I was going, I just walked, letting my awareness flow into the workings of my body, the feel of the concrete under my feet, the smell of the night air. I turned down one street and doubled back another, finding myself at last in an alley that seemed very familiar. I inhaled deeply and closed my eyes, searching my mind for clues to this place and remembered that I stood outside Larry Martin's old apartment building.

There was no police cruiser waiting outside the front door this night, as there had been that other time, no need for me to climb the wall and break into an open window. I walked around the side of the building and entered the front door.

I remembered his apartment number and in less than a minute stood outside the door. There was no good reason to assume that he still occupied this place, and yet there was really no reason for him not to. I knew better than most that the habits of a vampire die hard.

Listening at the door, I heard no sounds of life from within. I stooped over and put my face up to the keyhole, inhaling the scent of this place. It reeked of him. Larry Martin still lived here.

He'd grown more cautious, I thought, noticing extra locks on the door that had not been there before. Breaking them was possible with a few strong kicks, but the noise might attract the attention of his neighbors. Not really a likely prospect, but a possibility I didn't much care to test.

The longer I stared at the locked door, the more I knew I had to get inside. Then the answer hit me. The powers he used to enter my room were no different than the ones I possessed. I had transformed into a mist once before and I could do it again.

I closed my eyes and concentrated, trying to remember how the sensation of melting away felt. My body swayed slightly as I reached out to the air around me, willing it to flow through me, willing myself to dissolve into it. My arms and legs tingled and I felt a shiver sweep along my back. I emptied my mind of all thoughts of flesh and bodily contact; tried to will my body to merge and combine with the air around me.

But when I opened my eyes, I saw that I had failed. I was as substantive as I had been before the attempt. Laughing bitterly at myself, I remembered lines from Hamlet, "O, that this too too solid flesh would melt . . ." and ". . . 'tis a consummation devoutly to be wish'd . . ."

"Damn." I walked away and down the front steps of his building back to the street, talking to myself. "That's what you get for trying to hold onto this body for so many years, Deirdre. When you want to get rid of it, you can't."

"Oh, I don't know," came a familiar voice behind me, "as bodies go, it's certainly one I'd like to hold onto."

I spun around. "Mitch!" I threw myself into his arms and kissed him, then snuggled into his familiar suit coat. "How on earth did you know I was here?"

"Coincidence?"

"Not on your life." I hugged him again and noticed that he was wearing his shoulder holster and his gun.

"Armed and dangerous, tonight, are we?"

He shrugged. "I thought it might come in handy. So when I was over at the old apartment I picked it up."

"Did you see Chris?" I asked anxiously. "Is he still upset?"

"One crisis at a time, Deirdre." Suddenly all the life went out of his eyes. "But, yeah, I saw Chris. We can talk about it later, okay?"

"Fine. So tell me how you knew I'd be here."

"Well," he took my arm and led me back up the steps to Larry's apartment, "actually, I got back to the room earlier than I expected and saw the note on the floor. I know you all too well by now, Deirdre, and knew that you would attempt to meet the threat head on."

"I failed. Miserably." We now stood outside the same door and I gave it a feeble kick. "Couldn't even get in the damn door."

He smiled down at me and kissed the top of my head. "So I gathered. He's not home, is he?"

"No."

"Good. That makes this much easier." He

pulled out his gun and fired at the locks. The noise of the shots echoed through the hallways, but not one person stepped out to see what was happening. Mitch looked around a second before reaching down and turning the knob then gave me one of his mischievous smiles. "God, I love this city."

Twenty

We entered the apartment. It was filthier than I remembered. "I find it hard to believe that even someone as crazy as Larry would live here." I waved my hand in front of my nose and coughed. "It's more than foul."

Mitch scanned the place. "I don't actually think he lives here. For one thing, there's no coffin. And Larry would most definitely opt for sleeping in a coffin. This is more of a hideaway, I'd suspect, and one that he hasn't actually used for a while."

"How can you know that?"

He pointed to the table surfaces. "By the fact that the dust is relatively undisturbed, for one thing. If he were here regularly there'd be cleaner patches, just from his touch."

"Then this is a waste of our time."

"Not necessarily. He keeps this place for a reason, I assume. If we can find that reason, then we won't have wasted our time."

I gave Mitch a wide, delighted smile.

"Why are you smiling?" he questioned. "Did you find something already?"

I nodded, still smiling. "Yes, I've discovered

that my detective is back. I missed him. He's been so busy trying to be a vampire, he forgot what he was good at."

"You don't get much of a chance to use police skills washing mugs and waiting bar in a pub, Deirdre. Not that I minded helping you out, but you know what I mean."

"Yes," I said, my voice saddened, "I do know what you mean. When all of this is over, my love, we'll have to see if we can find you a job better suited to your skills. I can always hire another dishwasher."

"So, what are we looking for here?"

"I don't have a clue. You're the detective, aren't you?"

"Yeah," he said with humor in his voice, "I think so, but this was your idea."

I kicked at a dusty pile of books. "I think I was hoping to find something that would explain how Larry managed to develop his powers to such an advanced stage in so short a time. He can't possibly have done it all on his own, you know."

"You think someone is teaching him on the side?"

"Yes." Suspicions of Vivienne instantly came to my mind, but I kept them there, knowing that they might be unfounded. Knowing also that they could easily be shrugged off as jealousy on my part.

"Who would do that? Not a Cadre member, certainly."

"Why not a Cadre member? Who else would know so much? Victor said that all of the notes delivered to the house leaders contained personal details that Larry should not have known. He must have a source of information somewhere."

"It would have to be someone fairly high up in the organization. How about Ron?"

I thought for a moment then dismissed the idea. "No, quite honestly, I can't see Ron having the initiative to stand against the organization. He's very dedicated to Victor. I think that only a very few of the Cadre would have enough gumption to plot something like this."

Mitch grunted slightly in what I took to be agreement and opened a box that had been placed under one of the end tables. I walked into the kitchen, shuddering at the number of roaches that scurried away at my approach. There was nothing here; with the exception of busy and thriving insect colonies, the cupboards and appliances were empty.

"Deirdre," Mitch called to me as I was leaving the kitchen, dusting my hands on my pants. "Did you ever think that maybe Max is helping him?"

I laughed grimly. "Very funny, Mitch. Max is dead. Buried. Even his ghost is gone forever."

"But," and he held up a black leather bound book with a triumphant smile, "his words aren't." He tilted the box he'd been examining over on its side so that I could see what it contained. "Do these look familiar?"

I felt like a fool. "Damn, Max's journals. I'd forgotten about them." It all fell into place.

Larry hadn't needed help from anyone; all he needed to do was read the words of the master. Max had been, by Victor's admission, the most powerful vampire the Cadre had ever known. No better teacher could be found anywhere, living or dead.

Mitch straightened up and lifted the box effortlessly. "Let's get these out of here and into a safe place before he finds out they're gone."

It wasn't until we were in a cab and halfway to Cadre headquarters that I thought to ask. "Where are we going to find a safe place, Mitch?"

"The holding cells, of course. Larry's crazy, but he's not stupid enough to return there." He patted the top of the box that sat on the seat between us. "Not even to get these babies back."

Mitch kicked open the door of Victor Lange's office and dropped the box of books on the floor. "Larry Martin is still alive, Lange. I'm afraid all your evidence to the contrary is useless. Even your eyewitness, whoever she may be."

Victor lifted his face to us and from the bloodstained tracks we could tell that he had been crying. "Jesus, Victor," I rushed to him and knelt next to his chair. "What's happened?"

"It was Ron."

"Ron?" Mitch's voice was gentler now. "What about Ron?"

"The body in the park was Ron's."

"Oh, God, no." I felt tears spring up in my eyes, for Victor's sorrow and for my own. Ron had been both my lover and my friend.

"Why would he do this to me?" Victor sobbed uncontrollably and I patted his shoulder, trying to offer what little comfort I could. "Ron was my son. No, he was even closer than a son; out of all my offspring, he was the finest and the best. How could he kill himself without even saying a word to me first?"

Mitch crossed over to stand in front of Victor's desk. "Ron didn't commit suicide, Victor. He was killed by Larry Martin."

"Larry Martin is dead."

I thought that if I had to hear those words from his mouth one more time I would scream. In deference to Victor's pain, though, I said nothing.

Mitch held no similar compunction. "Bloody hell, Victor, haven't you been listening? Larry Martin is still alive and kicking. Very much so. He is more powerful than you can imagine and capable of much more than the simple parlor trick he used to escape from your escape-proof cells. To top all of that, he is about as crazy as they come. And he seems to have found an easy, sure-fire way to kill vampires."

Victor rose from his chair, pushing me away. He took no further notice of me even when I rose to my feet and stepped back out of his way. He did look at Mitch and opened his mouth as if to say something, but closed it again, shaking his head. Shuffling past Mitch to the doorway, he seemed like an old, old man. I remembered that he had reacted this way after Max's true death; it had been a horrible sight then. But he had recovered quickly from that blow and his sanity had not been affected. Apparently, Ron's death stole not only his vitality and youthfulness, but his mind and his ability to reason as well.

He turned back to us for a second, straightening himself up somewhat, almost returning to life. "Chase after shadows all you like, Greer. Go hunting for the ghost of Larry Martin if it makes you happy. You have my permission, in fact, you have my blessing." He laughed, a mocking cackle of his former strength. "For that matter, you can have my job. The Cadre is yours, now. Destroy it or save it, it's all the same to me. Ron is dead. And I," he sighed, a tired and sorrowful exhalation, "I have lived too long."

"Victor," I called after him, pleading for his return.

His lifeless eyes caught mine and held them. "I hope you understand that this is all your doing, my dear." The cruel words were delivered in a voice so devoid of emotion he might just as well have been discussing the weather. "Ultimately and undeniably your responsibility. That old bastard Max would have been proud of you." Victor looked away and around the office; the finality of the gesture tore at my heart. "I'll be in my room if anyone wants me."

The room was silent except for the ticking of

the clock on the desk. Mitch and I stared at each other for a while, then both turned when we heard footsteps in the hall. Vivienne rushed in, breathless and tearful. "Was that Victor?" she asked in disbelief.

"Yes, Vivienne, it was." I felt myself warming toward her, now that I realized that she might not be in league with Larry Martin.

"Mon dieu, what has happened to him?"

"Ron is dead."

She nodded solemnly, *"Oui,* so I heard. That is why I came down here to Victor. Oh, the poor man, will he be all right, do you think?"

"I doubt it," Mitch said with certainty.

"Then who will be in charge?"

Mitch cleared his throat. "Surprisingly enough, Victor gave the job to me."

I looked at Mitch and my laughter was hollow. "You see, my love, I told you we would find a job to fit your abilities. But I had no idea it would be so soon."

"I'm glad," Vivienne said with conviction. "It's no surprise to me. You are young and powerful, Mitch. We all know this and admire you. You were the perfect choice."

"Well," he looked embarrassed, but his tone was firm and commanding, "I don't know how perfect I'll prove to be, but I will try to get us all out of this in one piece. The first thing we need to do is call a general meeting."

"I'll gather the house leaders for you, Mitch." She glanced at the clock. It was barely one. "I assume you'll want them here tonight, before another sunrise."

"That would be best, don't you think?"

"It will be difficult, but I will try to get them all together. Shall I tell them the council room at four?"

"That sounds good. And thanks, Vivienne. Your support will be very helpful with the other leaders."

She laughed. "You're welcome, Mitch, but don't overestimate my influence with the Cadre. I am tolerated simply because of my age and my power. I am not as well respected as Victor, nor am I as feared as Max was. But I'll give whatever support I can. I enjoy my life too much to want to end up a heap of ashes on a park bench." She gave us each a small salute and rushed out the door and down the hall.

"Amen to that," I said.

Mitch walked over to the desk and sat down in Victor's chair.

"How does it feel?"

"Frightening. As if someone just told me I'd been elected president."

"Well, in a way, I suppose you have."

Idly, he flipped through the Rolodex on the top of the desk. "Yeah, I guess you're right. But you know as well as I that this isn't what Victor intended."

"True," I agreed, "but who better to fight a rogue than another one? And now instead of having the Cadre at our throats, we'll have them protecting our backs."

"I wouldn't be too sure of that, Deirdre. But it would be nice to think so."

I curled up in one of the side chairs at Victor's desk and took notice of the surroundings for the first time. The office was bleak and sparsely decorated, the walls were painted stark white and held only two adornments. One was a smaller representation of the large mural that hung in the judgment hall, depicting a medieval city by night. The second was the seal of the House of Leupold.

The desk was easily the most impressive piece of furniture in the room. Made of solid mahogany, it was massive and solid, the top surface highly polished, reflecting in its gloss a small brass carriage clock and the Rolodex that Mitch had been inspecting, along with a desk calendar, blotter and telephone. The chairs were high-backed and covered with burgundy leather, and I thought, wiggling slightly, very uncomfortable.

Through a door off to the right was another office. From what I could see, it was more modern and more comfortable. I got up from my chair and peered inside. This was where Ron had worked, no doubt. His death seemed unreal to me, and that fact saddened me even more. "Damn," I swore softly and wiped the tears away from my eyes.

"What's the matter, Deirdre?" Mitch got up from the desk and came over to me, draping his arm around my shoulder and pulling me close to him.

"Nothing. And everything."

"Strangely enough, I know what you mean." He went back to the center of the office and picked up the box holding Max's journals. "Let's get out of here, for now. I have no desire to spend the rest of the night pawing through Victor's desk."

"What are you going to do with those?" I asked him as we turned out the lights and left the office.

"For now, they'll stay with me. I'm the only one I trust enough to guard them. After the council meeting, we'll put them down in the cells. Although I'm really hoping I'll have a chance to read them soon."

We trailed back down the winding corridors to our room. I hesitated just a bit before opening the door; I no longer felt safe here. I wondered if I would ever feel safe again.

Mitch set the box of journals down next to the bed. "We'll catch him, Deirdre. And when we do, I'm going to kill him. You understand that, don't you?"

"I won't stop you this time, Mitch. And if there are consequences for his death, I'll take them, gladly. They'll be worth it if we can rid the world of this monster." I shivered as I caught a glimpse of the bouquet on the dresser. Then shivered again when I counted the red roses and found there were now only nine. "He was here again, Mitch, and there's another rose missing. One more rose, one more death. I wonder who it will be this time."

"No one, if I can help it."

"And if you can't, then what? At this rate I have only nine days to live."

"Deirdre, trust me. I won't let anyone hurt you, ever. Between you and me and the Cadre we'll find a way to catch him. I promise."

I said nothing, thinking that all I really wanted to do was to catch the next flight out of here. But I could not voice that thought. Running away, as desirable as it seemed, was not a good solution. Most of our current dilemma had been caused by my last escape from this city. This time I would stay and do it right.

"So," I said abruptly, changing the subject, "I take it you did speak with Chris."

Mitch ran his fingers through his hair. He was tired already, I could tell and the night was not yet over. "Yeah, I talked with Chris."

"And?"

He scowled. "And just like you might expect, he hates you for turning me into what I am. He says he'll try to kill you if he can; he seems to think that your death might return me to my normal state."

I laughed. "So now Chris wants to kill me, too? I'm becoming a very popular sport."

Mitch turned to me and grabbed me by the shoulders. "This is not a game, Deirdre. He's serious. I asked him to consider seeking therapy."

"Therapy? Mitch, he doesn't dare. If he were to tell anyone what his problem is, they'd lock him up in an institution and throw away the key. Just like they did to you."

"Except that because of that, there is now one highly qualified psychiatrist in the city who is also an expert on vampires. Or if not an expert, at least one who's open-minded on the subject."

"Sam." I was surprised I hadn't thought of him. "Of course. And Chris already knows him and trusts him."

"His first appointment is Monday evening at eight. Sam thought it would be a good idea if you could be there, not visible and not actually in the office with them, but on site somewhere so that you could be consulted if necessary. Although," Mitch twisted his mouth into a half-smile, "I suspect that Sam just wanted to have you there. He's a real fan of yours."

"Jealous?"

"Only a little bit. After the other day I have no doubts about you or your feelings for me."

I pulled in a deep breath and exhaled it, put my arms around him and hugged him tightly to me. "It's the same for me. But it's lonelier now, somehow, walking around in this body without you." I began to cry, long racking sobs that had been pent-up for way too long.

He rocked me back and forth for a while, stroking my hair. "I know, Deirdre, I know. Funny how it all worked out, isn't it? We share the most incredible bonding experience that could ever be possible, and we feel more alone afterwards than ever before."

After a while my tears subsided and eventually he moved away and looked down at me. "Look at you," he brushed his fingertips over my cheeks, "you're a mess. Why don't you get cleaned up and ready for the council meeting. I'm going to have a look at Max's journals."

Twenty-one

I'd always felt that there was nothing that a hot shower couldn't cure. I turned out the bathroom light and closed the door, stripping off my clothes in almost complete darkness. The only light was the small strip that shone under the door, a calming reassurance that Mitch was nearby.

Turning the knob to the hottest setting, I stepped into the tub and pulled the curtain shut. With the flow of the water over my body, I felt myself relax, felt a warmth spread through my chilled limbs. My mood lightened and I began to sing, softly at first and then with more confidence, enjoying the sound of my voice echoing off the walls.

"Pack up all my care and woe, here I go, singing low. Bye, bye, blackbird . . ."

I sang the whole song through twice, then once again. It had always been one of my favorites. The last time through, a lower voice from outside the tub joined in. "Make my bed and light the light, I'll arrive late tonight. Blackbird, bye bye . . ."

The addition of another voice made the entire

experience much more sensual. The steam seemed to grow thicker, and the water felt alive, as if it had hands that were molding and touching my skin. The fragrance of the roses from the other room filtered in and I inhaled deeply. "Ahh, love," I called over the sound of the water, "if you're going to join me, you'd better get in here now. We'll be out of hot water soon."

"That's an invitation I'd never want to turn down, Deirdre." Mitch's voice sounded different, higher pitched than usual, but I shrugged it off to the poor acoustics of the room. "But I'm afraid I have some serious business to conduct. I'll be back for you later."

"What?" I shook my wet hair and reached over to turn off the water. "What did you say? Mitch? Where are you going?"

My only answer was silence. I pulled open the curtain at the same time the door was opened and the light switched on. I blinked my eyes at the sudden onslaught, and peered around me. Mitch stood in the doorway, staring at the red petals scattered on the tile floor.

My eyes searched the room for a sign of someone else, but he had gone. Slipped in and out and delivered his message without either one of us knowing he was there.

"Bloody hell." Mitch reached out and folded me into his arms, paying no attention to the fact that I was sopping wet and soapy.

My teeth were chattering and my whole body shivered. Larry had been in here with me, sharing the intimacy of the shower. Had he reached out and caressed me, under the guise of water and steam and mist?

My mind screamed for escape. "We'll never win, Mitch. He's too powerful. If he can come in here, like he just did, without either one of us noticing, he can do anything. How can we ever hope to stop someone like that? We could go away, somewhere he wouldn't be able to find us. Build our powers together so that we could match him. But it's hopeless right now."

He shook his head. "I can't give it up, Deirdre. Can't just let him kill us all without a fight. There must be a way to stop him and we'll find out what it is." He reached over for a towel and wrapped it around my naked body protectively. "If it were just you and me, then maybe it would be different. But now I find myself responsible for the members of the Cadre as well. I cannot run away from this, as tempting as the idea is."

I sighed, the shivering subsiding as his arms and the towel warmed me. "I know, Mitch. I know. But I'm frightened. I've never been so frightened in my whole life. Because now I have something to lose, something which makes my whole existence worthwhile. Maybe Fred was right."

"Fred? What has he got to do with all this?"

"Nothing, really, except for what he told Mark."

"Mark?" His mind seemed to blank on the name for a second. "Oh, yeah, Mark. The bartender at the Ballroom. What did he say?"

"That when vampires fall in love, they lose

their edge and their instincts." I moved away from him, wrapped the towel completely around me and went out into the bedroom. Looking at the clock I saw that there were two hours left before the council meeting. "I need to think," I said. "I need to be alone."

"But you shouldn't be alone, Deirdre, who will protect you?"

"The same person who always has, Mitch. I will protect myself. If I can't do it, then quite honestly I don't deserve to live." I pulled the sweatshirt I had taken off back over my head and gave a low laugh. "It seems like all I've done all night is change clothes."

"I can't let you leave, Deirdre."

I zipped up my jeans and stepped into my boots. "You can't make me stay, either, Mitch. I have to go. I'll be back, probably in time for the council meeting. But if not, go ahead without me. This is what you're good at."

"But what if Larry finds you?"

I laughed and pointed to the roses. "He's not had any trouble doing that so far, has he? Don't worry about me, Mitch, you need to watch out for yourself. I'll be safe for a while. After all, I'm lucky enough to know exactly when my time is coming. Nine days from now, if we don't discover a way to stop him, I'll be dead. And all your promises and vows will not help."

I kissed him full on the lips. "Don't worry about me, my love," I repeated, "I'll be fine and I'll be back. I just need to approach the situation my way, not yours or the Cadre's. Do you understand?"

"Yeah, I do." He hugged me to him and kissed me back. "I don't like it much," he acknowledged his standard answer with a small grin, "but I do understand. Keep in touch."

"Always."

"Well, Deirdre," I said to myself as I hit the street, "where to now?"

I didn't have an answer for that, but I stood still for a moment, my face raised to the sky, my nostrils flared to better inhale the night air. Then I began to run. Abandoning all thoughts, I allowed my legs and my body to think for me, to carry me to where I needed to go. Street after street I ran, and block after block. Not knowing my destination, or even knowing whether one existed. It made no difference. I felt freed, as if I had just awakened from a coma and found that I was alive once again. I had been trapped within my thoughts, within my fears for too long, but now the spell had been broken and I was finally free.

My feet slowed finally outside a grim brick building, the institution in which Sam worked. I laughed. Obviously there was something here that kept drawing me back.

I flew up the steps and into the front door. "Hello," I greeted the sleepy nurse at the desk, "Sam's in, isn't he?"

She looked up at me with surprise. "Yes, he's here. May I give him your name?"

"No need," I walked past her, "I know the way."

Without even knocking I flung open the door to his office. He jumped up from his desk, then relaxed when he saw me. "Deirdre, what an unexpected surprise."

"For me, also, Sam."

He gave me a questioning look. "What can I do for you?"

"I don't really know right now. But something brought me here."

Sam looked puzzled. "Is it Chris?"

"Chris?" I didn't recognize the name for a second. "Oh, no, it isn't Chris. That's something to worry about tomorrow or the next day. For now, I just want you to listen while I tell you everything that's been happening. That's what you're good at. And maybe you can give me a new slant on things. See something from a human perspective that the rest of us can't glimpse."

I told him everything. It took me nearly three hours to recount the last week's events. By the time I had finished he had filled half of a yellow tablet with scribbled notes. He had interrupted when he needed to, attempting to clarify events and emotions. Finally we both seemed satisfied and he put his pen down.

"Busy couple of days, huh?" He smiled wearily. "I wish I'd had a full night's sleep to filter this on, but I think I have everything." He stood up from his desk and stretched, turning to the window and peeking through the venetian blinds.

"It's almost dawn, you know. Do you have enough time to get to shelter?"

I shook my head. "I doubt it. Do you have a bed here I can use?"

He laughed. "We've got plenty of beds, Deirdre, with doors and windows that lock tight. But I doubt it will serve as much protection for you."

"I don't need protection, Sam, I just need a sunless room. I can take care of the rest. But I do have one other request."

"What's that?"

"Stay with me through sunrise. If I have another vision, I want you to be there with me. Maybe you can find out something that I can't."

"No problem." He reached into his top desk drawer and pulled out a set of keys. "Thanks to the cutbacks in mental health these days, we have half a wing sitting empty. I can put you there, it's as safe as anywhere else."

"It will be fine, I'm sure. Shall we go?"

He started for the door, then turned back and opened one of his desk drawers and pulled out his portable tape recorder. I raised an eyebrow in question. "I thought that if you did have this vision, that I might hypnotize you afterwards. We can get much better detail this way. You know you can trust me; I've recorded you before."

"Well," I said with a shrug, "recording is one thing and hypnotism is another. But, I suppose it can't hurt to try. I'm not entirely sure that you can hypnotize a vampire."

"Of course you can." His voice held no doubts.

"You sound pretty sure of yourself, Sam."

"I am sure. From the story you told me, it's obvious that it's possible. It's just a matter of finding the proper method."

The room he showed me to was utilitarian. It had a small bed, unmade, but with bed clothes folded and set off to one side. The only other piece of furniture was a chair sitting in the corner opposite the bed. The room's most noticeable feature was its lack of windows with none facing to the outside and none in the door facing toward the hallway. Once the door was closed I would be completely safe from sunlight.

"Sam," I said with a sigh of relief, "this is absolutely perfect. Thank you."

Sam looked around and laughed. "If this is perfect for you, Deirdre, I'd sure hate to see what you consider substandard."

I laughed with him. "Perhaps perfect is not the proper word. Safe springs to mind and right now that is more important than decor."

"Oh, I see."

"Sunrise is close now." I sat down on the bed and pulled off my boots. Then I stretched out on my back and closed my eyes.

I heard Sam moving around the room. First he closed the door and locked it, then he pulled a chair over to the side of the bed. The pages of his notepad rustled and he clicked the pen several times, then scribbled on the paper, testing the ink.

"Okay," he said softly. "I'm here and ready. Is there anything else I need to do?"

I shook my head on the pillow. "Watch," I said, "and listen. If I attempt to leave the room, you can try to stop me. But not to the point of danger to yourself."

"You wouldn't hurt me."

"Not if I were aware of it, no. But these visions have been very powerful. I can't vouch for your safety. If it's a choice between me and you, save yourself." I gave a chuckle at those words; Larry was not the only one with a flair for the melodramatic. "Then again, I may just fall asleep and all of this will be for nothing."

"Even so, I'm sure it will not be a disappointment. How many doctors have had the opportunity to witness a vampire at rest?"

"If you had asked me that question three years ago I could have told you very few. But given what I've learned since then, that number is probably more than you think. The question really is how many doctors have known what they were witnessing?"

"That is always the question, Deirdre. Recognizing what the eye sees is more than half the battle."

"Shrink talk?" I gave him a quick smile.

"Common sense."

I shivered and he moved out of his chair quickly, deftly unfolding the blanket and covering me, before I had even realized I was cold.

"Your comfort is important if the hypnotism

is to succeed," he explained as he settled back down into his chair.

"Ah, thank you."

This particular section of the hospital was totally silent. The lack of windows helped alleviate the sounds from outside and the corridors outside the door were deserted. The only noise I could hear was Sam's breathing, quiet and controlled. And far from being a distraction, his presence was a comfort. I felt my body relax further.

"Sunrise is close," I whispered, afraid to break the spell of the silence, "I can feel it now."

Consciously, I made an effort to reach my mind out into the dawn. And felt the scream of pain slowly rise up within me to escape into the blinding and burning light of the sun.

Twenty-two

I woke to total silence. Sam slept soundly in the chair next to me. I sat up and looked around, tossing off the blanket. With no windows and the door closed I had no way of knowing whether it was an hour past dawn or before dusk.

Quietly, I reached over and turned his wrist gently so that I could read his watch, but even this touch woke him up. His eyes popped open and he gazed around in confusion, blinking his eyes until he saw my face.

"Morning," he said, standing up and rubbing the back of his neck, tilting his head from side to side until the bones cracked. I winced at the sound.

"Is it morning? I can't tell. This room is very effective."

He looked at his watch. "I should have said 'evening,' I suppose, since it's going on seven right now. And I know it's not the morning. You talked for almost an hour this morning after the sun came up and you didn't really settle in until well after eight."

"What happened?"

"Don't you remember?"

I shook my head. "No, not really. I remember the sun rising. And then nothing until just now."

"Interesting. Especially since I didn't tell you not to remember. Fortunately, I got it all on tape. And I think I might have even gotten some details that will help. But," and the look he gave me was sad and distant, "don't ever ask me to do this for you again. I found out things I didn't want to know."

He didn't answer my questioning look, but paced briefly around the room. "I guess you can't leave here until the sun goes down, huh? I sure wouldn't mind having a comfortable chair."

"No, I can't even walk down the hallway. But you can go and I'll come when I can."

He dismissed that idea immediately. "We'll listen to the tape first. That'll kill an hour and I'm actually anxious to hear it again. The voice on the tape was disturbingly familiar."

"Familiar? Why wouldn't it be? It's my voice."

"Well," Sam gave me a tentative glance as if he wasn't quite sure whether he should be frightened or not, "it was you, and it wasn't. I did manage to get through to Mitch though to tell him you were here and safe. And he let me know that your vision was true. Another vampire turned up dead shortly after sunrise this morning."

"Damn."

"That's what I said, too. But we'll listen to the tape and you can see why. You might want to get comfortable before I start this." He settled back into his chair, motioned me to the bed, and I lay

down again, on my back, my hands grasped behind my head.

At first the only sound on the tape was my
scream. It was terrifying. I could feel the pain all
over again, smell the burning flesh, feel the anger and the despair. I gasped in remembrance.
Sam just nodded his head.

"It stops soon."

And it did. But the echo of it would remain
in my soul.

The tape wound silently for a minute or two.
When Sam's soft voice began speaking, it did not
seem an intrusion, but merely a continuation of
the silence.

"Deirdre? Are you still in pain?"

"No, the pain is gone."

"Good. Now I want you to listen to my voice
very carefully. Listen and pay attention to every
word I say. Can you do that?"

"Yes."

"Good. I want you to imagine yourself in a
room of total white. The walls are white. The
floors are white. The ceiling is white. It is a room
of absolute safety, there is no harm that can come
to you in this room. Are you here now?"

There was a pause on the tape. Then my voice
came back, softer now, so soft that I had to strain
to hear it. "Yes, I am here."

"And how do you feel?"

"I feel safe."

"Good. When we start talking about something
that upsets you, that might make you want to
scream again, I want you to remember that you

are in the white room and that you are safe. No harm can come to you in this room. Do you understand?"

"Yes, I understand."

"Good. Now I want you to think back, before you screamed. Do you remember why you screamed?"

There was a silence on the tape. I could hear my breathing, labored and heavy, but I was not speaking.

"Deirdre?"

"Yes?"

"Do you remember screaming?"

"Yes." My voice filled with tension. Sam recognized it instantly.

"You are in the white room, Deirdre. No one can harm you here."

"I," there were a few short gasps on the tape until I continued, "I hurt. I hurt because I screamed. I screamed because I hurt."

"Do you hurt now, Deirdre?"

"No, the pain is gone. Because she is gone."

"Can you remember back before the scream?"

"Yes." I could hear the reticence in my own voice. My inherent cautiousness apparently overflowed into my subconscious, as well.

"Tell me what you were doing before the scream. Before the hurt."

There were four or five definite deep breaths on the tape. And then I began to speak. Sam was correct; the voice was mine, but it was not mine. I struggled as the tape played to recognize the voice.

"I'm with him."

"Who is he?"

"He's my friend. He treats me better than the rest. I'd like him to be more than my friend. I'd like him to be my lover, but he says it's too soon for that. He says that we need to move slow and that I need to prove how much I love him first."

"Who is he?"

"He's my friend. I don't have very many friends, you know."

"Yes, I understand that he is your friend. But what is his name?"

The voice on the tape giggled. "Larry, of course."

"Larry?"

"Yeah, Larry Martin. I do him favors and he stays my friend. I don't mind doing him favors usually, but I'm angry about the last favor he asked me to do."

"What kind of things does Larry usually ask you to do?"

"Usually he just asks me to do easy things. You know, like opening the door to let him in, or like putting the flowers in her room. One time he wanted me to go to Victor's office and steal some papers for him. And sometimes I just give him money. Those are easy things."

"And what was this last favor he asked you for? The one you're angry about?"

"He wanted me to tell everyone that I saw him die."

I motioned to Sam to stop the tape and he did

so. "Mitch should be listening to this. Whoever she is, she's Victor's witness."

"Does it really matter at this point? She's dead." There was an underlying emotion in his words that brought me up short. I had forgotten that this person speaking through me was one of the figures in the sun.

"Oh. I'm sorry. I didn't think." I felt myself blushing slightly. But the voice sounded so alive and enough like me, that it was hard to believe she was dead. "Please, start it again."

He wound it back just a little bit and restarted the tape.

". . . tell everyone that I saw him die."

"Why would he want you to do that?"

"He wanted everyone to think that he'd died so that they'd leave him alone. If they thought he was still alive, you see, they'd hunt him, and when they found him he'd have to go back to the prison in the cellar. I can understand that, I'd never want to be put down there. There's no air and no food and it's bright all the time. It's a horrible place; no one should have to suffer like that."

"So you did this last favor for him. Even though you didn't want to."

"Oh, no, I wanted to. I told him I understood and I would do almost anything for him. I didn't get angry until later."

"What happened later?"

"Well, later it all turned into a big deal. I had to speak to all the house leaders and swear an oath on my honor that what I'd said was true.

They kept asking me questions that I had a hard time answering, even though Larry and I practiced before."

There was a pause on the tape. "Go on," Sam prompted.

The voice sounded angrier when it spoke again. "All I figured I'd have to do would be to tell Victor that I had seen Larry sit on the park bench and wait for the sun. That I had watched him burst into flames. And that he was dead."

"Isn't that exactly what you did say?"

"Yeah, but I had to say it in front of everyone. And if they find out I lied about it, which they will, I'll be punished."

"How will they find out that you lied?"

"Mitch knows that I lied."

With her mention of his name I knew who she was. My eyes caught Sam's and he nodded. "Jean?" I mouthed the word and he nodded again. I sighed.

"And she'll know, of course. And if she knows, she'll tell Victor. They're very close, you know. Even though she killed Max, Victor still likes her. Almost everyone likes her. I think even Larry likes her, deep down inside, although he pretends that he hates her. It's not fair."

"Of course it isn't fair." I could feel the gentle tugging from Sam, attempting to keep her on topic. "But what about the testimony you gave? Did they believe you?"

"Yes. That was the easy part. I was upset anyway, that I had to tell his lies in front of everyone. So I just let them think that I was upset because

I watched him die. I was very convincing," the voice laughed, a whining little laugh that would have enabled me to identify her clearly if I had not already done so. "So much so that I said that I wanted to go away for a while. It was very traumatic to watch one of us die and I didn't want to talk about it anymore."

"And they believed you?"

"Why wouldn't they? What reason would I have to lie?"

"And then what happened?"

"I found out that somebody actually did die, that he killed one of us, so that he could escape. All of a sudden I was an accessory to murder. We fought about that, but eventually he convinced me that no one would ever know." There was a long pause on the tape and when the voice resumed, it was lighter, almost girlish. "We made love that night for the first time. And he told me he loved me and that when he left he would take me with him. And so I kept my mouth shut. It was in my best interest, anyway. I didn't want to be punished and I wanted to be with him. Almost all my dreams were coming true."

"And then what happened?"

"Then he killed again. When I asked him about it he denied it. It was just a coincidence, he told me. Ron had been depressed since she came back into town with Mitch. Ron loved her, you see, and he knew he couldn't have her." Jean sighed. "I know how bad it is to love someone, to know that you can't have them. And it's worse for us, because the pain lasts forever."

"I see. And you believed him?"

"Partway. I wanted to believe him. Then he asked to meet me and I said yes. I thought I loved him, you see, and I thought he loved me. We went to the park together and he'd brought a bottle of wine for me. And a blanket for us to lie on. A moonlight picnic he called it. I drank all the wine because he kept filling my glass and I didn't want to disappoint him. I didn't notice until it was almost all gone that he wasn't drinking any. And when I asked him why he wasn't, he just laughed at me. 'It doesn't agree with me,' he said. 'But it will work just fine on you.'

"Then I tried to stand up. I didn't like being laughed at, not even by him. And I couldn't move. All of a sudden I felt like my veins had been filled with glue. My blood had been slowed down. He looked down at me and laughed again. I asked him to help me and he reached down and picked me up. Carried me to a bench not too far away and sat me down. I still couldn't move but I watched him gather up the picnic stuff. He came back over to me and I thought he would pick me up again. But he didn't. He laughed again. 'You pitiful slut,' he said, 'how on earth could you think that anyone would love you?' I opened my mouth to say his name and my tongue wouldn't move. I wanted to spit at him and call him every name in the book, but I was totally and completely paralyzed. All that remained was my brain. And he walked away; he didn't even look back."

The tape wound out for a while and I thought it might be over, but Sam shook his head.

"What is your name?"

"Dr. Samuels, don't you recognize me? It's me, Jean, you know, the night nurse. But you knew that, you just wanted me to say it on the tape."

"Yes, Jean, I know you." On the tape, Sam's voice was sad, it almost sounded as if he were crying. I looked over at him this time and saw that he was.

"Jean? Can you tell me what happened next?"

"The sun came up and I died."

The tape ended exactly where it started, but this time there were two voices blended into one and the scream lasted much longer.

Twenty-three

"Jesus." I sat up on the bed, stretched out briefly and stood up.

"Yeah." Sam looked at his watch. "We can go to my office now. The sun is down. And you can tell me how Jean got involved in all of this."

I picked up the tape recorder. "May I borrow this? Just for the evening. It would save me a lot of talking and convincing. The Cadre is going to find this whole thing a little difficult to swallow."

"Be my guest, but don't forget to give it back, okay?"

I nodded my agreement and slipped the recorder into the front pocket of my jeans. "Thanks."

We walked down the hallway and returned to his office. He sat down behind his desk and glanced around. "On second thought," he got back up again, "let's go someplace else. I've been here for over twenty-four hours. They can do without me for a while. And I'm not actually on duty again for another four hours."

"Whatever you'd like, Sam, is fine with me." I leaned up against the door of his office. My voice sounded dull and I felt subdued, out of place. Listening to the tape, hearing Jean's story told in her words with my voice had been emotionally and physically draining. And even though I'd slept the entire day, I still felt weary.

Sam picked up his suit coat, checked his pants pockets for his keys and put an arm around my shoulder. He flipped out the light, led me out of the hospital, and helped me into his car.

"I thought we'd just go to my place, if that's okay?"

"Hmm?" I had been staring out the window, contemplating Jean's death and Larry's duplicity. "Bastard."

"What?" Sam's voice was shocked and I laughed.

"I'm sorry, I didn't mean you, honest." I reached over and laid my hand softly on his arm. "I meant Larry."

"Oh, well, then, that's okay. He is that."

He drove for a little while longer without speaking, concentrating on navigating the congested streets.

"Are you okay, Deirdre?"

"No, Sam, I'm not. Everything has gone wrong. I've unleashed a psychopathic vampire on the world. One who has no morals, no scruples. I have no way to gauge his powers, and I feel like I'm losing ground with each waking minute. You see, Jean was number three. Nine more and it will be my turn. And I'm not sure I'll be able to do anything to stop him when he comes for me."

He pulled his car in front of a high-rise apartment building. "We're here."

"Where?"

"My place. I asked you if it was okay."

I gave a tired laugh. "Any place is fine, Sam."

The attendant came around and opened my door, then held my hand as I got out. Then he went to the other side and collected Sam's keys.

I remained silent on the elevator ride to his apartment. He put an arm around me again when we stopped on his floor and led me down the hallway, then unlocked his door.

"Find a seat," he said, taking off his suit coat and draping it over a chair at his dining room table. "I'm going to have a beer. Would you like one?"

"Beer?" I said the word as if I wasn't quite sure what it was. "Sure, that would be fine." I sat down in one of his overstuffed chairs and curled my legs underneath me. Sighing, I stretched my head back over the neck of the chair, flipping my hair up and over the back.

"You drink beer?"

I smiled, remembering how he'd reacted when he first discovered that there was something different about me. "Yes, I can drink almost anything. And haven't we been through this before? That time over at Mitch's place when you thought I was an alien?"

"Yeah." He was bending over the refrigerator and brought two cans out. I watched him wipe the top of the cans with a towel. "That was a pretty stupid thing for me to say, wasn't it?"

"What?"

"That you were an alien." He laughed nervously. "I really felt like an idiot when I finally realized the truth." He reached up into a cabinet, brought down two beer mugs and came into the living room. He set his beer and mug down at the table opposite from where I was sitting, then turned to me. "Here you go," he said, handing me the mug first and then pouring half of the beer into it. He set the can on a glass end table next to my chair and rubbed his hands together briskly. "Can I get you anything else?"

"No, this will be fine."

"Do you mind if I order myself a pizza? I'm starved, but I don't want to eat it in front of you if it's a problem."

"As long as you don't expect me to eat some, it's not a problem at all. Besides, it's your stomach, go for it."

"Thanks." He picked up the phone, placed his order and sat on the couch across from me. He poured his beer and took a long drink. "Ah, that's better. I was getting pretty dry towards the end there."

"Yes," I cradled my drink in my hands and took a sip, "I felt the same. That was a pretty terrible session, I guess."

"Well, I could say that I've sat through worse. But," his eyes lit up in a smile, "I'd be lying. Although almost all of the serious discussions you and I have had have been of the same intensity. I have to admit that I was surprised."

"Why?"

He laughed again. "This is probably going to sound just as dumb and lame as the alien comment, but I can't help it. You're the first and only vampire I've ever met."

I interrupted him. "But you knew Jean."

"Yeah, that's true, but I didn't know she was a vampire until just this morning. That, as I'm sure you can imagine, was a huge shock." He shook his head and took another drink of his beer. "But, I'm getting all mixed up here. That's not what I wanted to say."

"Go ahead, Sam. Take your time. I'm listening."

"Okay then." He drained his mug and poured the rest of the can into it. "Since you were the first vampire I ever met, I just naturally assumed they were all like you. Not monsters, but civilized, gentile, beautiful creatures. Creatures trying to live in balance with humanity and the world." He chuckled, then his expression saddened. "I guess I got this idealized vision of what you were, and even though I knew that sometimes things went wrong with a few, like Max or Larry, I still thought of you all as gods, or super-human beings that could solve the world's problems. Disease, wars, poverty, famines, they were all in your reach to change. You are practically invincible, you never grow old or sick or die. Somewhere along the line I thought that there should be a higher purpose in a vampire's life than getting drunk in the park and killing each other. You, as a race or a species or whatever, have been given such a wonderful gift. Immortality could be such a blessing. But then I find out that vampires are driven by human emotions and in some cases the baser of those emotions at that.''

"So, you have been disillusioned. The godlike race of creatures that you thought would solve the problems of humankind, only end up adding to them.''

"Well, yeah, something like that. Pretty stupid, isn't it?''

"No, Sam, it makes perfectly good sense. We all waste our lives and my species is no different than any other in that respect.'' I took another sip of my beer and stared into the mug. "I'm not sure if I can explain it. But I'll try. The eternal years begin to weigh on you after a while. You can't stay in any one place for too long without people beginning to wonder why you haven't aged, why your lifestyle is different from everyone else's. So any thought of devoting a lifetime to a career of doing good for people is out of the picture. You cannot endure the daylight, so about fifty percent of your time is spent being pent up inside.''

"Yeah, I've been wondering about the daylight thing. Studies these days show that a certain amount of sunlight is important to human mental health. Some people go crazy after a while when denied the sun.''

I nodded. "I can't confess to knowing the origin of the vampire species, Sam, but I can vouch for the fact that I was once human. Most of the time I think that I still am. And I know that lack of sunlight is a problem for me. There are times when I long for it, when just the thoughts of being able to feel the warmth on my face can move me to tears."

"But that all still doesn't explain why you can't *do* something with your lives."

"No, it doesn't. That, I think, is the fault of the hunger. We are all driven by our need for human blood. It is an addiction of the worst kind. We cannot survive without it. And to get it we must prey on humans." I met his eyes and held him to me. "Don't ever make the mistake of underestimating that interrelationship, Sam. You and I may be friends, I may be everything that you said I was— civilized, gentile, and beautiful. But if you kept me locked in this room for more than a week, I would be hungry for your blood. If denied it for too long, I would eventually be forced to take it. We must feed, we crave the blood. Oh, I could make you believe that you wanted to give it, but it would still be a taking and a rape of your being."

We were both breathing heavy when I had finished. His was due to fear and excitement; I could smell both emotions clearly from where I sat. But my problem was different. To my embarrassment the talk of feeding had triggered my instincts. My gums were tingling and my canines were growing. I put both hands over my mouth to hide them, but he could not have missed the rush of arousal that shone in my eyes.

He drained the rest of his beer in his glass, and walked over to me, his eyes still locked in mine.

"Go away, Sam," I said, my words muffled behind my hands. "Go into the next room and stay away from me, until I've calmed down."

"How could you ask such a thing, Deirdre, when you're the hunter and I'm the prey? Would you turn down a willing sacrifice? I just want to know what it's like."

"Sam, please. I'm not really hungry."

He pulled my hands away from my mouth, and pulled me up to stand in front of him. "You once said you couldn't lie to me, why are you doing it now? Do you want my blood?"

"Sam," I tried to laugh to lighten the mood, but my voice shook and betrayed me. "You don't want this to happen, you really don't."

"Why not? Will it hurt?"

"No."

"Will it kill me?"

"No."

"Will it help you?"

"Dammit, Sam, yes, it will help me. You've sent me deep into the hunger now. I have no choice but to feed. Either on you or on someone else."

"Then feed on me. I'm here and I'm willing. And it will help me to understand, too."

"Dr. Samuels," I snaked my arms up around his neck and pulled his head down to my level, "I think you must be crazier than your patients."

"Don't talk, Deirdre. You've done nothing but talk about being a vampire since I've known you. Show me what it's like."

I hadn't had a willing victim in a long time. In fact, not counting Mitch, it had been since I had convinced Larry to let me feed on him in the cellars of the Ballroom. There was a heady sensuous feel in this man giving himself to me.

I put my mouth up to his neck. My tongue emerged to lick his skin, drinking and savoring the tang of sweat and salt. He moaned and held me closer to him, rubbed himself against me so that I could feel the extent of his arousal, his surrender. His hand came around behind my head and he tangled his fingers in my hair, holding my mouth to him.

"Oh," he moaned again, as I continued to lick the surface of his neck in preparation of my bite. Somewhere deep in the recesses of my mind I heard laughter. *So he wanted to feel the kiss of a vampire, did he? Then let's give him his money's worth.*

My hand reached over and pulled at his hair, bending his neck further down so that I could feed without stretching. I continued to lick him, and he began to stroke my back and my behind with his other hand. "Ahhh," I took my mouth from his neck for a minute and licked my lips. Then I brought my teeth full into him and he cried out. It didn't matter whether it was passion or pain, we were both too far gone to care.

My fangs split through the surface of his skin and I sucked on him, drawing his blood deep into my mouth, taking swallow after swallow of the bitterness of him. His body pounded up against me as I drank, and from his heavy breathing I knew that he was close to orgasm. And still I drank from him, deeply, taking much more than I needed, more than I had meant to take. He was gasping for air, but his hand was firm on the back of my neck, holding my mouth to him, asking me to take more and still more.

Then I felt the pulse in his neck falter and finally pulled my mouth away. He fought to keep me there, but now I was stronger. I had always been stronger, I realized. I could have resisted the temptation he offered, but I had wanted this seduction as much as he. I switched my grip from his neck to his shoulders and grasped him, probably with more roughness than was necessary, leading him to the couch, lying him down. I stood over him for a moment and shook my head in disgust. Then I bent down and checked his pulse. It was weak, but steady.

His eyes fluttered open and fastened on me. "I had no idea it would be like that," he said, his voice breathless and raspy.

"The hell you didn't, Sam. You brought me up here for this very reason."

"It's true," he said, sitting up and rubbing a hand over his neck, "that I wanted to see what it was like. If not to feed, then to be fed on. But I hadn't expected . . ."

"What hadn't you expected? You didn't think you'd like it? But I told you you would."

"No, you said you could make me like it, make me think I wanted you to feed. That's not what happened."

"No," I agreed, checking his pulse again, "that is not what happened. And what happened can never happen again."

"You're angry, aren't you? Why? You were only doing what you needed to do to survive. You were helping me with an important research question: Why do vampires not accomplish anything in their long life spans? And now I know. Or I think I do. That kind of experience can only lead to the desire for more. I would imagine after years, it would become overwhelming.''

"Yes. Isn't that what I said? You could have just believed me.''

He smiled up at me. "Don't be mad, Deirdre. I'm a doctor, after all. And a very curious one at that, or I wouldn't have become a psychiatrist.''

I smiled back at him in spite of my anger. "And curiosity killed the cat. You're lucky you didn't find some other vampire to do your research with. A response like yours could get you drained completely dry.''

The doorbell rang and he got up from the couch to answer it. "It's probably the pizza," he said, checking through the peephole. "Yep, dinner time for Sam, now.'' He opened the door, took the pizza from the delivery boy and held it out to me. "Hold this for me, Deirdre, while I pay.''

I walked over, took the box from him and set it on the kitchen counter. Then I opened up the refrigerator and removed two more beers. "Think fast," I called and tossed a can to him as he was closing the door.

''Hey!'' He spun around, caught it and laughed. "Don't shake up the beer.''

I went into the living room and curled back up into my chair, studying his movements through lidded eyes. His movements were quick and not luggish, which is what I would have expected. He came in and sat on the couch again, the pizza box in one hand and the beer in his other. He set the beer on the end table and pulled a piece of pizza from the box. "You're sure you don't mind if I eat in front of you?"

"Eat your pizza, Sam. Believe me, I'm not hungry."

Twenty-four

I watched him devour the entire pizza. He made no apology for his voracious appetite and for once I didn't mind. He had, after all, spent the entire day at my side, watching over me. He had brought me back to his apartment and fed me, as if he knew what I needed more than I did.

And his supposition was right. I no longer felt dull and sluggish. His vibrancy and life was now flowing through my veins, and I was renewed, reborn. I sipped on my beer and smiled indulgently at him as he wolfed down the last piece.

"Good?" I asked him at last, as he wiped away the tomato sauce that clung to his lips. He crumpled the napkin and put it into the empty box.

"It was wonderful. And I was starved. I mean I was hungry before, but afterwards . . ." He rolled his eyes and I laughed again. "I mean you want to talk about a gigantic case of the munchies, that one had to take the cake."

"Or the pie."

He groaned. "That was a very bad joke, Deirdre."

"Sorry, I'm not feeling particularly witty right now."

"What are you feeling?"

I could almost hear his shrink mode kick in and it annoyed me. "What's this all about, Sam? Feed the vampire, then analyze her? Pin her down on your charts for manic depression?"

"No, I just wanted to know how you felt. You seemed upset before we got here. I was curious to know if the feeding helped. Obviously not. I'm sorry I asked."

My anger disappeared as fast as it came. "No, I'm sorry, Sam. You didn't deserve that remark. I'm feeling better. Less anxious and more relaxed. Better able to cope with what's happening. How did you know?"

"That you needed to be fed?"

I nodded.

"I didn't, not really. But you were so pale and so tired, I figured it couldn't hurt. And guess what?" He rubbed his neck again where I had bit him, "it didn't hurt either one of us."

"Not physically, no. But I worry about the friendship and the professional relationship we had."

"We still have them. I gave you something you needed when you needed it. It didn't cost me much and was very pleasurable for me to give. Where's the harm in that?"

"No harm, I'm just not used to looking at it in those terms, I guess. Taking a willing victim is a lot more," and I felt myself blushing, "well, intimate than picking one from off the streets. It feels different."

"Well, if it makes you uncomfortable we won't make a habit out of it, okay?"

"Fine."

He rose from the couch and gathered up the pizza box and the empty beer cans. "Be right back," he said, "don't go away."

He put the garbage into the can in the kitchen then disappeared down the hallway. A few minutes later he came back, his hand fingering his neck still.

"Does that hurt?" I asked with concern. "If it does, it shouldn't."

"No, I was just looking at it in the mirror. Doesn't even make that much of a hickey. I'm betting that all traces of it will disappear in a day or two. You want another beer?"

I gestured to my full glass. "I don't need one right now, but thank you."

He glanced at the clock hanging on the kitchen wall. "And I have to go back to work in a couple of hours, so I'd better switch to something a little softer."

He went to the refrigerator and pulled out a can of ginger ale. "This is better."

Then he settled back in on the couch. "So," his voice was now professional, even the way he sat seemed different, "what do you think about the Larry Martin situation now?"

"I understand a little better now how he manages these murders, but that won't help us stop him, or even catch him. And it doesn't help at all with the powers he's developed. He's still capable of slipping into a room without anyone knowing he's there."

"Have you ever known a vampire who got paralyzed from drinking wine?"

I thought for a minute and smiled. "I never have. I've never even gotten drunk. Neither has anyone else I've ever come into contact with."

"Then Larry must be drugging these people. What sort of tolerance do you have for drugs?"

"Drugs? About the same as alcohol, I think. I haven't experimented that much with illegal drugs. Once, when I was attending night school at Berkeley I did drop some acid. It was a disappointment. I was hoping it would be an escape."

"And?"

I shook my head and gave a half smile. "Nothing. It had no effect other than the amusement I got from watching the antics of the other people. Marijuana is the same."

"How about prescription drugs?"

"What would I need prescription drugs for? I'm never sick."

"I would assume the same is true of over the counter items: aspirin, ibuprofen, cold medicines?"

"I don't need them so I've never taken them."

He leaned forward on the couch eagerly. "What's it like?"

"What's what like?" His question confused me. "I told you I don't take any of those, so I wouldn't know."

"No, what's it like to never be sick, to never have a headache, to never have a cold?"

I thought for a second. "I can't answer that one either, Sam. Because I don't remember feeling any differently."

"But you must have been sick sometime before you became a vampire."

I laughed at his choice of words.

"Was that funny?" He seemed offended.

"No," I lied and he raised an eyebrow. "Well, yes. It was the way you said, 'became a vampire.' Like it was an occupational choice I'd made somewhere along the line or I woke up one day and said 'I think I'd like to become a vampire now.'"

"Sorry. I didn't mean it that way."

"I know. Having a full stomach makes me giddy, I suppose. To answer your question, yes, I must have been sick before, but I don't have memories of it. Other than my pregnancy. I do remember that."

"Pregnancy cannot really be considered a sickness."

I laughed again, this time harder. "Spoken like a true man."

He blushed and I reached across to where he sat and patted his hand gently. "I was only teasing you. And yes, you're right about that one, too. But I remember that particular health occurrence very clearly. Is this leading somewhere?"

"I'm only trying to get some sort of feel for a vampire's make-up. If Larry is drugging his victims, it might help to determine what kind of drug he's using. For no other reason than that there might be an antidote. If he can't kill, he becomes less of a threat."

"That's true, Sam. I hadn't thought of it that way."

"What if we were to try a little experiment?"

I looked at him and smiled. "Another experiment? I would have thought that you'd have had enough research tonight."

"Funny lady. But I'm serious. Not tonight, though, since I have to be at work soon. But during the day, maybe. I could block off the room we were in today, administer different drugs to you and we could monitor their effects."

"How long would this take? It sounds like a long-term deal to me. Remember, I have only nine days left. And there are others who have even less."

"I have a theory that would probably cut back on the time actually needed. Whatever Larry's using, it would make sense that it's a drug that he's had firsthand experience with. I could get his records from his other institutional stays and see what he'd been prescribed over the years."

"Well, I don't know. It seems like a long shot to me."

"Yeah, I agree, it is a long shot. But what have you got to lose?"

I studied his face for a minute. "I lose nothing if we succeed. But if we fail, I'll have spent the last nine days of my life in a futile endeavor." I got up from the couch. "I'll mention it to Mitch and the rest of the Cadre. If they decide it's worth the risk, I'll consider it."

"That's all I can ask. Thank you."

"What do you get out of it, Sam?"

"Me?" He got up from the couch and put his suit coat back on. "I get to experiment on a real live vampire. It's the medical opportunity of my lifetime."

"But you won't be able to publish the results."

"Knowledge for its own sake is still a valuable thing. Come on, lady," he put his arm around my shoulder in a friendly gesture, "I'll give you a ride home."

Mitch was waiting for me at the back door to the Imperial. Sam pulled over and got out. "Told you I'd have her back safe and sound. And right on time."

"Thanks, Sam," Mitch called. I stepped out of the car and right into Mitch's arms. He kissed me like I'd been away for years and I returned the kisses gladly. I had missed him, and hadn't realized how much until I saw him again.

He held me out at arm's length and looked down at me. "You look great. Less frazzled than when you left and definitely better rested. So what happened? Sam told me on the phone that he thought he'd found out something that might help us. Something about how you were tuned in to Jean when she died?"

"Give me a minute to catch my breath, love. Oh, God, how I missed you."

He laughed down at me. "I missed you, too. But I didn't worry about you; somehow I knew you were okay." He kissed the tip of my nose and hugged me to him again. "But what on earth do you have in your pocket?"

"Oh, I almost forgot." I reached in and pulled out the mini tape recorder. "Sam recorded what I saw this morning. It's a very convincing session."

He took it from me and smiled. "Wonderful. I'm sure it will come in handy. Thanks." He kissed me one more time, then put an arm around my waist and we went inside.

When we got back to our room I noticed several things missing. I looked at Mitch. "Where are the flowers? And the coffins? I was just getting used to those."

"I had the coffins put into storage. Quite honestly every time I looked at them I got the shakes. This has been a bad enough nightmare without having to look at a constant reminder of impending mortality every day and night."

"Yes, that's how I felt, too. Thank you. But what about the flowers?"

"I had them moved into the council room. Some of the leaders didn't believe my story of how a rose would disappear with each death. They're each going to take turns sitting with them, 'just to see what happens.'" He barked out a laugh. "Damn bloody fools, they'll sit around debating what to do until they're all just heaps of ashes. And it would serve them right."

"I take it you've been having a difficult time convincing them of the dangers."

"Difficult doesn't even come close to describing it, Deirdre. But I want you to tell me everything that happened while you were gone. And what has Sam discovered?"

I stretched out on top of the bed. "Why don't we start at the most important thing first? Larry has discovered some sort of drug that can paralyze a vampire."

"A drug? But how is that possible? I thought we were immune to the effects of drugs and alcohol."

"Apparently so did everyone else, except for Larry. Sam thinks, or hopes, that he is using a drug that he'd once been prescribed during one of his many institutional stays. Something that he might have had already and discovered its effect on himself by accident."

Mitch thought for a minute. "That makes a lot of sense, but how will Sam know what drug it is? I've seen Martin's record, he's been in and out of those places since his middle-teens. The list of drugs he's taken over the years has got to be fairly impressive. How does he plan on narrowing it down?"

I sat up and scrunched back into the headboard, bending my knees and hugging them to my chest. "He hopes to experiment on a willing guinea pig."

"No," Mitch said emphatically. "I won't allow him to experiment on you."

I narrowed my eyes. "Excuse me? You won't

allow it? I see that being appointed the leader of the Cadre, even temporarily, has gone to your head. I will most certainly consider your opinion in this, but in the end the final decision will be mine. I trust Sam not to hurt me."

He had the good sense to hang his head just a bit. "I didn't mean to come across so authoritative, Deirdre. But the thoughts of you putting yourself into danger for this organization really bothers me. These are the same people who would have willingly locked you away . . ."

"Yes, Mitch, we've been through all of that over and over again. And I have to admit that I feel the same way at times. My fondest dream right now is to get this all taken care of and move far beyond the reach of the Cadre forever."

He chuckled a bit and walked over to sit next to me. "I like that dream."

"I thought you might. But we can't do that now; like it or not we have made a commitment here. And I intend to stand behind my promises, whether or not those who extracted those promises are worthy. Sam said something today that really hit home." I tried to paraphrase his many questions into one. "He wondered why, with all of our eternal life and our powers, we don't try to make a bigger impact for good on the world around us."

"To be honest, Deirdre, I have wondered the same thing."

I gave him a rueful smile. "I would have expected no less from you, my love. You are still very new at this."

He shot me an angry look. "Now that's hardly fair . . ."

"I don't mean that to sound patronizing, Mitch," I interrupted. "With only a little more than two months under your belt, you have made great strides. You are an excellent example of what can be done." I reached over and squeezed his arm. "Especially when you start with prime material. But your thinking is closer to Sam's at this point than mine is. His question took me completely by surprise. And made me take a hard look at my priorities."

"There's nothing wrong with your priorities."

"Yes, there is. I've been fending for myself for so long that I sometimes forget that the world out there is not just for my taking. I can't make a difference to the problems of disease and war and famine. But I can make sure that I live up to my promises." I made a face at him. "You can probably wave the flag now, if you want. That was an incredibly maudlin speech."

"Not maudlin at all, Deirdre. It's just unlike you to take the big view. Not that I didn't think you cared about those things, but that you had distanced yourself from them."

"Distanced is a good word. We are a very insular breed, so totally convinced of our superiority. I suspect that we need to have a Larry Martin come along every so often and shake us up. Living forever can make us entirely too complacent."

"And danger can make us reckless. Do you really intend to have Sam run his little experiments on you? What if something goes wrong?"

"If something goes wrong, then I die. I don't want to die, Mitch, and I don't intend to die. But if it happens at this point, no one can say that it wasn't long overdue." I leaned my head up against his arm. "I don't mean that to sound cruel, Mitch, I don't want to leave you. I love you. But you must see that, if I don't take this chance, it's possible Larry Martin will find a way to kill all of us. And I would be just as dead either way."

Twenty-five

Mitch looked at me, his eyes glowing with passion and pride. "You're right, Deirdre. I'm sorry that I was being so obstinate with you. If you feel this is something you have to do, then do it. I'll support you one hundred percent of the way."

"Thank you."

"I'm probably just jealous anyway. You seem to have accomplished more in your time away than I have. All I've managed to do is make a large number of the house leaders angry and upset. And believe me, you don't want to make these people angry." He ran his hand over his face. "I haven't shaved since you left, haven't showered either. These people can run you into the ground with their pettiness and their disputes."

I took a long look at him. Despite his complaints, he was smiling and seemed relaxed and fit. "And you're loving every minute of it all."

"No, I'm not." His voice held a touch of laughter.

"Tell the truth, Mitch. You've been having a good time."

"Well, at least I feel like I'm accomplishing

something more than balancing the bar tab every night. I got them to agree to post a guard at all the possible entrances to this place. I got them to agree that they would not go out except in pairs. And I got them to accept this as a sort of martial law period." He laughed out loud this time. "Now that was an accomplishment."

"Martial law? What exactly does that mean?"

"Basically, that anyone who steps out of line has to deal with me. No questions, no complaints. My decision is law. That's probably why I came down on you so hard about this experiment thing."

"It's perfectly all right, Mitch, I understand. I didn't really mean that remark about how being leader has gone to your head. You're not like that. I don't think you ever will be."

He kissed me and jumped up from the bed. "And now for the surprise." He started to remove his clothing, a self-satisfied smile on his face. "In the midst of everything else, I learned one other thing. I guess I should say that I'm ashamed to admit that this is what I'm most proud of. But," and he stepped out of his pants and his briefs, "that would be a lie."

I started to laugh. "You learned to take your clothes off? I could have taught you that. So who's your teacher?"

"Wouldn't you like to know?" He gave me a mock glare and I laughed again. He looked so wonderfully ridiculous, standing there, stark naked, his hands on his hips that I couldn't help myself. I laughed until tears started to stream down my face.

"Shut up, woman," he was trying hard to control his own laughter. "This is no time for levity. Now watch."

He closed his eyes for a minute to concentrate. When he opened them again, they were unfocused, staring off into the distance, as if he were seeing into another world. Then I saw the outlines of his body blur, change and I realized he was in another world. He moaned and fell to the floor on his hands and knees. A shiver began to run up his back, his skin texture changed and silver, wiry hair began to cover him, starting from the middle of his back and spreading all directions. He lifted his head and gave a wordless cry that turned into a howl as his face changed shape, and animal features quickly superimposed themselves over his familiar ones. He shuddered once and howled again and the transformation was complete.

What had once been Mitch was now a very large, very frightening silver-coated timber wolf. I shrank back just a little on the bed and he turned his head to stare at me, a wild and feral look in his eyes.

"Mitch?" I saw recognition begin to grow in his eyes. He padded over to me and sniffed at my outspread hand. Then he jumped up onto the bed and lay down next to me. I stroked his head lightly and closed my eyes. I could feel the essence of his soul within the body of the animal and I relaxed totally. He lifted his head to my face, his tongue out slightly, panting, exposing a set of truly dangerous-looking teeth. But the eyes were the eyes of the man I loved and I felt no fear. I hugged him around the neck and whispered into his pointed ear.

"Very nice, my love. You make a superb wolf. But can you change back now? I want you to teach me that clothes trick."

The wolf shook his head ever so slightly and sat up, giving my face a sloppy lick. Then he closed his eyes again. This time the outlines of the wolf faded into nothingness, curling into a mist that slowly wound its way to the center of the room. And coming out from within the mist, as if he were walking through a tunnel, was Mitch. Then the mist was gone, as quickly as the wolf had disappeared and he stood in front of me again, in all his naked glory.

"So what did you think?"

I knew he was very pleased with himself. And I was very happy in his pleasure. That he could learn to do this so quickly, so effortlessly was amazing. I held my arms out to him. "I think I love you, Mitchell Greer."

"Aw, shucks, ma'am, I'll bet you say that to all the wolves." He approached me with a wide grin spread across his face; I could plainly see the wolf buried deep within him. And what had once appeared to me to be a denial of our human nature now seemed normal and natural.

"So are you going to teach me the clothes trick or not?"

"My pleasure, Mrs. Greer."

"And mine, my love." I lay back on the bed and he removed my clothing slowly, one piece at a time. When I was finally naked, he covered me with his body, pinioning my arms with his hands, and my legs with his. I put up a mock struggle and he growled at me.

"So, now that you are the prisoner of Mitch, the grand exalted poo-bah of the Cadre, wolf and mist extraordinaire, what will you do? Try to escape?"

I put my mouth up to his ear and bit gently on the lobe. "Never," I whispered, "but you must be careful at all times that I don't turn the tables on you. Then you'll be my prisoner."

The phone rang and we both jumped. "Damn." He rolled off of me and reached for the phone. "Yeah? Okay, I'll be right there." He slammed the receiver down.

"Bad news?"

"Another rose has disappeared from the vase. Right under the nose of the guard, who saw nothing. Now the leaders are willing to listen. Sorry."

"It's fine, Mitch, I understand. I think I should come with you this time, don't you? Because if they're willing to listen, I have things to say they need to hear."

The Cadre's council room was amazingly normal in its furnishings. I suppose after my exposure to the judgment center I was expecting trappings and ostentatiousness. Instead, this room was a typical conference room. No different from the one at Griffin Designs or many other places I had been. It held a long chrome and glass table, surrounded by chairs with chrome frames and black leather seats and backs. In one corner was a credenza which held a pitcher of ice water, some glasses and a telephone. And of course the vase of roses.

I went over to it and counted. There were, indeed, only eight red ones left and they were starting to look bedraggled and dry. The black rose bud had still not opened. Mitch sat down at the short end of the table away from the door and motioned for me to take the place to his right. As I did so, he pulled the tape recorder from his pocket and set it on the table. He sorted through the sheaf of papers he'd brought with him and only looked up from them when the other members began to file in.

Vivienne came first and she threw a kiss to me as she sat down to Mitch's left. I had never learned the names of the other members, but since none of them looked at me when they entered, it did not seem to be an issue. Mitch could tell me who and what they were at a later date. They were a gray and lifeless group at best, no less bedraggled than the roses in the vase. They took their places around the table without a word to each other. That the seat next to me was left vacant came as no surprise.

Victor was the last to arrive. He sat at the opposite end of the table nearest the door. I tried to catch his eye, but he avoided all direct contact with everyone. He kept glancing at his watch and then at the door, mumbling to himself the whole time. I noticed that the others kept their distance and wondered why Mitch had even invited him. He couldn't possibly follow the discussion, much less have anything to add or suggest.

But to my surprise he opened the meeting. "Call to order," he said and his voice was strong. "Are all houses present?"

Mitch spoke up. "All houses present."

"Good," Victor said. "As soon as Ron gets here we can start." At the mention of the name, a muted whisper rose from the others for one brief second.

"Victor?" Vivienne's voice sounded soft and concerned. "Ron can't be here tonight, he asks that we go on without him."

"Fine," he said, his voice quavering a bit. He put his hands on top of the table and leaned in toward us. "Where are my notes? I can't run this meeting without my notes. Ron knows that."

This time Mitch interrupted him. "Ron left the notes with me, Victor. Now with your permission we will start."

Victor nodded regally in Mitch's direction. "If you would read them for me, young man, I'd be very grateful. My eyes are not what they used to be."

Then, as if the meeting were over, he got up from the table, pushed his chair back underneath and left the room.

They all watched him leave and then turned their attention back to Mitch. He cleared his throat and began.

"Three sunrise deaths have occurred. Does anyone still believe that these deaths were suicides?"

The woman sitting next to Vivienne spoke. "Since I was the one who fought most adamantly against you, Mitch, I have to admit that the third death has convinced me. Two suicides, two mornings in a row could be coincidence. But three? No, I will now agree that these are murders and should be punishable as such."

Mitch glanced around the table. "Anyone else want to make a case for these deaths being suicides?" He paused and searched the faces of the others. "Okay, then, we're all agreed."

The man two seats down from me spoke next. "So we've agreed that the deaths are murder, that doesn't prove who is responsible. It could just as easily be any of us as this Larry Martin person."

"I have a witness of sorts to one of the deaths." Mitch turned to me. "Deirdre, can you relate what happened to you the past three mornings?"

I stood up from the table, feeling at more of an advantage that way, and told them of the visions I had seen. These actually proved nothing but my sensitivity to the events. And prepared the way for the recording that Sam had made that morning.

"Mitch will play the tape from the session this morning after Jean's death. I will come back when it is through and answer any questions you might have."

"Deirdre, you're not staying to hear the tape?"

Vivienne asked the question we had set up ahead of time.

"No," I said and walked to the door, "once was quite enough, thank you."

I had at least three-quarters of an hour before the tape ran all the way through. Although I had prompted Vivienne to ask that question, it was absolutely true that I never wanted to hear the tape again. So I took the elevator upstairs into the Imperial and sat down in the near-empty bar.

The bartender smiled. "Red wine, right?"

"Yes, thank you. Slow night, tonight?"

"About par for a Sunday."

"I guess it is Sunday, isn't it?"

"All day," he laughed and handed me my glass. "You're from downstairs, aren't you?"

I took a long sip of the wine. "Yes, my husband and I are staying here for a while, as Victor's guests. Why do you ask?"

"Well, I know it's none of my business, but there's been some talk today. About Victor and how he's sick and might be closing the place. This is a good job with great tips and I'd hate to have to go somewhere else."

"Victor is very upset about the death of a close friend. But I haven't heard a word from him or anyone else about the Imperial closing. I think your job is safe for now."

"Thanks."

He started to wash glasses, but I was aware of his curious glances in my direction.

"Big goings-on down there this weekend."

"Really? I can't say that I've noticed. I've not been in that much. You know how it is when you're from out of town, lots of people and places to visit."

"Yeah, sure, that's how it always goes. So where are you from?"

"Here actually, but I've spent most of the past two years in England."

"And you came back for business?"

I shrugged and finished my wine in one drink. All of his questions made me nervous. "Half business, I suppose," I said, sliding from the stool and laying a bill on the bar. "And the other half is none of yours. Good night." I smiled pleasantly at him, but I knew he got the hint.

"Night, Miss Griffin," he said, as I walked away.

I didn't notice that he'd used my name until I was already on the elevator.

The tape was very close to the end when I arrived back at the council room. I could hear the uncomfortable blend of Jean's voice and my voice in the hallway.

"Dr. Samuels, don't you recognize me? It's me, Jean, you know, the night nurse. But you knew that, you just wanted me to say it on the tape."

"Yes, Jean, I know you. Jean? Can you tell me what happened next?"

"The sun came up and I died."

Our scream echoed down the hallway until

Mitch pushed the button to cut it off. I heard him clear his throat. "How about if we take about a fifteen-minute break and then reconvene?"

The leaders filed out of the room even more solemnly than they entered. But each one who came through the doorway made a special point of noticing me. Some nodded or said hello, some actually came over to me and shook my hand or patted my shoulder. Obviously the tape had affected their opinion of me, favorably.

I went back into the room. Mitch and Vivienne were still sitting at the table, staring at the tape recorder. When they looked up at me, their faces were bleak and unbelieving. And I could tell that Vivienne had been crying. But she smiled at me, then got up without a word and left the room.

"Jesus, Deirdre."

I moved behind him and rubbed his shoulders. "That was my reaction, too. Horrifying, wasn't it?"

"Yeah. The whole experience was a shock. And I know Larry Martin, know what he's capable of. And still . . . poor Jean."

"Yes. But it seems to have served its purpose. I think the Cadre will listen to anything you have to say now, Mitch."

"I think you're right, Deirdre. I just wish it hadn't been necessary."

Twenty-six

The Cadre had surprisingly few questions when they sat back down. Mitch mentioned the drug experiment to them and how I had volunteered. The project received their unanimous approval. Not that I felt that I needed their okay, having already committed to the endeavor in my mind and heart, but I appreciated their support. And said so.

The woman next to Vivienne spoke up again. "What else can we do to protect ourselves and our house members?"

"Just what we've already discussed. Stay indoors as much as possible and when you do go out to hunt, do it in pairs if you can. Report any stranger found in Cadre territory to security immediately. I think that it's possible that Jean might not have been the only plant Larry had here, so screen your people carefully. And as ridiculous as it might seem, don't accept a drink from anyone you don't know. If he can't get the drug into your system, he can't kill you."

"Can't kill us that way, you mean. There are still many other ways to skin a cat."

Mitch looked at the man who spoke. "True,

John, very true. So watch your backs. And trust no one but your closest and oldest friends."

"Mitch?" I felt uncomfortable speaking up in this group, but I wanted to mention what had just occurred with the bartender.

"Yes, Deirdre?"

"Does anyone know the status of the Imperial employees? How much of Victor's life they're privy to? And how much do they know or should they know about this setup down here?"

"Good question. Does anyone have any answers?"

"I've often wondered about that myself, Mitch," Vivienne said and was met with agreement all around the table. "Unfortunately, the Imperial was always Victor's business and he preferred to keep it that way. As Max did with the Ballroom of Romance. Why do you ask, Deirdre?"

"When you were playing the tape I went upstairs for a drink and the bartender was too curious for my tastes. And as I left he called me by name. I hadn't given him my name, nor had I ever seen him before."

"Do you know his name?" Mitch's voice sounded more worried and less in control than it had before.

"No. Now that I think about it, he wasn't wearing a name tag."

"What did he look like?"

I thought for a minute. "Young, good-looking, nothing remarkable or out of the ordinary." I found to my surprise that I couldn't pull his face to mind. "Light hair, I think, but dark eyes."

"Ah, well, I'll have security look into it." He pushed back his chair. "If there are no further questions, I think we should adjourn." He yawned and stretched. "I haven't had a chance to shave, shower or welcome my wife back home properly." His statement drew a few chuckles from the leaders before they sobered again. "Just remember the basic security methods and you should be fine. We'll meet again tomorrow night, same place, same time."

It took another half hour for the meeting to die down completely. The leaders all had individual questions they wanted to ask of Mitch or of each other, questions that had not seemed important enough for a council meeting venue, but were important enough to delay our departure. Finally the last of them were gone.

Vivienne stayed by Mitch's side the entire time, but for once I found her presence comforting. I knew that he admired her and he'd be less than a man if he didn't find her desirable. If something should happen to me, it was good to know that he wouldn't have to be entirely alone.

Mitch came over to me, as if he'd been able to read that last thought in my mind. "Now that Cadre business is taken care of, I believe that you and I have some catching up to do. Let's get out of here." He pulled me to my feet and we started out the door.

"Have fun you two," Vivienne called after us,

"and try to be a little quieter this time. Some of us need our beauty sleep."

Mitch turned in the doorway. "Ear plugs are hardly a new invention, Ms. Courbet. I suggest you invest in a few pairs."

Her delicate, metallic-sounding laughter followed us down the hall.

"You like her, don't you?"

"Yeah," Mitch replied. "I like Viv a lot. She's really pretty different than she seems at first. When you get to know her better, you'll understand what I mean. And she thinks the world of you."

"Of me? Why on earth?"

He smiled a little sadly. "She takes this blood ties thing very seriously. As ridiculous as it might seem to us, she really does consider you her long-lost sister."

"So, can I assume she's the one who taught you the clothes trick?"

He opened the door to our room, held it for me to enter. "Clothes trick?" He blinked his eyes for a minute, then a smile crossed his face and he laughed. "Oh, the clothes trick. Yes, she's the one who taught me."

"Did you take off your clothes in front of her?"

"Well, it was either that or allow the ones I was wearing to get shredded to bits. But it was nothing sexual, I swear."

I wrapped my arms around his neck and kissed his chin. "Mitch, you'll disappoint me if you say you aren't attracted to her. How could you not be? But you can find a woman desirable without having to make love to her, can't you?"

"Of course I can. That particular situation has only been a problem one time in my life—the night I took you back to my apartment for the first time. Do you remember? I was so nervous and you were so jumpy."

"Well, of course I was jumpy. I was trying to keep you from discovering my deepest, darkest secrets."

"Secrets? There was another secret besides your being a vampire?"

"Naturally. I didn't want you to know that I was falling in love with you."

"That soon?"

I reached up, and cupping his face in my hands, pulled his lips to mine. "Oh, yes, my love," I murmured between kisses, "that soon."

"You never did get to shave, did you?"

We were both lying on our sides, his chest pressed up against my back, our legs curled together. He rubbed his chin against my shoulder, and I feigned a wince of pain. "What makes you think I need a shave?"

"The fact that I don't have a square inch of skin on my body without beard burn is a pretty good indicator."

"Poor baby," he continued, rubbing his chin on me. I giggled then sighed.

"What's wrong, Deirdre?"

"Nothing, really. What time is it?"

"Why? Do you have a hot date lined up or something?"

I pushed myself up on one elbow and looked at the clock. "As a matter of fact, I have to be with Sam at the hospital in about an hour. I'll have to leave soon to avoid getting caught in the sunrise."

"Bloody hell." He sat up abruptly. "I'd forgotten all about that. Do you have to go today?"

"The sooner I go, Mitch, the sooner we'll be done. And I promised Sam I'd be there."

"What kind of security arrangements have you made for yourself?"

"Security arrangements? None, of course. Why would I be making security arrangements?"

He grabbed my shoulders and rolled me to my back. "You can't go out by yourself, especially at this time of the night."

"Why not?"

"Why not?" He pushed me back into the mattress. "What do you mean, 'why not?' You were at the meeting, you heard the rules. Stay in as much as possible and if you must go out, only do it with an escort."

"But the black rose is still in the vase. I should be safe for at least the next eight days."

"Fuck the black rose. You don't really think that Larry would miss the opportunity to kill you earlier than planned just because a black rose is still around, do you?"

"No, I suppose not."

"Then I'll ask you again, Mrs. Greer, have you

made security arrangements for this little trip of yours."

"No, sir, I haven't. Can you help me?"

"Well, it just so happens that I know this ex-police detective who's absolutely crazy about red headed vampires."

"He sounds nice, tell me more."

"I think if you asked him very nicely, maybe with a kiss and a declaration of love, that he might be interested in providing you with an escort to your destination."

I smiled up at him and kissed him. "I love you, Mitch."

"That's pretty good, but not perfect. I think you're going to need a little more practice."

I glanced over at the clock again. "Some other time, Mitch. If you're going to get back here before dawn we'll need to leave here fairly soon."

"Damn. You're right. I'm sorry."

"Don't be sorry. Let's just make sure you have enough time to get back here."

As it turned out Vivienne was waiting for us at the elevators. "I knew you'd be leaving soon," she said, kissing me lightly on the cheek, "and I figured you were like me and would completely forget about our new security measures. So I thought I might go with you. Perhaps your doctor would like to experiment on me, too."

I looked at Mitch and he nodded. "That would be wonderful, Vivienne. With two of us, the whole thing should go much quicker."

"Thanks, Viv." Mitch ruffled the top of her hair. "I was going to take Deirdre over and then come back here, but this is much better for everybody I think."

Vivienne laughed. "Of course it is. You should never be in such flagrant violation of your own rules, Mitch."

"I wasn't violating the rules."

"Oh, but you were, *mon cher*. You seem to have forgotten that if you took her there you would either have to stay there until she is done or come back by yourself. And traveling alone is not permitted."

"But that doesn't apply to me." He was growing angry and I shot Vivienne a warning glance. Teasing was fun, but did have its limits.

"Mitch," I placed my hand on his arm, "you need to be as cautious as everyone else. Maybe even more so because we're all relying on you. But it doesn't matter now, I have my escort and Sam will have two of us to work on. It couldn't have worked out better if we'd planned it this way."

"If you're both happy, then I have no complaints. Let's see if we can get you two guinea pigs into a taxi and into the laboratory before the sun comes up."

Sam was waiting at the door of the institution for us. We both got out of the taxi and he smiled and gestured at the lightening sky. "Cutting it a little fine, aren't you?"

"Oh, Sam, don't you know that living dangerously keeps you young."

"Oh, is that what does it?"

"Absolutely. And I've brought you another cold body to experiment on. Vivienne Courbet meet Dr. John Samuels."

He took the hand she held out, "Sam to my friends if you don't mind."

"*Enchanté,* Dr. Sam. It is an honor to meet someone who is so willing to help our kind."

"Ready, willing, and able." He glanced at the sky again. "But I'd better get you inside to safety right now. If anything happens to you while you're under my care I have no illusions about what Mitch will do to me. That kind of living dangerously can put you in an early grave."

He opened the door. "Deirdre, why don't you go in first and get settled in? I'll show Ms. Courbet around a bit and we'll meet you at the room."

"If it's all the same to you, Sam, I think she should come with me. She needs protection as well."

He blushed. "Of course. I'm sorry, I don't know what I was thinking of. You two go on ahead and I'll find an extra bed."

Vivienne took hold of my arm and we went down the hallway to the deserted wing. When I figured Sam was out of earshot I turned to her. "Maybe he didn't know what he was thinking about, but I sure did."

She giggled. "As did I. Because I was thinking the same thing. He's a very beautiful man, Deirdre. I can't believe Mitch would allow you to be alone with him for too long."

"Why not? I allow him to be alone with you. And minus his clothes."

She blushed, "It's not what you think, Deirdre. I like Mitch very much, but he's your husband and you're my sister."

I stopped. "You don't need to explain anything to me, Vivienne. I trust Mitch." I gave her an affectionate look. "And I'm learning to trust you. Anyway, we are here." I opened the door and let her enter first. "I'll admit that it's not a very pretty room, but it's completely shielded from the sun. We're as safe here as anywhere these days."

I walked in behind her and saw that Sam had refurnished the place a little. Instead of the small chair, there was now an overstuffed armchair, next to it was a square end table on which a row of pill bottles were arranged along with a pitcher of water and several glasses. And although the bed was still the narrow hospital one, it was now made and had two pillows at its head instead of one. On the top of those pillows rested a single red rose.

My heart started to race and I felt Vivienne's startled gasp next to my ear. When we heard footsteps in the hallway we both turned around and snarled in unison.

I can't believe. Myah would about going to the wall from 15 feet...

"Sure, sure, I called him once alone with you and maybe his father."

She choked. "It, but I am to. I just started buy dlly. My heart from me to my eyes. and young of I and trial.

she... of she will said this replica to she wanted. I tried hard to do something here.

Twenty-seven

Sam entered the room. "I have an orderly bringing an extra . . ." He stopped in mid-sentence and looked first at me and then at Vivienne, taking in our defensive stances. "Something wrong, ladies?" Nervously, he backed off just a little.

My voice was stretched and anxious. "There's a rose on the pillow, Sam."

"Yes, I know." His tone was so matter of fact that I wanted to strangle him. "I put it there."

Vivienne let out a long breath and I felt the tension flow from my body. Unfortunately for him it was replaced by anger. "You put it there? Dammit, Sam, take it away. Now. You should have know better than that."

"Better than what? For Christ's sake, Deirdre, it's only a rose."

"Didn't I tell you how Larry was keeping track of his kills with roses?"

"Oh." The color drained out of his face and he rubbed his hands over his eyes. "Jesus. I'm so sorry. I guess I wasn't thinking. It seemed like a welcoming gesture, somehow."

I shook my head.

"Don't worry about it, Dr. Sam," Vivienne sat

down in the chair, "it's over and done now. We had a shock, that's all. Deirdre doesn't like shocks. And these days, neither do I."

A metallic squeal came from the hallway and an orderly entered the room wheeling another narrow hospital bed. "Where do you want it, Doc?"

"Anywhere," and he looked over toward us, "unless the ladies have a preference."

"Anywhere is fine by me." I said, my good humor returning. "What do you think, Vivienne?"

She waved her hands in the air. "Anywhere is also fine by me."

"Thanks," Sam said dryly. "You're both such a big help."

The orderly set the bed up on the opposite wall and left the room. Sam went over and closed and locked the door. We grinned at him and then at each other. I saw the mischievous glint in Vivienne's eyes and knew that no matter what, it would prove to be fun to watch her work him over.

Sam looked at his watch. "Sunrise time. You ladies might as well settle in. It's going to be a long day."

I slipped off my shoes and crawled into the bed. Vivienne did the same but with a giggle. "We should have brought our nighties, Deirdre. We could have had a pajama party. Did you bring your pajamas, Sam?"

"No, I'm the doctor, I'm not allowed to wear pajamas. Deirdre, how do you feel? Have the visions started?"

"Not yet, Sam. Maybe there'll be no visions this morning." But even as I said it, I knew I was wrong. The fourth rose had been taken and the fourth vampire would die. Once again I pushed my consciousness out into the dawn and braced myself for contact.

When I finally made contact, it was weaker than any of the others. It was the same feeling, the same scenario, but watered down as if layers of insulation had been interposed between my mind and the pain. And then the tenuous grip I had loosened further and I lost the vision completely.

I sat up in bed. "I think there was something, Sam, but it was so very far removed, that I'm not entirely sure it actually existed. It may have been nothing but my imagination this time."

"Oh, well," he said, sympathetically, "you can't be right every time. How about you, Vivienne? Did you get any visions, clear or otherwise?"

"I'm afraid I didn't. But then I didn't have them with the others, either. Perhaps I'm just not a vision kind of person. In fact, when I closed my eyes and tried to get a vision, the only one that came was that of you, Dr. Sam, *sans* pajamas."

"Right." He took her teasing good naturedly. "Let's talk drugs. I thought I would start with the more common tranquilizer families today. We might even get through them all, since I now have two lovely volunteers instead of one."

"What exactly will we need to do, Sam?" Vivienne waved to me from her bed and gave me a sly wink. "Will it involve long needles, electrodes, or being strapped down?"

"No, nothing like that."

"Ah, too bad." Her voice was totally believable, but I could see her face. I stifled a laugh.

"What?" Sam spun around and she tried but failed to compose her face into the disappointed expression that her words required. "Oh, I see," he said, "teasing the doctor again. Ms. Courbet, if you would like needles or electrodes or black leather straps I'm sure we can reach an amiable agreement."

"No," she said, somewhat chastened, "that's not really necessary."

"So I thought." He turned his back to her again. "To get back to the original question, all I will be doing is giving you each a pill and studying your reactions, if any. Before that, though, I will need to administer a small physical examination. Not anything terribly involved, simply a recording of vital statistics: body temperatures, pulse rates, reactions. General medical background. Who wants to be first?"

"Let Deirdre go first. If she lives through it, I'll be next."

Sam opened his black bag and came over to stand by the side of my bed. "She's charming, Deirdre, under what rock did you find her?"

"Be nice, Sam," I advised him as he poked and prodded at me. "She does have a temper, you know."

"She's not the only one." His teeth were

clenched together and he held an instrument with a small knob on the end of it.

"What's that?"

"A new kind of thermometer. You insert the knob into the ear. It will record body temperature in three to four seconds."

He put a hand on the side of my cheek and attempted to take my temperature. After much longer than the time he'd specified, he took it back out of my ear and hit it on the back of his hand. Then tried again, still with no result. "So much for modern technology," he said in disgust, put it back into his bag and pulled out another instrument that I understood. "Open up," he said and plopped it under my tongue. "This one will take 3-4 minutes, but at least we'll get a reading of some sort."

After he had finished with me, he did the same series of tests at Vivienne's side. Finally, when he'd written all the numbers and result on his charts, he turned to the row of pills. "Now, let's see." He made a show of picking out exactly the right pill for each of us. "Ah, here we go, how about a nice little black and green one for Deirdre?" He handed it to me, along with a glass of water and I swallowed it. "And," he carried a glass and a pill across the room to Vivienne, "here's a nasty little red and white one for Ms. Courbet."

"Why thank you, Sam." She took the pill from him and looked at it intently before popping it into her mouth and swallowing it without use of water. "I see that your adjectives work properly, even though your instruments do not."

"Quite to the contrary, it's not my instruments that are at fault, but the person whose temperature registers below the normal range."

"Touché," she said with a smile. "I think we have had enough sniping, don't you? I promise to be good if you do. So now what happens?"

"We wait."

"Wait? I'm not very good at that. What are we waiting for?"

He sighed. "I thought you knew what you were getting into here, Vivienne. We wait to see if you have an adverse reaction like total paralysis to the drug. If it does not happen within four hours, we try again."

"This could get very boring, Sam, and very quickly at that. Have you brought any games for us to play?"

"I think you play enough games on your own, Vivienne. You certainly don't need any encouragement from me."

"Sam," I called him from across the room. "Can we sleep?"

"Only if you don't mind being woken up every fifteen minutes or so."

"You know," I said, looking at the many bottles of pills displayed on the table, "this could take more time than any of us actually have. Is there any way to streamline the process? Take the pills closer together, perhaps? Or narrow down the infinite choices?"

"I've thought about all of that, Deirdre. If you

take more pills than one every four hours we'd have no way of knowing whether an adverse reaction was caused by the particular drug, or by a combination of it and the previous ones ingested." He straightened the row of pill bottles and sat down in the chair. "And I've already tried to narrow down the choices. They must be drugs that would have routinely been prescribed for somebody of Larry's mental health background and they would have to have been available during the years that he spent time in hospitals."

I sighed. "I should have known that you would be thorough about all of this. I don't mind for me so much, I rather enjoy the peace and quiet, but my little sister is not quite as tractable."

Sam gave a laugh. "So I've discovered."

"I will have you know, Dr. Sam, that I am not her little sister, I am her big sister. Deirdre's a mere babe in arms compared to me."

Sam perked up slightly. "How old are you, Vivienne? If that isn't too rude a question to ask of a beautiful woman."

"I don't mind, I'm not ashamed of my age. Why should I be? I still occupy the body of a nineteen-year-old. I was born in March of 1698."

Sam gave her a long and very pointed look. Then he whistled between his teeth and she laughed. "Thank you, Sam. Even after three-hundred years a girl likes appreciation from a healthy and handsome young man."

We all waited in silence for a while. Until Vivienne sat straight up in bed. "*Mon dieu*, this will drive me crazy and you will have your adverse reaction in a lot less than four hours. Is there nothing for us to do? And if so, do we have to lie around like lumps for the rest of the day?"

Sam looked over at her and so did I. "I never said you had to stay in bed the whole time. And as far as something to do, I did have them bring the VCR and some appropriate movies for us earlier this morning." Sam got up from the chair, went to the closet in the side wall and wheeled out a cart containing the television, the VCR, and his determination of appropriate movies.

I sat up and swung my legs over the side of the bed. "Movies? What kind?"

Vivienne was faster than I. Before Sam could even plug in the equipment she was examining the boxes. When she finished, she looked up at him and smiled. "Dr. Sam, I take back every insult I have thrown your way today. If this is your assessment of appropriate viewing for two female vampires, you are one very sick person. And," she blew him a kiss, "I think I love you."

"Deirdre, come here and see what he brought for us." She waved her hands excitedly. I came over and knelt next to her on the floor and she pushed the boxes into my hands. "Look, here's 'Love At First Bite' and 'Buffy, the Vampire Slayer' and 'The Fearless Vampire Killers,' along with a whole bunch more. Sam, where did you get all these? I can't believe that these are standard fare for a place like this."

He looked slightly embarrassed. "I brought these from home; I've been acquiring quite a collection the past year or so."

"Interesting," I said very quietly to myself. "But where are the alien movies, Sam?"

Our eyes met and we laughed.

"Aliens?" Vivienne missed the private joke completely, of course, but she was too preoccupied with the movies to even notice. "Pooh, who needs aliens when you can have Louis Jordan? Oh, I don't know which one to pick first. Deirdre, you pick. Which is your favorite?"

"I've never seen any of these."

"What?" Both she and Sam looked at me in astonishment. "You've never seen any of these?" Vivienne spread the boxes out on the floor. "These are all the classics."

"Oh, I did see that one in black and white many years ago." I pointed to the box with the picture of a hideously deformed vampire. " 'Nosferatu.' It was too sad for me."

"Well, if you don't like sad, my melancholy friend, then I have the perfect movie for you." She selected one and put it into the machine.

Vivienne and I watched the movie four times in a row, curled up together in her narrow bed, interrupted only by Sam's occasional physical checks and new pills. The only adverse reaction we reported at the end of the day was that our sides hurt from laughing. And every time I did my best George Hamilton imitation by waving my hand and saying, "It's a creature of the night, it flies," we would be assailed by uncontrollable hysterics.

When Sam announced that the sun had set and

that Mitch was waiting for us outside, I was disappointed that the day had ended.

"Will I see you ladies tomorrow?" Sam asked as he escorted us down the hall toward the lobby.

Vivienne gave me an encouraging look. "I will come if Deirdre does."

I sighed. "I'm not sure, Sam." The previous day's fervor for this experiment had waned when I viewed the prospect of spending whole days confined here, without sleep, without Mitch. Maybe Sam was right in his assessment of vampires being selfish and uncaring. Or maybe I was just tired.

"Deirdre, is there any special reason why you don't want to continue?" He rubbed his hand over his neck.

"Not really, Sam. But it seems like we're searching for a needle in a haystack here. There are too many choices and so few days left. I'll let you know."

"Fair enough. I hope you both come back."

Twenty-eight

Mitch was holding a cab for us in front of the hospital. "I hope you don't mind that I didn't come inside to get you." He held the cab door open for us; Vivienne hesitated just for a moment, then got in first. I followed her, Mitch sat down next to me and closed the door. "That place gives me the creeps." His eyes sought out mine and I caught a brief glimpse of the haunted visions he had experienced there.

"I understand, Mitch." I took his hand in mine, brought it up to my mouth and kissed the palm before bringing it down to rest on my thigh.

He patted me briefly. "So, how'd it go in there today?"

Vivienne smiled. "It wouldn't exactly be my first choice in how to spend my time. But Deirdre and I enjoyed the movie."

"You saw a movie? I thought you were supposed to be testing drugs."

"We were, Mitch. The problem was we could only test one drug each every four hours. We couldn't sleep, couldn't leave the room. It was frustrating."

"And a waste of your time, I would think. Did you find anything out?"

"Not a thing."

"Sam's nice, though. And Deirdre finally got to see 'Love At First Bite.'" Vivienne chuckled to herself. "You two should really leave your bedroom every once in a while. There's a world out there, you know. See a movie, take in a show, ride a roller coaster, do something for God's sake. You both need to realize that there's more to life than blood and sex."

She smiled at us, then, to soften her lecture, "Not that there's anything wrong with blood and sex. Except that I can't quite decide which is the proper order."

"Will you be going back there tomorrow?" Mitch asked.

"No," I was sure now, "it really is a waste of our time. We could test these drugs from now until next Christmas and it wouldn't really do anyone much good. Sam was very persuasive when he first spoke of it."

"He could persuade me to do almost anything," Vivienne interrupted.

"Yes, well, but the truth of it is that I think he's just trying to conduct his own personal research on vampire physical make up. And there's nothing wrong with that. But now is not a good time."

"There never seems to be a good time for anything these days," Mitch agreed. "And when we have time on our hands we don't ever seem to use it the way we should."

"That's life," Vivienne chimed in. "The way it always has been; the way it always will be. And believe me, I've seen enough time go by to know."

"By the way," Mitch leaned forward in his seat to talk to her, "Deirdre is interested in learning a few of the tricks you've been teaching me."

"Mitch, you're no gentleman. And you promised you wouldn't tell her. What must she think of me now?"

"Well," I stretched the word out as long as I could."

"No, no, don't tell me, Deirdre. I'm sure I don't want to know. Do you really want to learn these tricks? I don't mind teaching you, we could start tonight if you like. I'm sure that you're just as quick a learner as your charming husband."

The smile faded from my face. As much as I'd enjoyed my time with Vivienne, I didn't really want her company every waking moment.

Mitch jumped in with an enthusiastic, "That'd be great." So I smiled and nodded and accepted the fact that tonight at least would be spent learning her tricks. If I could actually learn them. Although I'd transformed twice already, it was not a conscious effort. And my one attempt to do it on purpose failed miserably.

"Sure," I said, my voice not as eager as it could be, but pleasant enough. I'd finally admitted to myself that these skills could be useful and that I was being incredibly stubborn attempting not to learn them. And they'd certainly had a good effect on Mitch. "Let's do that."

The cab pulled up in front of the Imperial.

"Good, then that's settled. The two of you come to my room around ten; we'll have some wine," she gave a deep chuckle, "and do a few tricks."

The first thing I did when I got back to our room was collapse into one of the armchairs.

"Tough day?" Mitch came up behind me and rubbed my shoulders.

"Not exactly tough, but exhausting." I stretched my legs out and wiggled back into his strong hands. "Oh, that feels good."

"You and Viv seem to be getting on pretty well, though." He brushed my hair over to one side and kissed the back of my neck. It made me shiver as always and I put a hand up to stroke his cheek.

"I think that I like Vivienne better these days, but she can still get pretty wearing after a while. She seems to have this need to be constantly on display. It's endearing in one way and damned annoying in another."

Mitch laughed. "Yeah, I know exactly what you mean. To be honest, I could have done without her company tonight."

"But, Mitch, you were the one who sounded like you were interested. I was just going along to be amiable."

He snorted. "Oh, hell, I only sounded interested, because I thought you wanted to spend time with her."

"Well, it won't be that bad. She serves a decent wine."

"And teaches a decent trick."

"This is terrible. She's a vibrant, beautiful, and powerful woman and we're talking about her as if she were a not-so-bright relative to be tolerated."

His hands continued to work their magic on the tense muscles of my neck and back. "You know what it is, don't you?"

"No, tell me."

"You and I are complete in ourselves. We don't need the companionship of others anymore, because we have each other. And we always will. So the intrusion of someone else is just that, an intrusion."

"I fed on Sam the other night."

"What? Where'd that come from?"

"An intrusion. He wanted to know what it was like, the taking of blood. And he pushed me past my endurance and I fed on him."

Mitch's hands stopped their massage. "You didn't sleep with him, did you?"

"Good heavens, Mitch, no. I couldn't do that to you."

"Then why is it an issue? I'm not trying to imply that you're lying or that it should be an issue. I'm just curious why you'd bring it up."

I shook my head. "I don't really know. There's something about feeding on someone who wants you to that just feels strange." I twisted around in the chair so that I could see his face. "You know what an intimate experience it can be, even with a stranger. But to know the person ahead of time and to have them practically beg you to bite them, well, like I said, it just feels strange."

"Is that why you aren't going back there tomorrow?"

"Partly," I admitted. "And it really does seem like a waste of time. What good does knowing the drug Larry's using do? It's not going to stop him."

He walked away from me and went to sit on the bed. "There was another murder this morning."

I nodded. "Yes, I felt it. Although it was vague this time, nothing at all like the experience with Jean, thank God."

"Yeah, that was a rough one. They all are in their own way. And I feel like I'm failing horribly at this. All of my attempts to beef up security and keep people safe just aren't working."

"Who was it?"

"Someone who should have known better. John Harwicke, one of the house leaders."

"I only met him last night. He was the skin-the-cat guy, wasn't he?"

"Yeah. That was him." Mitch rubbed his forehead and then ran his fingers through his hair. "The trouble, Deirdre, is that I don't have a clue what to do next. It seems too much like playing into his hands to just sit and wait for him to come after us. Yet that's exactly what we're doing. All of us. Hiding in our warren, shivering in fear of the great and powerful rogue." He got up from the bed and paced the room. "People are starting to treat that damned vase of roses like the holy grail or something. They stop by the council room as if it were a sacred shrine and count the roses. One of the guards told me that some stop by five or more times a day now."

I shrugged. "Why don't we just throw them out? Where is it written that we have to play by Larry's rules? Maybe we don't need to play at all."

He stopped pacing and looked at me, a broad smile growing on his face. "Damn, Mrs. Greer, you know, that is one hell of a suggestion. I think I'll do just that."

"Glad to be of service, love. While you're doing that, I'm going to shower and change my clothes so that we can go to Vivienne's. But we won't stay long."

"We couldn't stay too long in any event. There's a council meeting at two that I have to run. And you know, now that we're cleaning house, I suspect these meetings may be something else that goes the way of the roses." He grimaced. "The damned things are totally redundant anyway. We have the same agenda, night after night. I tell them the same things over and over and they just don't listen."

He came over to me and gave me a quick kiss. "I'll be back in just a few minutes. Save some hot water for me."

I was out of the shower before Mitch returned, wrapped in a towel, using another to dry my hair. He burst into the room with a wonderful glint in his eye. "God, but that felt good. I took the goddamned flowers and the vase to the dumpster in the back of the restaurant. I ripped each one of them to shreds and sprinkled them on top of somebody's uneaten dinner. Then I took the vase and flung it against the alley wall."

"Wonderful. If nothing else, Mitch, at least you feel better about it all. That can only help."

He did a double take, noticing my apparel for the first time. "You're out of the shower already? Nothing went wrong, did it?"

I got up from the bed, walked to the dresser and picked up my hair brush. "No, nothing was wrong. I just didn't feel like a long shower tonight. And," I intercepted his skeptical glance, "I admit I felt just a little edgy about what happened last time. It still scares the hell out of me that he can just come and go as he pleases. But right now it also makes me angry. And I think the anger is winning."

"Okay, that's great. I'm sorry I missed the shower with you, though."

"Have one by yourself. Take your time, use all the hot water if you want. I'm going to get dressed in a minute." I looked at the clock. "I might even stop at the bar for a drink before we go to Vivienne's room. You could meet me there."

"Will do."

I finished brushing my hair and started to dress. Mitch was singing in the shower, and although it was often hard to tell just what he was singing, this one was faintly recognizable as "Born To Run." "Appropriate," I laughed and took a fresh pair of jeans from the dresser. Then put them back. I'd been wearing black jeans for too long, I decided. Time for something a little brighter. I removed the red velvet dress from the armoire and pulled it on over my head, smoothing it down over my hips.

Slipping my feet into my black high-heeled pumps, I walked into the bathroom. "Hey," I called in to Mitch, "I'm almost ready to go. How are you doing?"

"Just fine. It's sort of nice to not have to share the water."

"That's what I thought." I got my makeup out of the medicine cabinet, but knew I couldn't put it on in here. "Steamy enough for you?"

"Yeah. Now get out of here, woman, and let me take my shower."

I made do with the small mirror over the dresser, put a little rouge on my cheeks, applied some mascara and fluffed my hair just a bit. "See you up there," I called loud enough for him to hear over the running water, picked up my purse, and left the room.

The bar held a lot more people than last night, but I managed to claim a small table in the corner from a couple who were leaving for dinner. Curious, I checked around for the bartender I'd met last night, but didn't see him. It was possible, I admitted to myself when the waiter brought me a glass of wine, that I was being overly paranoid. The man last night may have just been a talker, and he could have overheard my name mentioned elsewhere. The entire atmosphere of the Cadre, I decided, was intended to breed suspicion and paranoia. I'd be happy to see the last of them when we finally were able to leave.

Despite my newfound positive attitude about Larry Martin and his reign of terror, I still acknowledged that I, at least, could not leave here until he was eliminated or neutralized. He was, as I had said so many times, my responsibility.

I settled my chair back against the wall and watched the people around me. That had been one of my favorite pastimes before I became involved with Mitch, the Cadre, the whole terrible mess that had begun in a Kansas cornfield so many years ago. Actually it had been started long before then, with the carriage wreck that had killed my husband over a century ago, the scent of his blood that had drawn the attention of Max. I sighed. I still missed Max. He'd been there for so long for me and I'd relied on him without even knowing that I did.

But Max was dead and so was the past. It was time to start looking to the future. I was jolted from my thoughts by the arrival of the waiter with a glass of wine I hadn't ordered.

"It's from the young man at the end of the bar."

I was afraid to look for a minute, but eventually my eyes traveled to where the waiter had pointed, expecting to see Larry Martin standing there. Instead I was delighted to see Christopher Greer.

I flashed him a bright smile and waved him over, before I remembered what Mitch had told me the other day. Chris wanted to kill me so that his father could return to a normal life. I panicked slightly, but it was too late to take away the smile and the wave. Chris was already moving toward me, weaving his way through the tables and the people.

"Hi." His voice didn't sound like the voice of someone who wanted to kill me.

"Good evening, Chris. Join me?"

"Where's Dad?"

"Oh, he'll be on his way fairly soon. Last time I saw him he was singing in the shower."

"Oh, no, Dad was singing?" Chris pulled out a chair and sat down. "When I was a kid that used to drive my mother crazy. What song was it?"

"Hard to say," I smiled at him and took a sip of my wine, "they all sort of blend together. Does it matter?"

"Sometimes you can gauge his mood by the song."

"That must be a corollary to the fact that he only orders a scotch on the rocks when he's angry."

"Yeah. Funny isn't it, how all our little day to day habits can sometimes say more about us than anything else? Like how I knew you were in a good mood before I even sat down."

"Me? Really? How could you tell?"

"You were studying the people around you.

When you're not happy you tend to stare into thin air."

I took another sip of my wine. "I'm afraid I don't know enough about you to guess your moods, Chris. You'll have to help. What kind of mood are you in? Happy? Sad? Murderous?"

He jumped guiltily at the last word. "Dad told you I said that?"

"Well, you can't blame him too much, I suppose. He's been very worried about you, and how you seem to refuse to accept what has happened. There's not really anything that can be done to change your father back at this point. And even if there were, I'm not sure he'd thank you for it."

"So what did you say when he told you I wanted to kill you?"

I glanced up at him and smiled. "You won't like it, I'll bet."

"I'm a big boy, Deirdre, I can take it."

"Oh, it wasn't all that bad, Chris. You don't seem to understand that in spite of how you feel about me, I like you. You're a good kid and a good son. Most of the time." He blushed at that and I smiled at him. "First thing I did when Mitch told me that you'd vowed to kill me was laugh. And then I said something about how attempting to kill me was becoming a very popular sport."

"Why? Who else was trying to kill you?"

"Else? Are you still angry with me?"

He shook his head. "Nope. And you know, I'm not sure I ever was angry with you. Dad, yeah, for leaving town and not telling me what had happened. And myself, for not being able to accept you, when it's obvious that you make him very happy."

"You saw Sam tonight, didn't you?"

He gave me a sheepish grin very similar to his father's. "Yeah, you can tell, can't you?"

"A little. There's nothing wrong with that, though. Sam's a good doctor and I'm glad he's helping. If you had tried to kill me, it would have been a very difficult thing for Mitch."

He laughed. "To say nothing of how difficult it would have been for you."

He motioned the waiter over. "Another Coke for me, please and a glass of wine for the beautiful lady."

I smiled at him.

"Well, you are. And I'm sorry I said I wanted to kill you. I'd been drinking heavily ever since you and Dad got married. I got a little crazy, I guess."

"It happens." I took a sip of wine.

"So who is trying to kill you?"

"Larry Martin."

"The bastard that tried to kill Dad?"

I nodded. "One and the same. Trouble is he's already killed four vampires and everyone around here is just a little tense about the situation."

"So what are you going to do?"

"If you'd asked me that question a day or so ago, I wouldn't have been able to answer. Now it's easy. I'll get him before he gets me."

"When you get him, save a piece of him for me, okay?"

I toasted Chris with my glass of wine. "You've got a deal."

Twenty-nine

Chris got up from the table and put some money down to pay the bill.

"You're not leaving, are you? Don't you want to stay and see your father?"

He shook his head. "Not tonight. I really came to find you, to apologize for how shitty I've been with you. You can't help what you are. I think I always knew that, but it took me a while to really know it."

"Well, I'll tell Mitch that I saw you and that everything is fine. Then he'll have one less situation to worry about."

"Okay. Thanks for being so nice about all this."

I rose, moved around the table and gave Chris a hug. "No problem. Now if you'd shown up with a hammer and a stake that would have been a different story."

He laughed and hugged me back. He even kissed my cheek lightly. Then he walked away and I sat back down, sipped at my wine, and watched the people around me.

Five minutes later, Mitch showed up.

"You just missed Chris," I said when he sat down.

"Chris was here? Tonight? Wasn't he supposed to have an appointment with Sam?"

"Yes, he stopped here on his way back."

"I see that you're still alive. Either you did some real good sweet talking or he feels better."

I gave a small laugh. "He feels better. I save my sweet talking for handsome police detectives." My eyes swept over him. He was wearing a pair of tight jeans, with a button down shirt and his suit coat. I wondered how many people knew that the suit coat meant that he was wearing his shoulder holster. "You look very nice tonight. Almost good enough to eat."

"Don't start, Deirdre," he said with a mock groan, "we have to go to Vivienne's pretty soon."

"But we don't have to stay, do we?"

"No, but then I have a council meeting. What's gotten into you these days anyway? You're even more amorous than usual."

"Are you complaining?"

"Never." He reached over and took my hand. "But there's just not enough time in the day to take care of everyone else and satisfy your insatiable appetites."

"Ah, but that's why there are nights."

"Okay, okay." He stroked the sleeve of my dress. "I'll try to make room in my busy schedule for you."

"Why thank you, Detective. That's very kind of you."

"Kind, nothing. Whatever's gotten into you

has also gotten into me. It's like I can't get enough of you."

"Living under a death sentence might have something to do with it. And the fact that we actually spent time away from each other. To say nothing of how you've been romping naked with blond French women."

He chuckled. "That does tend to have an interesting effect on the male libido."

"No doubt. And speaking of which, I guess we should be moving along. She'll have everything ready for us and we won't be there."

But when we knocked at her door, there was no answer. We knocked again and called her name and still there was no response. "Maybe she forgot," I said.

"Viv? Forget something?" He cocked an eyebrow at me. "You must be joking. That woman never forgets a thing."

"Well then, maybe she found something more interesting to do than endure a visit from an old married couple."

"Yeah, that could be it. She might even have taken her own advice and gone out to ride a roller coaster. But I don't like it, her going away and not letting us know."

"Mitch, my love, I would back Vivienne against an entire army of Larry Martins. She'll show up a little later on, with a saunter in her step and a smug smile on her face. Let's go back to our room so that I can have one, too."

* * *

When she didn't show up for the council meeting Mitch tried to hide his concern. The leaders were more despondent than usual due to the death of John Hardwicke that morning and were not noticing anything. Several of them argued that he shouldn't have removed the vase and the roses without first seeking full approval. The rest simply sat, completely demoralized. Mitch outlined his plan for not having a plan. He compared Larry to a terrorist, who gets just as much delight in watching people scurry around in terror as he does from blowing up buildings.

"We don't want to feed off his behavior." Mitch told them. "We need to deal with him in a rational and sane manner, rather than running around in panic."

"Are you saying we shouldn't worry about him at all? That the danger is over?"

"I'm saying no such thing. Just don't let him preoccupy your thoughts. He's only one man, after all. We allowed him to frighten us and I suspect he loved every minute of it."

It was not terribly surprising that the Cadre members found Mitch's speech distressing. They wanted him to tell them what to do, they wanted rules and regulations to follow, even if they were outdated and useless. The Cadre had become so used to taking orders from Victor that they'd lost all of their initiative. I looked around the table before we left; these were the dinosaurs of our breed, I thought. And they were not necessarily at fault. The organization that had brought them together for mutual protection had turned most of them into cowards.

As we walked out of the room I found myself remembering Sam's thoughts that every so often a Larry Martin is needed just to shake things up.

We checked Vivienne's room one more time. There was still no answer and Mitch's look of worry increased.

"She'll be okay, Mitch," I said, "you can almost count on it."

"I hope so. I've grown pretty fond of her these past couple of days. She just seems so small and frail and innocent."

I started to laugh as we went back into our room. "We are talking about the same woman, aren't we? Vivienne Courbet? She might be small, but she is far from frail. And innocent?" I put my hand over my mouth to control my laughter. "She's got you completely fooled, Mitch, if you can even voice such a thought."

He gave me a sick little grin. "You're probably right."

"Probably, nothing. You should have heard her today at the hospital. I thought Sam was going to hit the ceiling." I stopped for a second. "Sam."

"What about Sam?"

"Vivienne is with Sam tonight; I'd put money on it."

"Do you really think so?"

"I have no doubts about it whatsoever. Trust me on this one, Mitch, I know I'm right."

"Fine. I'll quit worrying then. I just hope you're not too disappointed."

"Disappointed? Because Vivienne is with Sam? Hardly, my love. I think they make a lovely couple."

"No, disappointed because you didn't get to learn any tricks tonight."

"I've never cared about the tricks, Mitch. If you can and want to do it, that's fine. There may come a day when the changing is important to me. I can learn then. And you can teach me."

"So, what shall we do now that Ms. Courbet has stood us up?"

"I think we should just go to bed. I didn't get any sleep today at all. Every fifteen minutes or so, Sam would come around and test our non-existent reactions. I'm tired. I just want to stretch out and sleep for about a year."

"Bed it is then."

I didn't actually sleep much that night. Mitch and I lay together and he began to talk. About his past, about his failed first marriage, about his childhood hopes and aspirations. And he talked about Chris, especially when he was younger.

"He used to have these horrible tantrums. We never knew what they were about. I'm not real sure he did either. We tried everything we could to stop them. We bribed, we pleaded, we yelled, we even spanked. None of it did any good. Then one day he threw a real fit. He and I were shopping somewhere and he flung himself to the floor, screaming bloody murder. I couldn't take it anymore, I didn't want to deal with him at all so I just turned my back on him. He quit screaming until he crawled around my feet to sit in front of me. He started back in and I turned around again. We did this about four or five times and he stopped. Completely. Never had another tantrum afterwards. Kids are strange sometimes, we expect them to think like us and they never do."

He talked most of the night and I said little. I just snuggled in closer to him, my head resting on his chest, listening to his rumbling voice.

And at sunrise I had no visions. It was as if the symbolic gesture of destroying the roses had broken the spell on me. I sighed and curled deeper under the covers, sleeping at last.

When I woke the next evening I felt fully rested. Ready for almost anything. Mitch was up and moving around in the bathroom. I could sense the activity above me in the restaurant and the occupants in the rooms surrounding us slowly coming to life. "Mitch?" I called loudly so that he could hear me.

"Yeah, babe, what do you need?"

"Nothing, I guess. I just feel like we should be doing something. About Larry."

He walked out of the bathroom, naked except for a towel wrapped around his neck. He still had a spot of shaving cream close to his right ear. I rubbed my finger in the same spot on my own face and he wiped it off with the end of his towel.

"Yeah, I've been thinking that, too. It's one thing to say we won't allow him to panic us. And another to just let him run wild. We still have to stop him, you know."

"Exactly. Did you ever get a look at Max's journals?"

"I scanned some of the more recent ones, yeah. They would make interesting reading some day and they explained a lot about how Larry accelerated his power. But they didn't have any practical solutions for this kind of situation."

"Too bad, that would have been nice."

"That's what I thought, too. But I'm afraid we're pretty much on our own with this one."

As if on cue, someone knocked on the door outside. "Deirdre, Mitch, are you there?" It was Vivienne.

"I told you she'd be okay, didn't I?"

He took the towel from around his neck, wrapped it around his waist and opened the door.

She flew in to the room. "Sorry I stood you up last night, but another opportunity arose and I figured you'd understand."

"Hello, Vivienne. And how is Sam?"

"Sam's wonderful." Her voice sounded wistful. "But how did you know I was with Sam?"

I shrugged. "I just did. Mitch was a nervous wreck about you not being here, though. Next time leave a note."

"Yes, Mother."

Mitch laughed and Vivienne looked over at him and whistled. "Nice towel, *mon chou*.

"Thanks, Viv." He walked over to the dresser and got some clothes.

"No need to get dressed on my account, Mitch," she said with a sly smile. "I've seen you naked before."

"But not in front of my wife and not quite this soon after sleep. I'll be more comfortable dressed."

"Fine, but I want to go on record as saying I'm disappointed in you."

Mitch just smiled and shook his head, took his clothes into the bathroom and shut the door.

"He's no fun."

"That's a matter of opinion, Vivienne. So what's the big deal that you had to come knocking on the door so early?"

"Tonight I decided you are going to sell me the Ballroom."

"Just like that?"

She smiled. *"Oui,* just like that."

"But what about Larry Martin? We have to do something about him."

"Larry Martin will be around to deal with later on. His type does not go away. And a night out won't hurt either you or Mitch. Perhaps we will even find him there, at the club."

I had never expected that I would feel sentimental about the Ballroom of Romance. But as our taxi pulled up in front, I was surprised to find myself crying. The Ballroom had been a staple of this city's night life for over twelve years.

And for a good part of those twelve years it was like my second home. But everything changes and the Ballroom was a part of the past.

There was no crowd outside the door as there would have been in years past. But it was still a good location and pulled in a lot of people. Vivienne was going to get a very good bargain.

Mark saw us enter and met us at the door. "Evening, Vivienne, Deirdre, Mitch. How's business?"

"That's what I need to be asking you, Marky."

He tilted his head a bit. "I won't even ask what that's supposed to mean. I'm glad to see the three of you, though. Especially you, Mitch. Fred's missing."

"Missing?" Fred never struck me as the kind of person who would just pick up and leave. "When we were in here last you said he was on vacation."

"And he was. From the club, that is. But he stayed in town instead of going away. He would call me every night, here, after we closed out to see how we did. But the last time I heard from him was Wednesday night."

"Maybe," Mitch said, glancing around, "he changed his mind and went out of town anyway."

"That's possible, I suppose. But his vacation was over on Sunday, he should have been back by now."

"Have you contacted the police?"

"No," Mark said, "that seems so drastic."

Mitch nodded. "And a waste of everyone's time at this point, unless you have reason to believe that he was kidnapped or a victim of foul play. Do you have reason to believe that?"

"No, I sure don't. I suspect he'll turn up soon.

"Could be. Keep us informed, though."

"Will do. Now, do you all want to sit at the bar or at a table?"

"Actually, Marky, we didn't come to party. We came on business. Do you have an office somewhere we can use?"

He laughed. "Very funny. Just tell me if you want a table or do you want to sit in the bar."

"Seriously, Mark," and she certainly looked serious, "we need a place relatively quiet so that we can conduct business."

"You, Vivienne? Sorry. You and business do not mix."

I smiled. "Not yet anyway. But you should watch how you speak to the new owner, Mark."

"Vivienne? You're buying the place?"

"*Oui*, I am. Down to every rat's whisker and roach's leg."

"Well, if that's the case, then you can use Max's office."

"Max's office?" The words gave me a chill. I'd never expected to hear them again.

Mark noticed my reaction. "Weird, isn't it? Max has been dead for over two years and most of the staff here now never knew him, but that room will probably be called Max's office forever."

I smiled. "A living legacy. Max would have appreciated the gesture."

"Consider it done, Deirdre." Vivienne extended her arm and we shook hands. "I'll even have a plaque made up to put on the door. Something ornate and gothic feeling. Max's office will go down in history."

Thirty

The deal could not actually be finalized that night, because neither Vivienne nor I had our attorneys present. And sadly enough we discovered that we shared the same attorney, Ron Wilkes, and he was dead.

So we did very little business, but we did party. We stayed late into the night, paying the band extra so that we could dance. Vivienne discussed her plans for remodeling and redecorating eagerly. The new name of the club would be Dangerous Crossings and it would have a definite S&M theme.

"You're going to turn the Ballroom of Romance into an S&M club?" Mark had finished the last of his duties and had joined us around the table.

"No, no, you don't understand." Vivienne sighed, she'd attempted to explain this repeatedly throughout the night. "It will not be an S&M club, but it will be decorated like one. People love this stuff whether they would ever use it or not. Black leather and chains and studs. And crucifixes."

"Crucifixes?" I asked her, laughing at the

thoughts of a vampire opening a club with crucifixes hung on the walls. "How on earth do these
fit in?"

"You'll see," she said mysteriously. "It has
something to do with the name of the club. It
has something to do with what we all are, deep
inside."

Right after she made that last statement, Mitch
got up from the table. "Nothing personal, Viv,"
he said, reaching over and patting the top of her
head, "but that about does it for me. I need to
get back soon. Anyone else want to go?"

I stood up. "I'm with you, Mitch."

Vivienne remained at the table with Mark and
one of the band members. "I'll stick around for
a while, if you don't mind. I want to snoop into
things around here that are none of my business."

"Be my guest, sister. My business is your business."

"So what do you think of Viv's plans for the
club?" Mitch asked me, as we got into the cab.

"I think they're strange, no question about
that. I also think that she's right and that after
opening, Crossings will probably be one of the
more popular night spots around here. She'll get
rich."

"Do you mind?"

"That Vivienne will get rich? No."

"No, do you mind that she's taking what must
be an icon in your life and completely changing
it."

"No," I told him emphatically. "Life is change

and growth. To expect anything to remain static for too long is ridiculous. The Ballroom of Romance has been dead for years. It's time to bury it and move on."

"I'm starting to feel that way about this whole city. I want this all to be over. We have to find Larry Martin and finish this, once and for all."

"I agree, Mitch, but how do you propose we go about it? Take out an ad in the personals? 'Would Lawrence Martin please present himself to Mr. & Mrs. Mitchell Greer so that they can kill him and get on with their lives.' "

He laughed. "You'd certainly get points for being original. And it could be that the direct approach might be the best one, especially when dealing with Larry. But how do we lure him out?"

"I have no idea," I admitted as the cab pulled up to the Imperial. "Let's sleep on it."

When I woke the next afternoon, I woke to an empty room. Mitch had been with me when I fell asleep, I knew. But he was gone now. I got out of bed and pulled on a pair of jeans and a t-shirt, slipped on my boots and went in search of him. The hallways were completely deserted and had an eerie feel to them. But I could hear a low undercurrent of voices coming from somewhere on this floor. I followed the sound and ended up at the door into Victor's office. I knocked softly and when there was no answer I opened the door and walked in.

Mitch sat at the desk with the phone to his ear.

He looked up and smiled at me, beckoning me to come in closer. He looked tired, but seemed happier than when we had gone to sleep last night.

"And they seem to help your anxiety?" he asked the person on the phone. "Uh, huh, well if that's the case, then keep taking them. It's no shame, son, to take help when it's needed."

"Tell Chris I said hello."

"Deirdre says hello, Chris. Yeah, she told me she saw you and that the two of you have made peace. I'm proud of you for that. Thank you."

I watched the expression on his face change as he listened to Chris.

"No, I do not think that's a good idea. And it's not even necessary. I'm close anyway. Some of the leads I've found this morning have paid off. I now have a general idea of where he's hiding. And an idea on how to lure him out."

"Larry?" I mouthed the word and he nodded. "You've found Larry?"

He nodded again. I felt a flash of relief combined with a rush of fear. He'd found Larry. And had a plan.

"I promise I'll keep you informed. If you'll do the same. Okay then, you have a good evening and I'll talk to you later."

He hung up the phone.

"How's Chris doing?"

"Better. Much better. Sam's got him on some sort of antidepressant now. Chris says they help immensely."

"And you've found Larry?"

"Not yet, but I'm close. Very close." He opened his top desk drawer. "Look what I found outside our door when I came out this afternoon." He pulled it out, a black rose.

"He hasn't forgotten me. How sweet."

"More importantly, he hasn't forgotten the game. I keep forgetting that Larry is no more than a child in some respects. I keep expecting him to make sense. Why did he back off when I threw away the roses? They were nothing more than a bit of melodramatic decoration to us. But they were important to him, because they were part of the game."

"So he quit killing us when we quit paying attention?" I thought about that for a while. And shook my head. "Sorry, I don't quite get it."

"Neither do I, yet. Except for the gut feeling that I'm right. That black rose outside our door is an invitation to play the game again. And we're going to accept it, but on our terms."

"But we don't know the game."

"Oh, but we do. It's king of the mountain. That's why he uses his powers so flagrantly. He wants to be the best. Larry Martin, King of the Vampires."

"Why don't I like the direction this is taking, Mitch?"

He gave me a sheepish grin, "Because you know me too well. I'm going to step forward and offer Larry the chance to be the best, by beating me. If Victor hadn't stepped down, it would have been him."

"So how do we issue the invitation to him?"

He picked up the black rose. "We send this back to him. He'll want to know if finding this has frightened you or made you mad or sad or anything else. So he'll be around waiting for our response."

"Which is?"

"Basically, it's meet me out behind the school after class and we'll see who's the best. Although for Larry it needs to be dressed up just a bit."

We worked until sundown on our response. It was simple enough to seem totally transparent, melodramatic enough that he couldn't possibly resist.

Eventually the note that we stapled to the rose read: "Enough. Let's settle this the only way it can be settled: Single combat, winner take all. Tonight at midnight in the Ballroom of Romance."

"And if he doesn't get it today?"

"Then we just keep trying until he does."

I threw the rose into the dumpster at sunset. I didn't have to feign my apprehension, although it was purely for Mitch and not for me. And I didn't stay around to see if it was picked up. I didn't really want to know.

After that all we needed to do was wait. I called over to the club and told Mark, since Fred was still missing, that we would be closed this evening due to the impending sale and the staff should take the evening off with pay. He could go home or do anything he wanted as long as he was back at the Ballroom by eleven-thirty, waiting for us by the private entrance.

Back in our room once again, Mitch did not turn on the light, but locked the door and reached for me. I made a feeble attempt to push him away.

"Don't you think you should save your strength for the confrontation?"

He laughed. "As if making love to you could do anything but increase my strength. I need the time with you, Deirdre, the unity and the closeness. It may be our last time together."

"Please, love . . ."

"Face the facts, Mrs. Greer. Larry Martin has more powers than I could learn from Vivienne in a year. There's no bloody way I can hope to match them, or even come close."

"Then why meet him? We could leave, now. The Cadre is in such a shambles with Victor the way he is, they would never know. Or even care."

"But we would know. And we would care."

I sighed. He was right; I knew we couldn't abdicate responsibility, but the temptation to turn and run was great. And the risk of losing Mitch was too real.

He raised an eyebrow at me. "If I don't meet him now, Deirdre, I'll have to do it some other time. How many more deaths do you want on your conscience?"

"None," I agreed, "but most especially I do not want yours."

He pulled me to him and held me close, stroking my hair. "I don't want to die and I don't intend to. I'll live through this, I promise you. Have I ever broken a promise to you?"

"No." I buried my head in his shirt to hide my tears.

"That's right. I don't plan on starting now."

"But you said this might be our last time together."

"Oh, that. I meant tonight." His words were light and reassuring, but his voice was choked. I lifted my head, our eyes met and in his I could read determination, fear, love.

"Well, then," I said, attempting to keep my voice light, "that's an entirely different story, isn't it?"

We filled the waiting hours making love. At first I still protested that he should save his strength, but eventually I could not deny that I wanted him as much as he wanted me. Finally, I gave myself entirely to the experience, savoring and treasuring each caress, each kiss, each stroke.

A wildness filled us both, as if our humanity fell away from us. Perhaps it did. I felt, in the touch of his tongue, the mouth of the wolf on me, felt the hair on his head thicken under my fingers. My nails dug into his shoulders and arms like the lethal claws of the cat, leaving bloody ruts that I licked clean and watched heal. We had no voice, we had no breath, but we had bodies that melded and fit so closely I could not tell where I left off and he began.

Mitch buried himself inside me; he threw back his head and howled. The sound of his passion made the hair on my body stand on end and I growled my response. Frantically, desperately, we strove, grappling together, biting and licking, riding out each shuddering wave before being overwhelmed by the next. Then he slowed his thrusts, a deliberate gentling, but still diving deep within, wrenching orgasm after orgasm from my shivering body. His breathing grew deep and labored and I knew he was close to his own climax. I opened my eyes, to see his, glowing silver-blue in the darkness of the room.

Suddenly, as his seed filled me, we exploded into one another. We were one in body as we had been one as a mist. Blended and combined, never to be separated again.

As we rolled from one another, and lay panting on the bed, I did not feel an absence. I knew he was with me still, and would be with me for the rest of our days.

I also knew that there would be no difference between his death and mine.

When we arrived at the Ballroom the place was black, the front of the building locked up solidly. But Mark was there to let us in.

"What are you two up to?"

"We're taking inventory."

"Oh, sure." He winked at Mitch. "Do you need anything else?"

"No, go on home and have a good evening."

I waited until I heard the back door close before speaking. "Do you think he'll actually show?"

Mitch laughed. "I'd be very much surprised if he isn't already here." He took off his suit coat and flung it over one of the tables. I was surprised to see that he wasn't wearing his holster, even though I knew that the bullets would not permanently harm Larry. Then I nodded and smiled, knowing that he had sufficient confidence in his own powers to do without it was a comforting thought. He embraced me briefly then walked to the center of the dance floor.

"Hey, Martin," he called, "did you hear me? I know you're here, why don't you just crawl out of whatever hole you're hiding in and get this over with."

Thirty-one

I heard a hiss behind me. We spun around to see a cloud of mist approaching. And as on the occasion that I had seen Mitch do this, locked within its center was a figure. The cloud stopped moving and the figure grew larger, finally coalescing into the familiar features and body of Larry Martin.

He bowed to me and smiled, exposing his canines fully, then reached into the already dissipating mist to produce a black rose to throw at my feet.

"Deirdre, I'm glad you're here, too. It will make it easier to find you when I'm done with Mitch." He turned away from me to Mitch and held out his hand. They shook hands briefly, only the veins that bulged and twisted under the skin betraying the strength of their grips. Then they each took a deep breath and their eyes locked together.

I had seen Mitch do this on the plane with Victor and knew that he was good. Taking a few steps back I positioned myself so that I could watch the action but not interfere with either's direct line of vision. It was dark on the dance floor, but I could see the tension in each of their faces and bodies.

By the set of Mitch's shoulders I could tell that he was straining hard to maintain his erect posture. Larry too seemed to be tiring, his tension showed in the constant clasping and unclasping of his fists. The pungent, tangy smell of their sweat fell around them, forming an almost tangible curtain and Mitch's shirt was drenched. The contest seemed to last an eternity, many hours of them staring, boring deep into each other with their inhuman stare.

Finally, Mitch squared his shoulders and took a step forward, and then another, his gaze never faltering. Larry held his eyes up, but with each step Mitch took, he took one backwards. All it took was one bad step for Larry to lose his balance. He went to catch himself and in so doing, he dropped his eyes.

I wanted to cheer, but knew that was only the preliminary round. They wasted no time getting to the next game. Mitch stepped forward and grasped Larry by the shoulders. Larry did the same. Neither of them moved a muscle visibly. But I knew that they were pushing against each other as hard as they could. The tension in their necks and backs gave the motion away. They stood like statues in the center of the dance floor, striving, but not moving, each trying to dominate the other through sheer strength.

A small quiver shook through Larry's body and the shape of his face changed, almost liquefying, as if it were a reflection in turbulent water. I blinked my eyes and when I opened them again, the figure standing there was not the same. The features of Mark were superimposed over the more familiar ones of Larry Martin. Then in a blur he became the unknown bartender at the Imperial, then Fred, and finally, incongruously matched with the male body, my face appeared.

I gasped involuntarily, but Mitch was unsurprised by the events and maintained his position and his grip. Perhaps, I thought, he knew that these powers were possible. Whatever the reason, his unwavering concentration seemed to distress Larry, who gave a disappointed grunt and resumed his own form and face. Again, hours passed, but the transformations must have sapped some of Larry's endurance. With one burst of strength, Mitch finally pushed Larry back a step and that round ended.

I gave a sigh and let out a relieved breath.

"Fuck." Larry's obscenity echoed in the empty room, "This is bullshit, Mitch. Let's get to the real contest."

"Fine by me."

If their combat hadn't been so deadly serious I might have laughed at this point. Mitch's earlier assumption that this was similar to a schoolyard vendetta proved to be true.

But children in school were not equipped with the weaponry exhibited here. In a flash, both men were gone and in their places stood snarling animals. Mitch's silver timber wolf was familiar to me. Larry's form was darker and harder to distinguish, until his high laughing bark gave him away. The hackles on both of their necks rising, the wolf and the hyena circled around each other warily. The hyena leapt first, attempting to sink his yellow teeth into the silver flank of the wolf's back right leg. Contact was made, but a sharp back kick from the wolf dislodged the hyena's bite. If the contest had been to first blood, Mitch would have lost. But we all knew the contest was to the death.

They squared off, again and again, each scoring a succession of minor wounds that healed almost as quickly as they were inflicted, each managing to protect their vital areas, faces and necks. Their snarls and howls grew loud in that space and I wanted to cover my ears. I wanted to intervene, but knew I couldn't. My human form would be no help in this situation, and my animal form was totally inaccessible to me.

Finally, after many feints and false passes, the wolf that was Mitch spun around in a flash of silver and sunk his teeth into the hyena's throat, Larry's throat. His yelps of pain filled the air, but Mitch continued to hold tight, dragging him back and forth. Blood spurted out from between the wolf's lips, he lifted his enemy high in the air and tossed him into the corner of the dance floor.

As the wolf came forward again licking the blood from his mouth, the hyena hunkered down, whimpering slightly. His body shivered and shuddered and shifted in its form. With a rush of giant black wings a large black buzzard flew up from where the hyena had landed. The wolf howled his frustration at his prey escaping and lunged up into the air, snapping with powerful jaws at something he couldn't catch.

I held my breath, not knowing if Mitch had achieved mastery of a flying form. The buzzard flew down at the wolf, long lethal talons extended, slashing at the eyes and sensitive nose. The wolf crouched low as if to avoid the claws, then with nothing but the strength of his hind legs launched himself high in the air to grasp Larry's neck between his teeth again.

They both fell to the dance floor but the wolf maintained his grip and flung the buzzard back and forth until his body went limp and the light in his eyes died. The wolf dropped his enemy and threw his head back and howled in victory.

I felt the hair raise on my arms and I let out the breath I was holding. The wolf turned to me, silver-blue eyes gleaming in the dim light. Then his outline blurred and within seconds a naked Mitch was standing in front of me, wounded and bruised, but healing and well.

I threw my arms around his neck and hugged him to me. "Well fought, my love, well fought."

Our only error was inexperience. A sinister hiss came from the seemingly dead body of the buzzard and Mitch spun around, to see the buzzard dissolve into a mist and drift off. As it dissipated, Larry's voice echoed through the empty club. "It's not over yet, Greer. If I can't kill you I can at least kill your son."

Mitch stared at me, defeat reflected in every part of his body. "I lost. And Chris is dead."

"No," I screamed at him, "you can't give up now. Follow him as a mist and stop him. I'll be there as quickly as I can."

He hesitated only a minute then began to flow into the mist form, disappearing after Larry, driven by his urgency to save his son.

I started to run and burst out of the back door of the Ballroom, tearing off down the sidewalk and toward Mitch's old apartment. I noticed as I ran that the sky was already lightening with the approaching dawn. How long had they fought? It seemed like no time at all, it seemed like forever. My pace quickened; now I was not only racing to Mitch's side, I was running a race with the sunlight. A race I knew I would lose. I stopped and gripped my hands together, feeling a cry of despair rage through my body.

Helpless, angry, at the end of my rope and my life, I screamed my distress. And then it happened, my mind remembered the accidental transformation I had made, duplicated the event. I was almost instantly a lynx again and I ran, my powerful leg muscles propelling me forward in giant bounds that covered more ground than my human legs could ever hope to achieve. Still the distance was almost too great for me. I approached the steps of the apartment building just as the rising rays touched the sky. But the front door was closed and I was trapped outside. In desperation I drove my body up against the door time and time again, each lunge stronger than the last. Finally the door weakened and fell in. I bounded up the stairs and into Mitch's apartment.

He sat on the living room floor cradling Chris's body on his lap. I looked at him, trying to put words into my stare. Mitch shook his head and tears began to stream down his face. "He's dead, Deirdre. Chris is dead."

My tail whipped in anger and my head snapped back and forth searching for the enemy that caused so much pain. "Where is he?"

"In the bedroom," Mitch said. "Unless he escaped. He was acting strange."

I sprang though the bedroom door. Larry was sprawled on the floor, twitching slightly. He'd managed to drag himself out of the sunlight coming through the window, his hair still smoldered slightly from where it had made contact. I paced back and forth for a minute, growling slightly, not wanting to approach him, but knowing that I had to drag him back into the light. The light would kill him.

I attempted first to push him, placing the top of my head on his shoulder. When that didn't work, I sprang around him and sunk my teeth into his bare leg and began to drag him inch by inch into the sunlight.

"Deirdre, no." Mitch stood in the doorway, a horrified expression on his face. I felt the sun burning into my fur and the flesh underneath, but still I pulled on Larry's inert body. Blood from his leg filled my mouth with a strange medicinal taste and I felt my tongue go numb. It did not matter, nothing mattered but Larry's death. I kept pulling until finally his body lay fully in the sunlight. As did mine. The air was filled with the pungent smell of burning flesh and hair.

I tried to crawl away but found my limbs were paralyzed. All I could do was lie on the floor next to my fallen prey and die with him.

Mitch moved into the room, crossing the sunlight himself and pulled the spread from the bed and flung it over me. He darted in and out adjusting a fold here and there until my body was fully covered. Then I heard him move slowly into the other room and fall to the floor.

When I next became aware it was dusk. And I was once again back in my human form. I cautiously lifted the spread from my head then tossed it off completely when I saw that the room was in near darkness. Next to me was a pile of charred bones and ashes, all that was left of Larry. I stood up, my limbs stiff, the healing burns on my body crackling with each step. But I was alive. Something I had not expected.

I walked slowly to the other room. Mitch was rousing now, also covered with burns. Chris's dead body lay where Mitch had dropped him to save me. Tears formed in my eyes and I let them fall. Mitch lifted his head and saw me. He struggled to stand and when he succeeded we stumbled toward one another, grasping each other in a sorrowful embrace.

"It's over, my love," I whispered with a parched voice. "It's finally all over."

And yet, the scars that had been formed would take more than a lifetime to heal.

Mitch and I lay in the dark room in the institution for a week under Sam's care for the severe burns we sustained. After a time, and a little bit of blood-sucking on his own, using needles instead of fangs, Sam was able to explain why Larry had collapsed after draining Chris, and why I had gone into partial paralysis after biting Larry.

"It was that anti-depressant I'd given him," Sam said, "Amitriptyline. A standard drug, and widely administered when Larry was undergoing his years of treatments. One of its side effects causes a drastic change in blood pressure and blood sugar contents. Interesting. I wonder how many other drugs of its type would cause the same effects."

Mitch looked up at him from the bed. "We're not going to find out now." The intensity of his voice was enough to make Sam back off.

"Well, I wasn't suggesting that we experiment at this point in time. You two are healing miraculously, but are still in no shape to act as my guinea pigs."

"Good. And I would appreciate it if you keep to yourself the knowledge of how this drug works on us."

Sam laughed. "Of course, Mitch. I'm not likely to call up the pharmaceutical company and say,

'Oh, by the way, please add stopping vampires cold to the list of possible side effects.'"

Mitch chuckled weakly. "No, I guess you wouldn't."

We had few visitors. Vivienne stopped by every night, whether to see us or Sam, I wasn't quite sure. But it didn't matter, her lighthearted chatter was comforting, as was her obviously growing relationship with Sam. They positively glowed when they looked at each other. Mitch and I laughed about it after they left the room.

"I guess we should be upset," I said, reaching a hand over to him from my bed, "both of our 'friends' deserting us and finding someone new."

He returned the squeeze of my hand. "As if I had a need for anyone but you."

Mitch's ex-wife came by often, Chris's funeral arrangements quite rightly preoccupying her thoughts and conversations. I stayed out of their discussions and their arguments, feigning sleep when necessary. Over and over she would demand an explanation. And Mitch would only sigh and shake his head.

"Later, Barbara," he would say wearily, "let's just get through this and we'll talk about it later."

Chris was eventually buried in the same cemetery in which Max lay. It was a fitting end to the cycle. His death was tragic and unnecessary, and I ached for Mitch's grief. But it seemed to punctuate the ending of that portion of our lives; it sealed us closer, if such a thing were possible, into the existence of vampires, blocking us forever from humanity.

The night we were scheduled to leave we made the trip to the cemetery. Chris's grave lay not too far from Max's, so after I made my goodbyes, I walked away and allowed Mitch privacy with his son, and found myself in front of the marker that read "Father."

"It's over, Max," I whispered, hope replacing the grief in my voice. "It's finally over. Now I can live unhaunted by the past."

Mitch came to me after a while, his face streaked with blood-tinged tracks. We stood silently for a while, looking at each other.

"Let's get out of here." He wrapped an arm around my shoulder and we supported each other to the front gate where a cab waited to take us back to Cadre headquarters.

We stayed for only a while, having very few friends left to bid goodbye. Vivienne rode with us to the airport, sitting between us, holding our hands in hers.

When the cab stopped, she looked at us both. "Are you sure you can't stay on for a while? Everything is in such a shambles. They want me to take charge of the Cadre. *Mon dieu,* who would have ever thought it? I knew I'd stayed here too long."

"You'll do fine, Viv." Mitch reached over and ruffled the top of her hair. "I have faith in you."

"Strangely enough," she grew serious, "I'm looking forward to the challenge. But I have some big shoes to fill."

"And Victor?" I asked. "How is Victor?"

She shrugged her shoulders. "Who can say?

Sam thinks he may be able to help him. But Victor has lived a long time and he's tired. As we all are. This is a shock to many of us, finding out after so many centuries that we're not totally invulnerable."

"It takes some getting used to, I guess," Mitch said.

She asked the cab driver to unload our luggage and stay to return her to the Imperial. We climbed out of the cab and waited awkwardly at the baggage check-in.

"So will you stay and help?" She didn't look at either of us, but fastened her gaze on the driver moving the suitcases out of the cab trunk.

"Vivienne, we can't." My voice was sad.

"Ah, well, I knew that, I suppose. But keep in touch when you can. There will always be a place for my sister and her husband in my life." She smiled and laughed, kissing us both full on the lips before getting back into the cab.

We boarded the plane, and waited for take-off, not speaking. Once we were in the air, I sat back in my seat and gave Mitch a smile.

The lights of the city disappeared quickly underneath us and we flew into the night to a brand new life.

Epilogue

With some of the proceeds from the sale of the Ballroom, we bought a large cabin in Maine. Nestled deep in the forest there, it is a welcome haven, an oasis from the death and destruction we underwent those awful few weeks. Our meager needs are easily supplied, a fully-stocked wine cellar and fully-stocked refrigerator, the bags of blood courtesy of Sam. He has promised to come back with the spring thaw to bring another shipment.

Mitch and I are finally at peace, finally happy. We have each other and we have the vastness of the woods to run, wolf and lynx, when we so choose. The beauty of the night seen from animal eyes is beyond description.

Deer and moose live wild here, they sense our difference, and allow us to approach them, even in animal form, allow us to feed on their blood if we so wish.

Mostly we sit by the fire, staring at the dancing flames. There is no need for speech between the two of us now, so completely are we merged, as if Mitch and I were one body, one soul.

If we desire human contact there is a cabin

three miles down the road. A lone woman lives there; she too seems to be around only at night. We know she is there, sitting on her porch, watching the night. We can scent her blood, her perfume, the smoke of her cigarette curling in the cold air and somehow through the darkness she can see us.

Always, when we visit, she shakes her head, amazed at the sight of two such incongruent animals running together. "There's a story there," she says, pitches her cigarette onto the ground, goes inside and closes the door, leaving us alone in the night once more.

About the Author

Karen E. Taylor lives with her family in Imperial, Pennsylvania. *Blood Ties* is the third installment in her *Vampire Legacy* series, which began with *Blood Secrets* and continued with *Bitter Blood*. Karen is currently working on the fourth book in the *Vampire Legacy* series, to be published by Zebra Books in October 1996. Karen loves hearing from her readers and you may write to her c/o Zebra Books. Please include a self-addressed stamped envelope if you wish a response.

HORROR FROM HAUTALA

REAL HORROR STORIES!
PINNACLE TRUE CRIME

SAVAGE VENGEANCE (0-7860-0251-4, $5.99)
By Gary C. King and Don Lasseter
On a sunny day in December, 1974, Charles Campbell attacked
Renae Ahlers Wicklund, brutally raping her in her own home in
front of her 16-month-old daughter. After Campbell was released
from prison after only 8 years, he sought revenge. When Campbell
was through, he left behind the most gruesome crime scene local
investigators had ever encountered.

NO REMORSE (0-7860-0231-X, $5.99)
By Bob Stewart
Kenneth Allen McDuff was a career criminal by the time he was
a teenager. Then, in Fort Worth, Texas in 1966, he upped the ante.
Arrested for three brutal murders, McDuff was sentenced to death.
In 1972, his sentence was commuted to life imprisonment. He
was paroled after only 23 years behind bars. In 1991 McDuff
struck again, carving a bloody rampage of torture and murder
across Texas.

BROKEN SILENCE (0-7860-0343-X, $5.99)
The Truth About Lee Harvey Oswald, LBJ,
and the Assassination of JFK
By Ray "Tex" Brown with Don Lasseter
In 1963, two men approached Texas bounty hunter Ray "Tex"
Brown. They needed someone to teach them how to shoot at a
moving target—and they needed it fast. One of the men was Jack
Ruby. The other was Lee Harvey Oswald. . . . Weeks later, after
the assassination of JFK, Ray Brown was offered $5,000 to leave
Ft. Worth and keep silent the rest of his life. The deal was ar-
ranged by none other than America's new president: Lyndon
Baines Johnson.

*Available wherever paperbacks are sold, or order direct from the
publisher. Send cover price plus 50¢ per copy for mailing and
handling to Kensington Publishing Corp., Consumer Orders,
or call (toll free) 888-345-BOOK, to place your order using
Mastercard or Visa. Residents of New York and Tenne͏͏
must include sales tax. DO NOT SEND CASH.*

REAL BONE-CHILLING STORIES
FROM PINNACLE TRUE CRIME